"What if you could be young again, if only for a week? That is the provocative question explored in this touching novel by Don Trowden and Valerie McKee. *Young Again* is also a delightful love story, filled with insights about family, aging, religious faith, and the importance of music for human flourishing."

— Michael Kinnamon, author of *Summer of Love and Evil*

In *Young Again* the authors weave a heartwarming tale of inter-generational magic, love, respect, and support. Carefully crafted characters, vivid imagery of the American South, and a close-knit Black community all come together around music as young Mabel performs jazz standards, surprising her audiences with a voice and skill level suggesting a much older soul. This novel keeps the reader engaged from the very first page until the last. I recommend *Young Again* for all those who enjoy a good fantasy, and don't mind shedding a tear or two."

— Wendy Shaia, author of *The Black Cell* (2022)

"There is a lot to like about 90-year-old Mabel, a sympathetically crafted character who is wise, witty, generous, and openminded. And, of course, very talented. She's seen it all and done it all, the embodiment of hard-won fortitude. Mabel's week, heaped high with blues and jazz and a side helping of classical music, unfolds in steamy, pre-Covid Mississippi. Rich in sensory appeal, abundant in authentic detail, this story showcases the authors' impressive ability to weave supernatural elements into the real world Mabel shares with the very human, and occasionally eccentric, characters who surround her. *Young Again* is an engaging story about romance, hope, and perseverance.

— Anna Blauveldt, author of *To Play at God* and *Kat and the Meanies*

"*Young Again* reminds us that only love can compensate for our losses, heal our hearts, and bind us together as a family."

— Otis Bullfinch, author of *Pursuing Daisy Garfield* (2023)

YOUNG AGAIN

A Novel

by Don Trowden and Valerie McKee

PUBLERATI

Trade Paperback ISBN: 978-1-7350273-5-7
Ebook ISBN: 978-1-7350273-6-4

Publerati donates a portion of all sales to help spread literacy. Please learn more at www.publerati.com

For the young at heart

"Age is not important unless you are a cheese."

Helen Hayes

"There's no excuse for the young people not knowing who the heroes and heroines are or were. I had spent many years pursuing excellence, because that is what classical music is all about. Now it was dedicated to freedom, and that was far more important."

Nina Simone

"Radical empathy, on the other hand, means putting in the work to educate oneself and to listen with a humble heart to understand another's experience from their perspective, not as we imagine we would feel."

Isabel Wilkerson

YOUNG AGAIN

A novel

by Don Trowden and Valerie McKee

FRIDAY

She gazes out from the stage relieved this will be her final performance. Everything in front of her slows; it's as if she's a bystander in a Renoir painting, both present and absent, the people at their tables rendered so well they seem to be in motion. The faces in this crowd are not all that different from what she remembers back in her day, except they are far more diverse. As much as things may change, they remain the same: the clinking glasses, the background chatter, the young couples so obviously in love. She turns and smiles at Leroy and Buzz, who have dressed in professional black attire for tonight's performance. She wants to do right by them, realizing they have no idea this is the last time they will perform together. She spots Richard through the darkness seated at the far end of the bar. He smiles, mirroring her resigned acceptance, aware that what they shared this week came at a price not yet knowable.

Charles Schmidt is going over program notes with the sound engineer, his recording equipment set up in the middle of the club. Wade Ferguson steps onto the stage and squeezes

1

Peggy's hand, grateful his club is receiving national exposure. She takes her seat behind the Steinway and adjusts the long red gown to free her pedal foot. Schmidt holds up his right hand, counting down slowly from five to one, lowering his arm signaling for Wade to make the introduction. He taps the mic: "Good evening, ladies and gentlemen. Welcome to Wade's in Clarksdale, Mississippi, birthplace of the Delta blues. Tonight's performance is being recorded, so I ask that you please remain quiet, withholding any applause for the end of each song. And now, it is my special privilege to present the Peggy Winston Trio."

LAST SATURDAY

Mabel splashes water from the faucet onto a face she does not recognize. The reflection in the mirror is at odds with how she sees herself, her once-freckled caramel skin now an ink blotter of dark stains. The bags beneath her eyes extend down to her cheeks in an apparent hostile takeover. She sees her great-granddaughter standing behind her, reflected in the mirror, her expression combining curiosity and sadness.

"Good morning, Grammy May," Priscilla has just arrived with her father.

"Hi, honey. Will you just look at this hot mess?" Mabel tugs at her Afro as if pulling shrubs from the garden. "My hair looks like the ventricles of a heart, these two bushy sections split right down the middle. I look like a sheep dog."

Priscilla hugs her. "Why don't you get it cut?"

"What's the point? It's not like anyone is actually looking *at me* anymore," she groans.

"Mommy kept hair products in her bedroom. Let me get them and see what we can do." She races off and returns with a wooden hair pick and a bright orange bottle of Cream of

3

Nature hair conditioner and detangler. Seeing her granddaughter Michelle's conditioner causes Mabel to tear up. "Oh, dear," she utters to no one in particular.

"Grammy May, come sit on the chair and I'll see what we can do with this," Priscilla looks cute in her yellow sundress, hair braided with the bright beads Michelle gave her for Christmas. Mabel sits and Priscilla begins twisting small sections of hair into manageable handfuls. She rubs cream into each handful, starting at the ends and working her way toward the scalp, using the hair pick to detangle.

"That feels so good, dear."

"Your hair is completely dried out," she massages more cream into the ends of each bunch.

"Did your mother teach you how to do this?"

"She did," Priscilla works with characteristic earnestness.

They remain silent for several minutes as Priscilla finishes pulling Mabel's hair into large braids, adding more cream to the dried ends. She takes one braid at a time and combs it out, until she is able to sculpt her great-grandmother's hair into a more uniform Afro.

John Anderson wanders in looking for his daughter. "Wow, look at you two."

Priscilla stands back, proud. "Much better, right Grammy May?"

"Yes, although I look like some old sixties radical, which at my age is probably not such a great idea."

"Maybe we can get your hair cut this week while I'm visiting."

John looks concerned. "I don't want you two driving much while I'm at the conference. Just to the diner and church, please."

They understand why he feels this way. His wife Michelle—Priscilla's mother and Mabel's granddaughter—was killed three months ago when a tractor trailer swerved in front of her as she drove to the supermarket. John and Michelle were hosting Ole Miss faculty friends for a cookout at their home. John, a sociology professor, is suffering from survivor's guilt, feeling he should have been the one driving to Kroger for more hamburger buns, not his wife.

Mabel once again utters: "Oh, dear."

The three of them head into the living room. Grammy May's modern home is tucked into a steep incline overlooking Sardis Lake, about an hour north of Oxford, Mississippi. She had the house built in 1968 as a reward for her stressful life as a touring musician. Louis Kahn designed the two-story home, which features floor-to-ceiling windows fronting the lake, and many surprising alcoves where one can escape to read. When Priscilla was two years old, she crowned her great-grandmother with the humorous name Grammy May.

5

Priscilla would stand for hours gazing at the Grammy Awards lining the shelves behind the Steinway piano. The name stuck and now everyone calls her Grammy May.

Priscilla, herself a child prodigy pianist, walks to the grand piano and plays a quick two-handed scale, eager to assess the quality of the tuning. Looking satisfied, she opens the sliding glass door to the deck and wanders outside into the hot July day, leaving Mabel and John inside.

"Are you sure you're up for this?" John asks.

"It will do us all good to take a break from our sadness."

Since her granddaughter Michelle's death, Mabel has been thinking about her own daughter, Violet, who fought a long battle with cancer before succumbing ten years ago. This barrage of women lost too soon seems cruel.

John interrupts her introspection. "You know, I can cancel my trip. Everyone at the university understands. Everyone at the conference in Germany will understand."

"No, you should go. You committed to presenting your paper, and need to focus on your career and getting the tenure you deserve. I don't want you giving them any reason to deny what's rightfully yours. Don't worry about us. We'll be just fine."

John hugs her, noticing how brittle she feels compared to when they last embraced at Michelle's funeral. Mabel turned ninety last month, and John worries how much longer she'll be able to live out here on her own. She has occasional help during the day to prepare lunch and to fill her complicated pill box, but complains about the germ-ridden parade of Occupational and Physical Therapists intruding into her personal space. John and Michelle had been discussing moving to the lake, with John commuting to the university three days a week, but that was before the accident. Now it's just John and Priscilla, and he doesn't want to disrupt his daughter's routine any further. He's been worrying about how to keep Priscilla with him in Oxford so she can attend school and be with friends, while also caring for Mabel out here in the sticks.

Mabel plunks herself down into one of the two sofas facing the large fieldstone fireplace. She had the sofas and matching armchairs slipcovered in green and brown tartan back in the seventies, but would like to choose a more modern fabric one of these days. John's attention is drawn to the shrine on the mantel in memory of Michelle, where he sees one of his favorite photos of his wife playing violin as a girl. He picks it up and runs his finger along the cool metal frame, longing to touch her one last time, to be able to say goodbye. Not saying goodbye seems so unfair and it doesn't help that he's fairly certain his final, somewhat irritable, words to his wife were to hurry back. Grammy May comes over and places her knobby hand on his shoulder. "Remarkable how much she looked like Priscilla back then," she takes the framed photo from him, tears welling in eyes.

"Exactly what I was thinking," John says.

Mabel stares off into the distance.

"Who's this?" John picks up a photo of a little girl playing with a puppy on the lawn in front of a ranch house.

"Oh, dear," Mabel sighs. "That's my daughter, Violet."

"Michelle's mother?"

"Yes."

"I've only seen photos of her as an older woman. She was a remarkable lady."

"Michelle never got over losing her mother," Mabel takes the photo from John. "And now she's gone too. It's not right, all these motherless children in our family. Oh, dear."

John puts the photo back on the mantel, carefully placing it where he found it.

Mabel turns to make sure Priscilla is beyond earshot. "How's she doing?"

"She's holding up as well as can be expected. She's tough like her mother, keeps her emotions bottled up. I, on the other hand, am not so strong. The thought of her growing up without a mother, with just me to raise her, is such a frightening prospect I don't know what to think. It feels completely unreal, as if Michelle will walk through that door at any moment and everything will return to normal."

"Well, with more time and space we'll all heal and you know that's what Michelle would want."

John sighs, glancing at his watch. "I wish I could spend more time with you but need to be off for the airport. I'll be home next Sunday in time for Priscilla's birthday on Wednesday. Are you sure you don't mind celebrating it here?"

"Of course not. It will be fun for us all. How old is she going to be again?"

"Twelve."

"I can't believe how fast she's growing up," Mabel says.

"I know, soon she'll be dating boys. God help me, then. Anyway, don't bother getting any food for her party as I'll go shopping in Oxford when I return. I'll need to pick up her friends Valerie and Susan and bring them here."

They join Priscilla outdoors, where she is leaning over the wooden railing lost in thought, the dappled light playing against her dress. She turns to face her father and knows without words he needs to be on his way. She feels that same sinking weight inside she knows well from her days leaving home for overnight camp. John stoops to her eye level, absorbing the sadness, and considers cancelling his trip.

Grammy May comes over and puts her arm around her great-granddaughter.

"I was thinking we could head into town and grab lunch

at the diner. Burgers and fries. Would you like that?" She knows the answer.

Priscilla smiles, Grammy May successfully refocusing her on something fun.

John rises from his stooped position and reassures his daughter. "I'll be back this time next week, don't you worry. I'll Skype with you every night and bring back one of those Steiff teddy bears I know you love so much."

She hugs her father and then he is gone. Grammy May points across the lake. "Look beyond the dock. I think that's a sandhill crane."

"What's a sandhill crane?" Priscilla asks.

"It's an endangered bird. Be a dear and pass me the binoculars from the table."

Grammy May presses the binoculars against her eyes, adjusting the focus. "Yes, it is," she exclaims. "Take a look for yourself."

"It's so beautiful," Priscilla says. "Why are they endangered?"

Grammy May gestures toward the outdoor chairs. "I need to sit down. My arm is killing me." She slumps into her chair as Priscilla listens to her father's car pull away.

"I'm sorry you hurt, Grammy May."

"Well, that's what happens when you get to be an old bag of bones like me," she manages a pained smile. "To answer your question, species become endangered through a variety of circumstances, some involving animal predators, others manmade. The good news is man is pretty good about identifying and helping endangered species make a comeback through controlled breeding and legal protections, and that's what the state of Mississippi has done to help the sandhill cranes. Maybe if you study science, you can help protect species, too."

"That sounds like fun."

"How was school this year?"

"Excellent. I had a science teacher I liked very much. Mrs. Ashton."

"And how are your piano lessons coming along?"

"Great. Professor Morehouse has me working on Chopin sonatas."

"Well, that's good to hear. I hope you'll play for me this week. I had the piano tuned for you."

"Are you still playing?"

"Oh, I wish I could but my arthritis is making it mostly impossible. And since my stroke last year, I don't have the same interest in music I once did. It's odd, but you play the same music over a long lifetime and it all becomes automatic. That automatic part of my brain must have been damaged because my fingers move differently than they did before, uncertain of themselves, if you understand what I mean.

Chords I played a million times over the years suddenly feel wrong."

"That's sad."

"Well, it's important to make the most of your youth my dear, and I'm so happy to hear you're sticking with your lessons."

Priscilla's hands hang loosely in front of her. "Is it true you played classical piano before going into the blues and jazz?"

"Yes, in fact I was among the first Black female classical pianists at Julliard back in the 1950s. But there was no path forward for me at that time, so I branched out and found my way playing blues and jazz in clubs around New York City. In hindsight, as much as it hurt, it was probably a good thing, given jazz and blues are the two genuine American musical art forms. It all worked out. Music made possible this wonderful life I've been so fortunate to live."

Grammy May stops abruptly and winces, a shot of pain passing from her neck to left shoulder and down to her elbow and wrist. She wishes everything were not so interconnected, that she might find relief from the electrical currents shooting across her body by short-circuiting some cluster of nerves, like flipping the breaker on the electric main. A few moments pass and the pain subsides as she struggles to sit upright in her chair, feet squarely planted before her in piano-performance posture. She reaches over and pats her great-granddaughter on top of her braided hair.

"You're so cute, Priscilla. I'm happy you're here. We all could use some cheering up."

Priscilla shrugs. "If you're not feeling well, we don't need to go to the diner."

"Nonsense. I just need to take an ibuprofen. Growing old isn't easy, dear. That's why you need to do everything possible to enjoy your youth. Oh, what I wouldn't give to be young again."

"I'm sorry, Grammy May."

"Don't be. I've lived a full life. I just wish I'd known what I know now back when I was young and stupid. Trust me when I tell you, being young and stupid is far more fun than being old and stupid." She chuckles at her little joke. "I would have been more assertive, that's for sure. Gotten more of what *I* wanted and not been so eager to please all those good-for-nothing men who were always telling me what to do. What to think. No doubt, there are things I would do differently given another chance."

"Like what?"

"Well, for starters I wouldn't have married Jerry."

"Why do you say that?"

"He was a drunk, who cheated on me from the day we were married. Stole from me and I just let him walk all over me because I was too afraid and weak to stand up to him." She pauses, not wanting to go down this recurring dark hole, one she does her best to keep to herself, not wanting to reveal how Jerry, on a drunken night, would slap her around and then force her to take on more rigorous tours despite her exhaustion. She should have married Kenny Taylor, the true love of her life, but that's all water under the bridge. Her arms are folded tightly across her chest, holding back the many hurts, the mere mention of her ex-husband firing up nerves. Her mouth turns down into an unattractive frown as she utters: "Oh, dear."

Priscilla doesn't know what *cheated* means in this usage, but understands intuitively it isn't good.

Grammy May continues. "I was so dumb back then. There were plenty of other gentlemen suitors who wanted me, some who became lawyers and doctors, important people. But they weren't Catholic so I wouldn't marry them. Nope, instead I ended up with that bloodsucker alcoholic who stole from my mother and me. Imagine that. Stealing from your wife's mother. Bad enough he stole from me, but I mean my mother, too? My mother only told me about it after we got divorced."

"But surely it couldn't have been *all* bad."

Grammy May manages a frail smile, trying to fight off the regrets eating away at her. "You're right, of course.

You're the apple of my eye," she pinches Priscilla's cheek. "As difficult as life can be, we have to maintain faith that events happen for reasons we cannot understand at the time."

Priscilla gazes at Grammy May, tears spilling from her eyes. "So . . . why did Mommy have to die?"

"Oh, sweetie. We're supposed to be having fun. Let's go to the diner."

"But I'd like to know why you think Mommy died. Why would that ever make sense?"

Grammy May beckons Priscilla to come sit closer. Priscilla snuggles against her great-grandmother's warm body, which smells of Garner's Garden Oatmeal and Honey soap, a favorite of Mabel's.

"We don't know, sweetie. That's the whole point. God has a plan for each and every one of us and we cannot know why bad things happen until many years have passed. But I have faith she died for some reason. Maybe she was needed in heaven to look after someone else who needed her more than we do."

Priscilla sobs against her great-grandmother, releasing the words she has yet to translate from feeling to expression. "I hope so. But that seems so unfair. Why does someone have to lose so someone else can win?"

Grammy May is reminded of her granddaughter's inquisitive nature when she was Priscilla's age. "I'm not sure why your Mommy had to die, but when I look at you I feel it might have happened to benefit you in some way. Maybe you'll grow up to be that much stronger and wiser as a result. Maybe you'll not take loved ones for granted, the way so many children and adults do. I don't know . . . maybe you'll grow up and cure cancer. Anything is possible for you my sweets and that was not the case for me or my mother."

Priscilla and Mabel pause as pleasing sounds from the nearby dock grab their attention. Several small boats are tied up at the neighborhood sailing school. The breeze is picking up, and the soothing sounds of clanking mast lines sing out like choir bells. There is an ineffable solemnity to the musical tones (the German word sehnsucht springs to Grammy May's mind from her classical music training), and they sit quietly with each other, two African American females descended from the same DNA, with so many shared emotions and thoughts passing down through the generations.

"Tell me about *your* mother," Priscilla wraps her arm around Grammy May's wrinkled neck, pulling herself even closer for comfort.

"Well, her name was Mary and she cleaned homes for rich white folks in Atlanta. She worked herself to the bone so I could go to college and then to Julliard. My father worked as a night watchman at a chemical company. It's difficult to appreciate, as we sit here today, that my mother's grandmother was the first freed slave in our family line. Her name was Mathilde and she lived to be 102 years old. Imagine that. God, please don't let me live that long."

"So, we're descended from slaves—"

"Why, yes."

Priscilla sits deep in thought. "I don't understand why there were slaves."

"It's complicated but as a general truth it involved money and power. Most everything does. There was a lot of cotton to be picked in the South and our ancestors did much of that work for free. They were brought here against their will in chains from Africa, sold as property, with families split up. Beaten into submission. Many murdered. Free slave labor built a great deal of our country. Slaves built the White House, did you know that?"

"No."

"Well, the good news is those old days are mostly gone and you have tremendous opportunities ahead of you. I want you to understand that life will present many hardships, but it's how you respond to those hardships that forms your character. When life seems overwhelming and you feel hopeless, just go outside and listen to the wind, or sniff some flowers, reminding yourself of what is important in life. Because it's been my experience that as long as we keep moving, just as the earth we stand on is always in motion, we

17

can leave the darkness behind and emerge into a new light offering new hopes and dreams. And it's important we honor the suffering of our ancestors who persevered in making our current lives possible. I still can't get over the fact we had a Black president. Did *not* see that coming. But, hey, enough of all this heavy talk, let's head into town and get lunch."

Grammy May drives slowly toward Sardis in her Volvo SUV, which feels like a tank to Priscilla compared with her father's small Prius. She can still get around quite well, as long as it's not some unfamiliar place or at night. Routine has become both her savior and source of boredom. There is little variation to her days: up early to get the newspaper from the porch and then have a piece of toast with tea; reading until noon; lunch with one of "the girls" who stop by, or pick her up to go out shopping; television in the afternoon; the nightly news, which depresses her but she's hopelessly addicted; game shows *Wheel of Fortune* and *Jeopardy!*, and then off to bed. If everything goes well, the next day will be exactly the same. On Sunday mornings she drives to church and lingers afterwards for coffee and conversation with the parishioners. There's always plenty of small talk about grandkids, the weather, and sports. The Ole Miss football team is one of the main forms of entertainment in the area but she doesn't give

18

one hoot about sports. She wishes she could still do needlepoint, but her arthritis makes it impossible. At least her eyesight is good enough to read books and magazines.

They approach the water tower in Sardis, the main feature rising above the sleepy southern town. They pass Dollar General and the public library. The grand Hefflin House, a Greek Revival mansion built during the Civil War era, stands out among the other ordinary architecture. It houses a museum filled with many artifacts from Panola County history. St. John's Catholic Church looms on Main Street and is the church Grammy May has been going to for most of her adult life, and she's looking forward to this Sunday when she can show off her great-granddaughter. She parks on the street in front of the Panola Playhouse. The Playhouse has been a local institution for decades and is the site of many excellent performances attracting people from around the county. Just up the street is the tiny Sardis Diner, which seats fifteen people at a time. They enter and sit in a back booth facing the street, beneath an air conditioner perched precariously from an overhead window. They have the diner to themselves, it being too late for lunch and too early for dinner. A waitress comes over to take their orders of cheeseburgers, french fries, and a chocolate milkshake for Priscilla, a decaf coffee for Mabel. The young waitress, who is working over her chewing gum—occasionally bringing it to the front of her teeth before her pink tongue emerges to drag it back inside—doesn't use an ordering pad, apparently able to remember whatever anyone orders despite the large menu. She prances away and their food comes out quickly, the only meal in queue.

Since her stroke, Grammy May has been on a strict Mediterranean diet, but she has decided to lapse for one day. "I know these aren't good for me, but I don't care. I've done my time, I deserve a few remaining pleasures," she dips two fries into ketchup.

Priscilla is happily sucking down her thick chocolate shake through a thin straw, the burger and fries waiting off to the side.

"This place brings back so many happy memories," Grammy May looks wistful. "I used to come here with Kenny Taylor in high school."

"Who's he?

"My boyfriend back then, my first love. He was a talented musician who played clarinet. He was so good, so smooth, sometimes he sat in with the professionals over in Clarksdale back in high school. But then he went away to music school in California and I have no idea where he is or if he's even alive."

"Where's Clarksdale?"

"Not far from here. The old Riverside Hotel was one of

the many juke joints where the blues got its start. James Cotton, John Lee Hooker, Muddy Waters. I saw them all back then and played with some of them once my career got going. You may not realize this, but Mississippi is the home of the blues, what's known as the Delta blues. There were many social clubs in Clarksdale where the music developed and spread north, mainly to Chicago and St. Louis. But the blues got started right here in Mississippi. Do you like the blues?"

"I don't know," she dodges the question, not wanting to be disrespectful. "I mostly like classical."

"What have you been listening to lately?"

"Rachmaninoff's piano concertos and new orchestral music coming out of Europe. It's called spectral music, where the composers alter the instruments to use the notes within the notes, if you will."

"Yes, I'm vaguely familiar with that genre. But I don't care much for it. Just too weird for me, I suppose."

There's a lengthy silence as they eat their food. The sun reflects off a juke box in the next booth and Priscilla slides over on her seat to avoid the glare. A young man outside on the street spots them and comes inside.

"Hi, Mabel. How nice to see you out and about."

"Hello, Doctor Roberts. This is my great-granddaughter Priscilla Anderson, John's daughter."

"Nice to meet you, Priscilla. I've heard a lot about you."

Grammy May dabs the cheeseburger grease on her chin with a napkin. "Please don't tell me you're stalking us, trying to keep me from enjoying my fries. I promise I've only been eating plants and fiber as instructed. What a way to finish off a life."

He smiles. "Remember, eat to live, *not* live to eat."

She laughs. "I've done a lot of living already so figure if I've made it this far, I can indulge every now and then."

"Well, I do worry about how high your triglycerides were the last time we did your labs, but as long as you don't make it a daily habit, you've come this far so I assume you have more miles on you. I'm just happy to see you in town. I can only imagine how tough this stretch has been."

The doctor is a dark-skinned Black man, with a neatly trimmed beard and high cheekbones elongating off to the sides of his head. His nose is broad and flat. He wears brown eyeglasses in heavy round frames, which enlarge his eyes and long lashes. He's new in town, recruited from Johns Hopkins for the local Medical Center. Attracting a doctor of his stature was a coup for the town and one many in Sardis cannot explain. Why would a promising young doctor want to work in rural Mississippi? Surely the cases were boring compared to what he had been trained to handle in an elite medical school. But he seems happy enough, despite the fact no one knows much about him. Mabel figures he must be lonely, living all alone in that big Greek Revival house on the edge of town. It can't be easy being new to Sardis, as most everyone knows everyone, and many of the same families have lived here for generations. Outsiders are not openly welcomed. Nothing much new ever happens in Sardis and there are no secrets.

"Is that a stethoscope?" Priscilla notices something shiny sticking out of his medical bag.

"It is," he replies.

"May I touch it?"

He hesitates, seemingly not eager to share his stethoscope with a young girl he does not know.

"Go ahead, let her touch it," Mabel remonstrates. "She's going to cure cancer someday, you know."

He passes it to Priscilla, who holds it for several moments in her delicate hands. She enjoys the feel of the cool metal, senses the scientific importance of this instrument crafted with care by people in a distant medical instruments' lab. Just holding it makes her feel important. She hands it back.

"Join us if you can, doctor," Mabel pats the seat next to her. "I was just reminiscing about my teenage years when I'd go listen to the blues in Clarksdale. Have you explored over that way yet?"

The doctor sits down next to Mabel. "Please feel free to

call me Richard. I'm still uncomfortable and fairly new at being called Doctor. Not sure I've earned it yet."

"By all means, happy to call you Richard. Do you go by Richard and not Dick or Richie?"

"Richie, that's funny. I'm going to need many more patients before anyone can call me Richie. No, Richard is just fine."

Mabel laughs. "Richard it is." She realizes he is a millennial, the younger generation, the children of the Baby Boomers, who have had it tougher than their parents in many ways, starting their adult lives with huge college loans to repay, living through the horrors of the World Trade Center attacks. She likes the few millennials she has met as they seem more socially and environmentally conscious than her own generation. She approves of their protests for racial justice. She sees them at the farmer's market when she goes Saturday mornings, young people returning to the land making and selling all kinds of interesting products: honey, cheeses, goat milk, kombucha, flower arrangements, as they stand at their stalls dressed in overalls, so young and idealistic. Sometimes she feels guilty for all the greed and eco-destruction her generation and those before have left to these kids.

The doctor continues. "Anyway, I've tried getting around as much as my schedule allows, but haven't made it to

Clarksdale. I don't believe the old blues clubs are there still, are they?"

"Sadly, most are gone. But there are plenty of newer ones doing very well from what I hear. I think the old clubs are now banks and parking lots. That's what life does to you. Can't even return to where your memories live because they've been paved over. So much beautiful old architecture should have been preserved but wasn't. It's a crying shame. Especially when you look at all those cheap cookie-cutter condos people overpay for nowadays. True craftsmanship died years ago if you ask me."

"I'm glad to hear the new clubs are doing well as I've been meaning to head over that way. I'm on vacation starting tomorrow, so might go catch some of the festival acts. Can you keep a secret?" he leans forward.

"Probably not," Mabel answers without missing a beat.

"I love the blues, especially Buddy Guy and Muddy Waters. I'm hoping there might be a club or two where locals can perform."

"What do you play?"

"The harmonica. And not very well."

Priscilla has moved on from her milkshake to the cheeseburger. "Grammy May told me she saw Muddy Waters play in Clarksdale when she was young."

His face lights up. "No way!"

"Yes way," Grammy May replies. "Many times, in fact. I even played with him when I got my start. He was very kind and introduced me to his musical friends. I wish today's stars were more generous in helping the next generation make their way. From what I can tell, everyone is constantly promoting themselves on social media, and those who've been lucky enough to be successful forget how hard it is getting started in the arts."

"Well, that's quite something," the doctor looks impressed.

Mabel continues. "Muddy wasn't well-known when I first started going to the old clubs. I can't remember the name of the one he played most of the time, but I can picture it like it was yesterday. You stepped down several stairs into a smoke-filled room, all hot and sweaty on a summer evening, glasses clinking as the music competed for attention. Plush red fabric on the surrounding sofas. Photos of musicians lining the walls, with all the men and women dressed to the nines and looking *mighty* fine. We'd get there early and sit right up front, just a few feet from the stage. When the greats played, like Muddy, people listened intently. No clanging glasses. No noise from out back. I wish I had known back then how lucky I was. When you're young, you just think life's gonna be that way forever. And then you start getting worn down, like a pebble on the beach, time mysteriously moving both too fast and too slow. It's true, that old saying that youth's wasted on the young." She sighs and gazes out the window lost in her memories.

"Doctor, why'd you pick Sardis of all places to move to?" Priscilla comes out of the blue with this matter-of-fact question that jars the adults back to the present. Priscilla is not one for small talk. Grammy May sits there recalling how her granddaughter had been concerned Priscilla's bluntness might cause her to have difficulty making friends.

"Don't be rude," Grammy May reprimands. "That's none of our business."

The doctor smiles. "No, it's fine. I was eager to make a fresh start and wanted to work someplace rural, someplace where the people truly need medical help. The cities have so many options. And I like it here very much."

"Oh, dear." Mabel sighs, lost in a past that doesn't jibe with her nostalgia. "You know, maybe we should take an old-timer tour of Clarksdale seeing you're on vacation. I can show you where some of the clubs were before I drop dead and it's too late. Assuming I can remember where they were. And we can check out some of the new musical acts. Been ages since I've seen any live music."

"It's never *too late*," he replies. "I'd love to explore with you if you truly mean it. How 'bout tomorrow afternoon, if you're free?"

She laughs. "You kidding? It's not like I have any grand plans."

Priscilla notices the scattered sugar wrappers in front of Grammy May. "Why are you adding so many sugars to your coffee?"

Mabel looks up with a slightly vacant look on her face. "Have I been adding too many sugars?"

"Yes, that's like the third packet you've added in the last few minutes."

"Hmm," she pushes her coffee off to the side. "I thought it seemed sweet."

The doctor realizes Mabel is in the early stages of dementia, made worse by her stroke. He doesn't want to make her feel bad about this so tries bringing the conversation back to their blues discussion.

"Well, Mabel, why don't I come pick you both up tomorrow at noon and we can head to Clarksdale and grab a bite to eat at one of the newer clubs. I'd like to tour the blues museum there, too, if you're game."

"Sounds like fun," Grammy May manages a hint of a smile as she stares at the torn sugar packets in front of her attempting to recall putting any one of them in her coffee. It's a complete blank. "Let me tell you youngsters something. It's difficult to accept how your mind lets you down when you find yourself suddenly old. Small things like forgetting if you

28

just shampooed your hair while staring at the shampoo bottle in the shower, wondering if you should do it again, if it *even* is again, and then having to say it aloud to make sure you remember doing it later. Same for all the pills I take. Or staring at your car keys on the counter, making an inadequate mental note to be sure to remember to get them when you leave, only to find yourself sitting in the car moments later without the keys. It's exasperating."

Doctor Roberts pats her hand sympathetically. "I'm sure it's not easy Mabel, but what a great life you've lived. I only hope I can feel as accomplished as you must, assuming I'm fortunate enough to live a long life."

Mabel smiles in the realization she has introduced a depressing mood to their otherwise fun outing. She rallies, resolved to be a good sport despite the way she feels.

Doctor Roberts glances at his watch and gets up to leave. "Well, I better be on my way. Don't want to keep my patients waiting. One might say my patients are lacking patience," he chuckles at his joke while Priscilla groans and Mabel laughs. "Until tomorrow, ladies." After he is beyond earshot Grammy May leans over to Priscilla and whispers, "My goodness, is that young man handsome or what. I can barely think straight gazing into those dreamy eyes of his. I don't care how many doctors there are in Mississippi, he's the only one for me."

******

That night, Mabel and Priscilla watch *Jeopardy!* after Mabel takes her nightly pills: one for the heart, two for high blood pressure, another for cholesterol, and several others that are large and difficult for her to swallow. She feels she is single-handedly keeping Big Pharma afloat. She tops off her pills with two ibuprofens to lessen the nerve pain shooting down her left arm. Mabel mutes the television when the *Jeopardy!* players introduce themselves, droning on and on in effusive gibberish about their *wonderful husbands* and *lovely wives*. She groans, rolling her eyes at this part of the program. "Just play the game. No one cares about your stupid husbands. Probably a bunch of drunks anyway." Once the game resumes, she turns up the volume and becomes frustrated at her inability to retrieve answers she knows, but can no longer summon. Priscilla sits quietly watching her, feeling sorry. She never wants to be old. When the show is over, Priscilla helps her great-grandmother up from the armchair and guides her to the bedroom at the far end of the house. Grammy May sits quietly on the edge of her bed looking ancient and lost to Priscilla.

"I'm so glad you're here, dear. It can be lonely all by myself."

"I'm glad I'm here, too."

"Why don't you go to your room and read if you're not ready for bed. I'm exhausted so want to turn in early. We've

30

got a big day tomorrow with Doctor Hunk."

"Okay, Grammy May," she leans in and kisses her on the cheek. Priscilla's bedroom is at the other end of the house on the lakeside. She slips into her pajamas and brushes her teeth in the adjacent bathroom, just as her mother would have wanted. She's eager to make her mother proud, to live her life in a way that will make sense of her tragic death. She needs to be more of a grown-up now; no one has asked this of her but she feels it intuitively. She slides between the cool sheets and lies in the dark listening to waves lapping against the shore through the open window. It's so quiet here, with no background sounds off in the distance, no highways with trucks rumbling along, just the lapping waves. She folds her hands and closes her eyes, praying as she does every night. "Dear God, I know you are looking out for me and helping my mother in heaven. I miss you Mommy very much. But I'm happy to be here with Grammy May and she misses you, too. So does Daddy. He's off in Germany attending a conference, but you probably know that. Please don't worry about us. We are strong, just like you. We'll be okay." She pauses and then continues. "God, there is one thing I would like to ask, although I have no idea if you can make this happen. Grammy May is in such awful pain and is feeling terribly old. I hate to see her this way. If only she could be young again, even for just this week while I'm here, that would be so wonderful.

31

Can you make that happen? Can you make her look and feel the way she did when she was a younger woman? I hope so. But if not, that's okay. I realize you probably have a lot you need to do for others in heaven. It's okay if you can't, really. But I thought I'd ask. I love you so much Mommy. Not a day goes by that I don't think of you." Tears spill down her cheeks as she composes herself. "Goodnight, God. Goodnight, Mommy. Amen."

SUNDAY

Priscilla awakens the next morning to a scream echoing down the corridor from the far end of the house. She jumps from bed fearing something terrible is happening to Grammy May, but what she sees upon entering her great-grandmother's bathroom is far from terrible. Grammy May is standing in front of the large vanity mirror gazing in disbelief at the youthful face beaming back at her. It isn't a young face but isn't an old one either; it's the face she remembers from when she was around forty years old, not yet beaten down by life's hardships. Grammy May flexes her hands and rubs her shoulders, searching for something that should be there but is absent. Pain. All the pain she normally feels in her elbows, hands, shoulders, back, knees, now miraculously gone. She sees Priscilla standing behind her and turns to face her. "I'm dreaming, right?" her look combines fear with elation.

"No, Grammy May, we're awake. It's a miracle. Thank you, God!"

"What are you talking about, girl? I'm losing my mind, right? Is this a nursing home? Am I dead?"

"No, we're at home. I can't believe it. I prayed you could be young again and it's actually happened."

"That makes no sense," Grammy May looks lost. "People can't just go to bed old one night and wake up the next morning young again."

"Well, *you* did."

Grammy May walks out of the bathroom into the living room and stretches her arms high above her head. "I can't believe how limber I feel. I can stretch. Look, I can almost touch my toes again." Priscilla bounds up and down on the sofa, as happy as she's been in months. Grammy May walks over to the Steinway grand piano and plays one of her classic hits, "Black Coffee," singing and playing perfectly. Tears stream down her face as she finishes playing, the music transporting her back to memories of the adoring crowds, the lavish lifestyle as she was escorted around the world for concerts. She had been someone, and she feels this deep inside, her old self-esteem now returning. She can smell the roses the venues would place on the piano when she played. She can see the enthusiastic clapping fans in the front row, Blacks and whites united by her soulful playing. She thinks people are basically good and music helps reveal that commonality. All this modern bickering, people just need to listen to more music and spend less time shouting at strangers on social media.

They are interrupted by the unexpected buzzing of the doorbell. "Who could that be?" Grammy May rises from the piano bench and heads for the door, where she spies her nosy neighbor, Alice Kramlich, standing outside holding a container of cornmeal. Alice avoids the sun and her skin is as white now as it was back in March. Mabel thinks this is because she had skin cancer five years ago, although she never came out and said so. She's wearing her floppy straw hat and dark sunglasses.

"Is Mabel home?" she looks around suspiciously after the door opens.

It takes Mabel a moment to realize Alice doesn't recognize her as a young woman. Priscilla races over to help.

"Grammy May is visiting my father for the week. This is Aunt Peggy, who's staying here babysitting me."

Alice leans in for a closer look. "My goodness, you're the spitting image of Mabel. I'm surprised she didn't tell me she was going away when I borrowed her cornmeal the other day."

"It came up quickly," Grammy May, now the fictitious Peggy, is searching for a credible response. She goes on: "Priscilla's father had some legal matters to attend to with Mabel, so they're in Jackson."

"When do you expect her back?" Alice attempts to push her way inside but is blocked by Priscilla.

"Maybe as early as tomorrow, it all depends on how long it takes to wrap things up."

"Hmm," Alice doesn't look convinced. "Wasn't that the piano I just heard?"

"Oh, that was me. I was playing some of Mabel's music," Peggy says.

"My goodness. You play and sing so well."

"Thanks. I took lessons with her as a child, and she taught me a few of her popular songs."

"Anyway, here's the cornmeal back. Please let her know my cornbread came out even better than usual. I brought a few pieces for her, but you might as well eat them."

"Why, aren't you kind," Mabel takes the cornbread wrapped in tin foil.

"They're nice and moist," she turns to leave.

"I'm sure we'll enjoy them," Mabel pushes the door closed. They look out the window to make sure Alice is heading home and not skulking beyond the door. "Phew, that was a close call," Mabel sinks into the sofa. "Thank goodness you thought up that lie. Where in the world did you come up with the name Peggy?"

"Why, don't you like it? *Peggy?*" Priscilla has a mischievous smile overspreading her face. "It's what I call my stuffed Piglet back home. Plus, I think you look like a Peggy. Smart. Pretty. *Young.*"

"My word, let's not waste time sitting around here. When does this spell wear off?"

"I don't know. I asked for a week."

Mabel's eyes wander out to the lake. "Let's go for a swim. My goodness, I can't recall the last time I swam out there." They race to their rooms and put on bathing suits. Michelle kept a bathing suit in her dresser and Mabel is pleased to see it fits her new slim body. She grabs beach towels and the two young ladies bound down the back stairway to the lakefront. They spread towels on the small sandy beach and wade into the water. Mabel dives in and swims out to the float. She laughs as she pulls herself up using the metal ladder. "I haven't been able to get up on this float in decades." Priscilla swims to join her and the two sit dipping their toes in the warm lake water. Priscilla gazes at her great-grandmother and says: "You're so beautiful Grammy May. I mean Peggy. I hope I look like you when I'm your age."

Mabel smiles. "I was quite the beauty, if you must know, back in the day. Especially when I was around twenty-five. There were always boys chasing after me. Those were some fun times, filled with promise. But as I look back, I'm probably just nostalgic in a way that doesn't truly capture the challenges of the era. We tend to romanticize the past as we grow old."

"Do you still feel old on the inside, but look young on

37

the outside?"

Mabel pauses as if trying to align her thoughts with her new feelings. "I suppose I feel mentally the same as I did yesterday, but now have my old body and health back. Look at my hair. It's the way it was years ago. My energy level is so much higher, I'm all wound up, I can feel my heart racing. There's so much I want to do this week while I have the chance."

Priscilla leans back, soaking up the sun. "I just remembered we're going to Clarksdale with the doctor today. Should we cancel?"

Mabel smiles, remembering their date. "Absolutely not. Let's just tell him the Peggy story and see how things go. The thought of hanging out with an attractive young man like that for the day, with me looking like this? DAAMN. We better head inside so I can find some clothes to wear. Thank goodness I didn't throw everything away and kept an old trunk in the attic."

At noon, Doctor Roberts stands at the front door taken aback by the beautiful woman who greets him. He attempts to contain his emotions, but hears his voice crack as he asks if Mabel is home. He smiles at Priscilla standing off to the side. The young Mabel speaks. "I'm Peggy, Mabel's niece. She was unexpectedly called away to Jackson on a family matter with Priscilla's father, so I'm here looking after her."

Priscilla pushes her way onto the deck. "Hello, Doctor Roberts. We're hoping you'll still want to go to Clarksdale to visit the clubs there."

Peggy chimes in. "Yes, Mabel has taken me to Clarksdale many times, so I told her I'd be happy to show you around in her absence."

"Yes, of course, that would be great," the doctor is struggling to regain control of his voice, which keeps modulating higher despite his efforts. "Truly wonderful." This Peggy woman is quite extraordinary, dressed in a floral blouse and yellow skirt revealing shapely legs. He can see the familial resemblance to Mabel, with the same intelligence and humor in the eyes. As much as he misses touring Clarksdale with Mabel, Peggy is an unexpected stroke of good fortune. She notices the way he looks at her now, very different from the way he looked at her yesterday. It's that long forgotten spark of sexual attraction coming from a man. Mabel feels that somewhere around the age of fifty she became invisible to men. Ralph Ellison may have written the classic novel *Invisible Man,* but he had no idea what it's like to become an invisible woman. Heads no longer turned when she passed. No man approached her with lame one-liners when she was out with her girlfriends. It seemed so unfair, as though she had served her purpose by attracting at least one man to procreate with, and then was put out to pasture with all the other spent cows. The men grew more distinguished with age, while the women sagged and wrinkled. The men divorced their wives to date younger girls eager for financial security. Mabel isn't sure how to feel about this sudden change in his attentiveness as she stands at the doorway, this handsome doctor barely capable of speaking when confronted by her resurrected beauty. But why not, she thinks, let's have some fun while we can. She flirtatiously extends her hand so the doctor can help her descend the steep steps to his BMW convertible. Priscilla follows close behind, amused by her behavior.

The drive to Clarksdale takes just under an hour heading west from Sardis. Clarksdale is a small town despite its large place in history as an important migration hub for Blacks departing the South for northern cities following the Second World War. Automation within the cotton industry, coupled with the return of Black GIs from the war, meant the odds of finding good work in the North were much higher than in the South. And, as if to drive the new realities home, the railroad station was right there as a constant reminder of new freedoms, the tracks heading north out of Clarksdale for Memphis, St. Louis, and Chicago. Priscilla's father's dissertation, completed at Columbia University, focused on the unique social and philosophical challenges faced by these poor rural sharecroppers, suddenly thrust into the industrial age of America's northern cities, where a new form of racism awaited them. John had spent many hours walking the streets of Manhattan's Upper West Side, deep in thought, keenly aware of his own ancestors who possibly walked these same streets, lonely, cold, and frightened for their lives. The railroad station is right smack in the middle of Clarksdale, offering a sad promise of escape and hope; sad because much of that hope was misplaced, the grass not necessarily greener on the other side, the sleepy southern beauty left behind not to be found in the cold northern cities. Mabel would have been eighteen in 1948, and as a girl from a middle-class family, was excited about starting undergraduate college next year. What she remembers about that time period is falling in love for the first time, with Kenny Taylor. She thinks 1947 might have been the year she and Kenny first saw Muddy Waters make his triumphant return from Chicago, playing new music on his shiny electric guitar, probably the first time she heard that instrument. Muddy grew up in a shack over on the old Stovall Plantation and there are Stovalls still in Clarksdale, as well as Messengers, who opened the first African American business in Clarksdale at the start of the twentieth century.

Doctor Roberts parks his BMW across from the Delta Blues Museum, which they agreed would be the best place to start their tour. The doctor exits the car so he can open the door for Peggy. She swings her shapely legs out the door and notices the look he gives her as he takes her hand and helps her from the low seat. Priscilla jumps out from the back seat, happy to be done with the car ride.

"Let me pay," he insists as they enter the museum, and Peggy doesn't protest.

Priscilla is carrying a pamphlet highlighting the museum's collection and is eager to see the Muddy Waters shack that has been preserved and moved inside the museum from the old Stovall Plantation. But upon seeing it, she is disappointed. It's not much to look at, but Peggy helps bring the display to life as she reads the sign: *McKinley Morganfield (April 4, 1913 – April 30, 1983), later known as Muddy Waters, is often cited as the father of modern Chicago blues. A native of Clarksdale, he used to play on the porch at the old Stovall Plantation. In 1941, Alan Lomax from the Library of Congress recorded him at the house."* She stops reading and turns to Priscilla: "See, some poor old sharecropper's son, dirt poor, followed his passions all the way to fame and fortune. Isn't that something?"

"You have a nice display here, too, Grammy—"

"Excuse me?" Doctor Roberts cuts her off, confused.

"Silly me . . . I meant to say that Grammy May has a nice display here," Priscilla covers up best she can. There is an awkward silence as the doctor glances at them in confusion.

"Well, I'll be sure to tell Mabel we saw her display when we speak on the phone tonight," Peggy adds.

The doctor gazes into Peggy's eyes. "It's truly weird how much you look like her. How did you say you're related?"

"I'm her niece, on my father's side."

"Well, the resemblance is uncanny. Where do you call home?"

"San Francisco," Peggy wisely picks a location far away in case he ever gets ideas about visiting.

"You like it there?"

"I *love* it. There's so much more to do in a big city than here in the rural south. I wonder why you chose to work here when I imagine you had other options."

The doctor sighs, casting a downward glance. She can see the pain on his face and attempts to change the subject. "It *is* a lovely part of the country, no doubt about it."

The doctor rolls his tongue around in his cheek, as if clearing out a bad taste before speaking. He lifts his head in a look mixing sadness and perseverance and says: "I came here in part to get away from my girlfriend. Ex-girlfriend."

"Oh, I'm sorry."

"Well, it's probably good for me to talk about it as I really need to move on."

"If I may, how long has it been?"

"Three years."

"No, I'm not asking how long you were together, I'm asking how long since you split—"

"Three years. Don't laugh, please. We were very much in love and I was jolted when she rejected my marriage proposal. She was the one true love for me and I don't expect to find another woman like her. So I'm down here hiding out for now, attempting to rebuild a new life. Fight or flight, I guess I chose the latter."

Peggy sees the tears in his eyes and reaches across to touch him on the forearm. "I'm so sorry. But, I don't believe there's only one true love for each person. Life is the sum of all the friends and loves we carry inside. Be open to finding someone new and it will happen when you least expect it."

He smiles. "That's a nice sentiment. Anyway, I used to think if I waited she'd date other men and realize we were the ideal match, but then I read she married last year, so the door is shut. Not only did she marry someone else, but he's an NFL quarterback who recently signed a contract for sixty million dollars. Maybe you've heard of him. Luther Buck."

"I'm not much of a football fan, so no, I haven't heard of him. But that's quite the name, if you ask me."

He smiles. "Tell me about it. The Luther part sounds about right."

Peggy cannot restrain her laughter. "I mean, Luther Buck sounds like a male stripper's name."

44

"Stop it," he manages a smile. "That would be Buck Naked."

She cannot stop, as she puts on a syrupy soap opera voice. "Luther Buck lowers himself over Tawny-Jo's heaving breasts revealing his hungry manhood."

"Stop, please. I'm going to bust a gut," he is bent over in hysterics. "Plus, we're standing here at a shrine to a great American musician. Show some respect."

They wander through the museum, past the guitar display where they stop to read about an Eric Clapton guitar and the influence of the Delta blues on Clapton, the Rolling Stones, and the many other famous rock-and-roll stars that followed. Peggy leans in pretending to read from one of the display signs: "Luther Buck was a poor good-for-nothing who was run over by the Clarksdale train one fine summer evening while attempting to tie his left sneaker. Once a great football star, Luther ended up dirt poor with no one in his life at all, no one to love him. His poor wife Tawny-Jo fell into a deep despair as she lived out her life full of regrets for rejecting the proposal of the famous Doctor Roberts, who cured both cancer and the common cold, all before the age of fifty."

"You're a funny one."

"Well, might as well laugh away life's pains, that's my view. Time is fleeting and there's no point wallowing in a past that can't be resurrected. Well, I suppose in some cases it can be—"

Priscilla laughs at their inside joke. They head off for the Charlie Musselwhite room, leaving the doctor behind wondering what exactly is going on with these two. He follows them and reads about Musselwhite, who was appropriately named given he was white unlike most of the musicians displayed within the museum. The doctor catches up to the ladies. "Turns out Musselwhite is from Mississippi, too. Maybe I made the right move coming here given all the musical celebrities."

Peggy laughs. "Yeah, right. Mississippi is *the* place to go if you're looking to become the next great surgeon or doctor or just about anything."

"Don't tell me you're one of those West Coast liberal EEE-lites," he exaggerates the first letter, poking fun at her.

"Damn straight I am, and a proud one at that. Don't be telling me you're one of those crazy—"

"Whoa, take it easy. My, you're a feisty one."

Peggy blushes in the realization she's once again gone and wound herself up over politics. Not a smart move when you've got just one week as a young woman and are lucky enough to find yourself in the company of a smart and handsome younger man. She rubs her right hand through her hair, and then redirects the conversation as one might expect when in the company of a distracted two-year-old. "It's such a beautiful day, what do you say we go for a walk around town and then grab a bite to eat."

The three of them step outside into the midday heat, the sun at the apex of its intensity beating down upon the sleepy southern town. They spot a young couple sheltering beneath a lovely willow tree in the park across the way. The couple looks to be deeply in love, hugging one another and laughing, oblivious to their surroundings, without a care in the world about what others might think of their public display of affection. Peggy remembers that feeling, the ones she felt way back in high school, when the world was her oyster, when endless possibilities of an unquestioned future stretched out before her like a path of smooth shells leading to the shore. She pauses to glance at the young lovers. She understands this young couple has no idea how difficult life will get, and if they did, how they'd probably never get up from their happy spot in the shade beneath the willow. Truth is, if people knew what was going to happen to them, nothing much would ever get done. She chuckles to herself at this thought.

The doctor interrupts her reverie. "It's too hot to be wandering outside for long. I see here on my phone that Wade's is the locals' preferred hangout for good food and music, so let's head over there."

They make their way through the bright midday streets, no shadows evident with the sun directly overhead, on down past the old Rexall drugstore, still in business on the corner despite all the chain store competition surrounding the town, past the post office where a wilted U.S. flag hangs listlessly in the breezeless heat. Peggy and Priscilla follow close behind the doctor, who taps his phone repeatedly along the way, looking up occasionally, following the map directions to Wade's with a surgeon's precision. Peggy can't help but notice he has a mighty fine butt, and she releases an involuntary *hmm, hmm*, becoming increasingly aware of the long dormant sexual desire rising up from its buried past. How she'd like to squeeze those tight buns given the chance. It's as if her physical being is experiencing a reawakening to those long-forgotten feelings of her youthful days as a touring celebrity, back when she was always faithful to her jerk of a husband because of her deeply held religious morality, except now she possesses the wisdom of an old lady short on time, who regrets not having had more sexual experiences. Back then, women mostly obeyed "their man" and didn't fool around, but nowadays, what she gathers from the modern sexual culture all around her—the culture of noncommittal hookups and rap songs with lyrics that shock her but that she understands as an artist, these lyrics both vulgar and poetic, making their way to eager listeners through our collective

48

protections of freedom of expression—she understands that feminism is inextricably tied to sexual freedoms, the same ones men have enjoyed forever. Her granddaughter Michelle turned her on to Cardi B, Gary Clark, Jr., and Drake, and she likes them all, but especially Drake. She understands this freedom of artistic expression better than most, given many of her early hit songs were considered too racy at the time. Why, back then, as people would say, *white people and Negroes shouldn't be dancing together, especially in the South.* So what did she do? Married a white man and did her best to ignore the many disapproving glances, the worst of these from avid fans, who upon seeing her husband join her after a set, would look aghast and slink away. But sometimes there were fights. She recalls remembering, sometime not long ago, as she was listening to ragtime records at home, about a story involving a studio musician playing a gig back in the Roaring Twenties, audiences of wealthy society folks and the all-Black performers, how this old-timer recalled a night at a club in Alabama when the drummer in the orchestra was flirting with some blonde girl in the front row, who apparently was impressed with more than his playing, and who at the end of the set walked up onstage in her fancy dress and jewelry and kissed him smack on the lips. All holy hell broke loose. He hightailed it out of there with rednecks chasing him into the rain for blocks before he got away. Mabel thinks, yes, there has been plenty of progress over the past hundred years, but there's still so far to go. She snaps back to the present and realizes she is lagging behind Priscilla and Richard. She catches up and a few blocks later they are facing a small nondescript building. Richard looks confused, the reality in front of him not matching what he envisioned on the map. "I guess this must be it, at least according to Google. Not much to look at," he is having second thoughts. A street person appears around the corner, pushing a shopping cart loaded with junk. He's an older white man, wisps of hair flying helter-skelter from his head, dirt smudged on tanned face. "Yawls thinkin' 'bouts headin' into Wade's?"

"Possibly," the doctor turns to face him. Peggy protectively takes Priscilla's delicate little hand, concerned they've wandered into a bad part of town.

"Well, you cain't do bettah than Wade's. Plus they've got some live music goin' on shortly."

"Thank you," Peggy replies as she whispers to Richard. "I'm thinking maybe we should go back to the blues club we passed on the main drag."

"SHE-it. You don't wanna eat that tourist monkey vomit swill they sehve ova they-ah," the old man pushes his cart closer. "If you axe me, Wade's has the best music and food in town. The catfish lunch special is to die for."

"Or maybe to die from," Richard whispers under his

breath.

"Listen up, how'd yawls like to help out an old street phil-os-o-phah. Everything in my cart is just a buck. I got this woman's brassiere that looks about right for this fine lady, if you axe me," his yellow teeth flash behind a mischievous smile. He leans in a little too close for comfort.

They stand back, mouths agape, as he hoists an old Playtex bra from the cart and dangles it in front of the doctor's face. "No, thanks, but here, let me give you a dollar," Richard reaches into his wallet, eager to put an end to this embarrassment.

"You showah you don't want to buy somethin'? I ain't asking for no charity, you know. I get by just fine on my own, workin' haad for each and every dollah."

The doctor scans the cart and sees a copy of *Man and His Symbols*. "How about I pay you a dollar for the Jung book?"

"Yes Sir-eeee," the old man reaches inside and passes the paperback edition to Richard. "That's a fine selection, one of my favorites."

Richard looks at the other books in the cart and sees they are all philosophy and religion books. Emmanuel Kant, Heidegger, Malcolm X, Freud, Nietsche, Thomas Merton. "That's quite a collection you've got there. Looks like someone was unloading their philosophy library and you hit gold."

"DAAMN, I didn't hit no gold. I'm always on the lookout for these books. You'd be amazed what you can find at the dump's bargain barn, or out on the streets when the rich folks are movin'. One thing I cain't stand, is people throwin' away great books."

Richard stands there for a moment attempting to size up this strange man, his blue eyes the color of Caribbean waters, his street talk at odds with his appearance. He hands him the dollar.

The old man continues. "Trust me when I tell you, this is the best food and music in town. Ordah the catfish lunch special."

They head into Wade's leaving the street person behind. As is true of many of the world's outstanding establishments, Wade's on the inside belies the rundown exterior. There is a small crowd enjoying lunch, lawyers and bankers, plus a few daring tourists with children who have ventured off the beaten path in search of local color. The inside is flooded in red chili lights strewn along the rafters, the walls covered in a proud selection of old Mississippi license plates, black and white photos of the town from the nineteenth century, and vintage guitars stuck to the wall next to the stage. The stage is small and features a Baldwin upright piano, a Ludwig drum set, and a vocalist stand, the current performers apparently on break. They grab a table a few feet from the bar and an elderly man approaches and fills their water glasses, inquiring if anyone wants cocktails or just lunch.

Peggy looks at Richard and they nod in unison that cocktails are a good idea. "How about two Manhattans for us and a ginger ale for the young lady?"

"Wait a minute," Priscilla objects, her matter-of-fact tone jarring him. "I'll have a root beer, please."

A few minutes later the drinks arrive and they all order the catfish sandwich with Havarti cheese, lettuce, tomato, and a spicy red sauce. Their lunches arrive ten minutes later and they order another round of drinks. Three musicians take the stage and play an impressive set of jazz standards, the female singer possessing a husky, sexy voice as she sings "You've Changed," a song Peggy knows well from her days hanging out with Sarah Vaughn. How Sarah could sing. What days those were, little did she know at the time, she was living through a heyday of the convergence of the blues with soul, rock, and jazz. The sandwiches are exceptional, with homemade chips and delicious coleslaw on the side. Apparently, the street person not only has great taste in books but also food.

"I'm glad we discovered this place," Peggy says as the song comes to an end.

"Me too," the doctor wipes his mouth and leans back in his chair feeling very relaxed and happy, loosening up from the drinks. The trio plays a few more tunes, culminating with an up-tempo version of "So Nice," a Gilberto standard Peggy has forgotten all about. The trio wraps up their set, and as the young singer walks past their table, Peggy looks up and says: "You sing beautifully. Thank you for brightening up our day."

"Why isn't that nice, thanks so much," she stops abruptly and motions to her bandmates to move along.

"I had forgotten all about the music of Gilberto. I used to play a lot of that Brazilian music including—"

"I didn't know you played," Richard looks up.

"Yes, I've been known to tickle the ivories on occasion."

"What a musical family you have," he says.

"Thanks."

Richard adds: "I wish I'd brought my harmonica with me so we could jam."

"Maybe another time or back at the house."

"Mind if I join you?" the singer asks.

"By all means," Peggy shuffles her chair off to the right so there is space for one more. "Do you perform here often?"

"No, in fact this is my first time playing here. I live in New York but had to come down to look after my father. He's not doing so well."

"Oh, sorry to hear that," Peggy pats her hand.

"My name's Lizzy Smith, thanks for letting me sit with you." She is one of those wan white girls who look like they

54

don't eat much. Her auburn hair is pulled back tightly into a bun, with a single earring dangling from her left earlobe. The right side of her face looks like it's doing a disproportionate amount of the heavy lifting in engaging with others; much like a stroke patient, her left side is less alive. There is immense light beaming from that ocean-green right eye, and Peggy takes an immediate liking to her. Peggy thinks Lizzy looks hungry so offers the other half of her sandwich, which at first she shakes her head no, but as Peggy slides her plate toward her, she accepts.

"They pay you well here?" Peggy asks.

"God, no," Lizzy wipes a crumb from her chin. "We get paid ten dollars per show. Plus, one drink each. This is my first and probably last show here. I need to find a real job. But I'm not sure how long I'll be in town. My boyfriend wants me back soon, and not with my father in tow. So that creates some problems, if you know what I mean."

"Sorry to hear that," Richard leans in.

The street person is causing a commotion by the entry door, mumbling something about self-reliance and the failures of contemporary civilizations. They turn to see what's happening and Lizzy gets up and rushes to the door. "Colin, come on, you're creating a scene."

"That guy just stole the bra from my cahht," he is sweating profusely as Lizzy leads him to the table.

"Let it go, it's no big deal."

"Some jerk in a MAGA hat," Colin looks like he's on a bad mix of speed and booze. Lizzy gestures toward an open seat and Colin sits down, staring over his shoulder at the entryway, neck twitching. They make room, all squished together. The acrid stench of chalky streets and his sweat takes any pleasure from their lunch.

Colin mumbles: "America is like a ship in a giant swell, rollin' left, heavin' right, people pukin' on each othah, day and night."

Richard laughs. "That ain't bad. You just make that up?"

"I'm a street poet, and don't you know it."

"Colin's an interesting man," Lizzy says. "I met him two days ago when I got to town. He's been helping me figure things out, plus he got me this gig," she passes what's left of her sandwich to him.

"Colin Lodge," he extends his dirt-smudged hand to Richard, who declines to take it.

"Be that way. I spose I wouldn't want to touch me neithah."

Peggy is squeezed between Lizzy and Colin. "Lizzy has such a wonderful, sultry voice," she says.

Colin leans in to take a closer look at Peggy. "Damn, you remind me of someone but I cain't for the life of me figure who. Have I seen you 'round?"

"Other than when we were walking in, no," she replies.

"Well, I'll be damned, you look awful familiah to me. You didn't teach at Haa-vid back in the sixties?"

"Afraid not. What makes you ask that?"

Lizzy interjects. "Colin was a professor at Harvard back then, or so it seems—"

"Really?" the doctor looks up in surprise. "What did you teach?"

Colin laughs. "Wud do you think a street poet who looks like this would have taught? Phil-ah-so-pheeee."

They laugh even though Doctor Roberts assumes he's joking. Yet those books in the cart make him wonder.

"I see you. I see you," Colin leans in. "Okay, so maybe it wasn't Haa-Vid, maybe it was Tufts. It was a long time ago."

"C'mon, Mad Professor. We should leave these nice people alone. Thanks for the sandwich and it was a pleasure meeting you all," Lizzy gets up and grabs Colin by the arm.

"Aren't you playing another set?" Peggy looks up, disappointed.

"Nah, we're done for the day. But if you play, you should. Just go ahead, they don't care here. During the day lots of people wander in and play. Most suck so you've got nothing to be embarrassed about. It's an okay piano."

Peggy looks down, shyly. "No, thanks, I'm really not any

good."

"What do you mean? You're great!" Priscilla is bouncing in her seat. "Please, play a tune for us."

"Yeah, c'mon Peggy, I'd love to hear you," Richard motions toward the stage. "Let's see how you stack up against your Aunt Mabel."

"Mabel Johnson!" Colin bangs his hand on the table so hard they all jump back. "Damn, that's who you remind me of, back when she was young."

"I'm her youngest brother's daughter," Peggy says. She realizes she hasn't thought up a last name and spots a pack of cigarettes on an adjacent table and continues: "Peggy Winston. I'm visiting from the West Coast."

"Well, you look just the way she did. It's uncanny. I used to go listen to her up in Bah-stin, when she played at the Jazz Workshop. They don't make 'em like that anymoah, that's for sure."

Richard is puzzled by this strange man, who has a certain patrician bearing despite the disheveled appearance and street talk. "Boston, you say. Interesting. And I suppose you're descended from the old Boston Brahmin Lodges?"

"Funny," Colin pulls back a bit, hands dangling between his legs as he gazes off into the distance. "Yeah, like a fancy Boston family Lodge would be down and out in Mississippi pushing an ol' cart around."

Peggy decides it would be fun to play in public again. "All right, I'll play just one tune. Lizzy, would you mind helping me adjust the piano mic?"

"Sure, hang tight Colin and I'll be right back." After Lizzy has gotten Peggy situated at the piano she heads toward the door with Colin in tow, but pulls up abruptly upon hearing the music. Mabel has launched into one of her classics, "Black Coffee," and she rocks soulfully on the piano bench with perfect posture, happily on stage for the first time in more than twenty years. Her fingers glide along the keyboard, the correct notes coming back to her easily, the muscle memory of so many performances and practice sessions taking hold. She loves this hit song of hers and plays quite possibly the best rendition she has ever performed live, due to the fact she knows she's an old woman getting another chance, if just for one week, and the old happiness she felt when playing is a happiness unmatched by any other. Music is deeply embedded in her soul. The people in the bar become quiet, listening intently, as she rocks slowly on the piano bench, her playing and singing several steps above the typical fare. The club owner stands off to the side of the bar, and when she finishes playing, loud applause rocks the club. She gets up from the piano bench, takes a very professional bow, and walks back to the table.

Colin says: "SHE-it, you sound *exactly* like the Mabel

Johnson I remember. Ain't that somethin' else, the musical gene and the way it runs through families."

"Don't be silly," Peggy sits down. "I'm no Mabel, even though she did give me lessons when she could."

"But she is her relative," Priscilla hammers it home, just in case he is suspicious.

Colin claps his hands. "Lordy, lordy, if you don't sound just like her. Wade," he calls out to the club owner, "you need to book this lady and fast. And don't be payin' her shit like you do everyone else. This is Mabel Johnson's niece. Imagine what a draw she'd be."

Wade strolls over. He's a bald white man with a long gray beard reaching down to the middle of his chest. His coal black eyes are slightly too close together. Peggy thinks he resembles an old southern rocker, maybe someone like Billy Gibbons from ZZ Top, whom she met years ago at the Grammy Awards. "Hey there, I'm Wade Ferguson," he introduces himself. "That was an awesome song, really enjoyed it. Might you consider comin' back and playin' this week when the crowds get bigger? The blues festival starts this weekend, so I'm expectin' decent turnouts this week."

Priscilla stands up. "What will you pay her?"

Wade is caught off guard by her question. He is a very tall man and gazes down on Priscilla.

"I dunno, how about $50 a night?"

"Or how about 40% of the door," she surprises him.

He lowers himself to size up this odd girl, his beard accidentally brushing her head. "My, aren't you one tough little negotiator. I can't be paying that much. No one gets that here."

Priscilla stands firm. "Then no one gets to hear the great Peggy Winston. Let's just get the check and go home," she starts walking away.

Wade doesn't quite know what to make of this spunky girl. He turns back to Peggy. "So really? You're related to Mabel?"

"I am."

"Well, I guess if I promote you that way we should be able to draw a good crowd, so how 'bout I give you 25% of the door?"

"She'll take it," Richard interjects, much to Priscilla's visible dismay.

"C'mon, doctor. Don't be caving so easily."

Peggy smiles. "Look, add in free meals for the three of us this week while we're here and I'll accept 25%."

"You got it. Come back tomorrow and I'll start spreading the word on social media and local radio. Plan to play two sets. One at five and another at seven."

"Will it be okay for Priscilla to come?" Peggy asks Wade.

"Sure. This is a family-friendly place. You can have dinner between sets. Kids are welcome as long as they're with their parents and behave."

Peggy pats Priscilla on the head and they turn to leave.

"We'll see you tomorrow, then."

On the way back to the car Peggy says: "I've got a whole lot of practicing to do between now and tomorrow night."

Richard, the perfect gentleman, opens the car door for her. "Let me pick you up and bring you home for your shows this week. This is the most excitement I've had in a long time. Man, I cannot get over how beautifully you play and sing," he closes her door and walks around to his side.

Peggy smiles demurely. The way he was just looking at her makes it clear he likes more than the way she plays the piano.

MONDAY

M abel is up early the next morning practicing scales and several of her hit songs, fingers gliding effortlessly and without pain up and down the keyboard of her Steinway grand. She wonders how much of the magic coming from her fingertips is of her own making and how much is coming from a higher power. She likes to think it's a bit of both. She gazes outside through the wall of windows facing the lakefront, and is dismayed to see several annoying streaks from the inadequate window washing she attempted last week, streaks she didn't notice then with her poor vision. But now that her senses have returned to their more youthful condition, these streaks jump out at her. Her attention drifts to the antique walnut table in the corner—a gift from her agent many years ago—and she obsesses over the dust surrounding her stack of unread magazines: *Variety, House and Garden,* and the *New Yorker.* She recalls trying more than once to cancel her subscriptions but has been unable to work her way through the maze of blocking systems and foreign-speaking humans put in place to minimize cancellations. The young man she finally reached at the *New Yorker* managed to guilt her into adding on three years at a 50% discount. He had said something along the lines of: *it's important now more than ever to support quality journalism,* and she couldn't argue with that, especially since she has more money coming in than she can possibly spend. Her music sales increased exponentially once Apple made downloading music so easy, and her recent royalties have been as high as they were back in the seventies. She knows how lucky she is, not having to worry about money the way so many of her elderly friends do, and she has been generous donating to many local and national charities focused on helping the poor and elderly.

Down the sloping lawn she sees the stump where a gorgeous magnolia once stood. Her landscapers were supposed to remove it two years ago but have either forgotten or have been taking advantage of her poor eyesight and declining memory. She misses working in the garden the way she once did, getting her hands dirty pulling weeds, planting annuals and perennials. She thinks she'll use some of this week of her newfound youth to tend to the garden. She is startled to discover she has finished the song "Misty" without paying any conscious attention to her playing, the notes deeply ingrained through decades of repeated practice and performance, all part of her autonomic functioning, allowing her to play while being mentally absent. She had relied on this ability to be simultaneously present and absent while grinding her way through several rigorous international tours during her heyday. She recalls how she tried to take breaks back then but there were so many people dependent upon her for their livelihoods, she always consented and soldiered onwards.

Mabel has played these songs thousands and thousands of times over the years without listening intently to her playing the way she did as a young musician. Now that she can play again, she decides to improvise, to play something completely new, something unique to her, without judging. She begins by playing some Scriabin she vaguely recalls from her classical training, and then branches off into an improvisation blending classical with jazz. Mabel explores extended chord structures, forcing herself to avoid anything she has played before, to truly try and find new ground. The piano sounds amazing to her as she bows her head down toward the keyboard as if asleep, feeling very much alive and aware as she takes artistic risks in ways she hasn't in decades. Her fans always wanted to hear the songs they knew so well, not experimentations. She had been pegged early on as a jazz and blues singer and was carefully managed by her record label to capitalize on this reputation, this easy familiarity, despite the fact she wanted to branch out artistically, especially after she had earned a small fortune. But the people managing her cared more about money than art. When she is done improvising, she reaches for a notebook and writes down some of what she just played for subsequent analysis and possible development into new music. It's been so long since she wrote music, and she can feel her heart beating steadily against her rib cage.

She gets up and sits on the couch facing the central fieldstone fireplace. She's amused and looking forward to playing in public again under the guise of this new Peggy Winston. She realizes she needs to be careful not to sound too much like the polished Mabel Johnson, so will be sure to add a few flubs to avoid scrutiny, although no one in their right mind would ever believe that through some divine intervention she has been made young again. It will be difficult not to play as well as the true Mabel, but given the unfortunate circumstance that the street person, Colin Lodge, recalls hearing her back in Boston, she needs to be careful. Maybe she'll try playing the new song she was just improvising and that way be likely to make noticeable mistakes. In fact, she should not be playing much of Mabel's music at all, and needs to develop her own unique songbook, so back to the piano she goes for the next two hours writing music.

Priscilla comes out of her room where she's been reading, and Mabel immediately stops playing, surprised to see it's now mid-morning.

"Priscilla, my word, I've lost track of time with all my piano playing. Have you had breakfast?"

"Yes, Grammy May, I walked right past you two hours ago but you didn't even notice, and I wanted to leave you alone to practice for the *Big Show* tonight," she teases.

"Be nice," Grammy May smiles as she takes her great-granddaughter's hand and leads her to the couch. She sees that Priscilla is carrying a small notepad.

"Have you been writing?"

"I've been working on a believable story for us to tell people who ask about you. *Peggy Winston.* I mean, have you even thought about all the questions you're going to be asked as the super-hot piano playing relative of Mabel Johnson?"

"Super-hot?"

"Yes, super-hot. Don't pretend you don't see it, too. And the way the doctor looks at you, well, we better figure out a good story to tell him at least."

Mabel realizes she has a point. She's been so excited about her return to youth she hasn't given much thought of how to deal with others. She taps her index finger against her chin. "I suppose you're right. So, what have you come up with there in your little notepad?"

"Well, it's good you said you're from San Francisco and only here for the week, so if you and the doctor get too close, he knows you'll be gone. So hopefully he won't want to get close, but judging by the way you were looking all lovey-dovey at each other last night, I have my doubts."

"Was it that obvious?"

Priscilla folds her left leg beneath her right in a frog position, adjusting herself on the couch. "Yeah, you both looked like one of those gross couples on "The Bachelor," a program I detest but one my mother always had on the tube."

Mabel looks sad, recalling how her daughter Violet watched too much television. She has never gotten over the guilt she feels for the lonely life young Violet was forced to live with her famous mother touring the globe. She tried to bring her on one or two tours a year so she could see the world and they could be together, but when Mabel finally summoned the courage to divorce Violet's deadbeat father, there was little choice but to send her off to boarding school. Mabel likes to think Violet enjoyed boarding school, and the truth is she did for the most part, but the disappearance of both parents when she was an awkward thirteen-year-old could not have been easy. Mabel thinks this experience was critical to the development of the tough veneer she noticed on her daughter's demeanor in subsequent years. Violet spent much of her childhood parked in front of the television and this was unfair. And now, just like that, not only is she gone, but so is Michelle. Tears well in Mabel's eyes.

"Why are you sad, Grammy May?"

She pulls herself together. "No reason. I was just remembering something. What were we discussing?"

"Your backstory, as the screenwriters might say."

She laughs. "Yes, of course. What did you have in mind? You named me Peggy, so why don't you take the lead."

Priscilla sits up straight, looking very serious. "Well, at first I thought you could be a technology lawyer working in Silicon Valley, but you don't strike me as the lawyer type. You're a little too pretty to be a tech nerd. So then I was thinking fashion model, but that seems like a stretch. Nothing personal—"

"Continue, please."

"So, then I landed on an airline stewardess. That way you're never in one place for very long and if someone goes digging into your past, you'll be more difficult to track down."

"And how do we explain my piano playing ability?"

"What . . . you don't think stewardesses can play the piano?"

Mabel realizes she's being a snob. "Of course they can. But how many can play as well as I do? Frankly, I've been worrying about my performances this week. I need to be good but not too good. You know what I mean? But let's continue along this path. Who do I work for?"

"I've got you pegged as a perky United Airlines stewardess. You know, beautiful, sort of unapproachable.

Not particularly bright—"

"I see you've really thought this through."

"I have. In fact, I looked at their routes and think we should say you work international flights, mostly to Asia. That way there's no reason for you to be back here in Mississippi."

"Right. So . . . what else can you tell me about Peggy Winston?"

"You and Mabel had a fight years ago and have not been close since. But with my mother's death, you've stepped up to help while she's grieving. This is why you volunteered to fly here to look after me this week."

"Yes, that makes sense."

"But when you were young, your family lived in Columbia, South Carolina, not far from Mabel's family in Atlanta, and Mabel gave you piano lessons when you visited. And then you studied her music over the years and learned to play many of her popular hits."

Mabel is gazing at the annoying streaks on the windows, determined to clean them before her week of youth is up. Assuming she only gets one week. She's not sure how she feels about staying young longer than a week. She glances at Priscilla and adds to the fantasy: "And, I also learned to play my own music. Yes, that works. I can play some of her songs and then some of these new ones I've been fiddling with this morning. In fact, I'm thinking my sets tonight will be partly her music and mostly my own new improvisations."

"Excellent idea," Priscilla gets up to answer the telephone in the kitchen.

"Who is it?" Mabel calls out.

Priscilla returns with the cordless phone and whispers, "It's the hunky doctor."

Mabel sits up and swipes her left hand through her hair, amazed not to find the tangled mess, but instead her former short-cropped Afro. She's been thinking it would be nice to get her hair done this week for one of the shows. "Hello, Richard," she says. A lengthy silence ensues and then she continues: "Sure, if you want to come by and make us lunch, I won't stop you." A few moments pass. "Oh, my. Pasta Puttanesca sounds fabulous. Let me make a salad. Okay, we'll see you at noon."

Richard arrives at noon with a full grocery bag and follows Mabel into the kitchen. She senses him behind her, admiring her figure. This is a feeling she has forgotten, being sized up by a man, and she's ambivalent, on the one hand enjoying feeling attractive but on the other hand remembering what a nuisance men can be, how needy and grabby. Mabel is impressed with the #metoo movement and was harassed many

71

times in her past by agents and record producers, but always had to stay quiet to avoid retribution from the men holding all the power. She respects the many brave women who have come forward after years of repressing the hurts they experienced at the hands of powerful film producers, news anchors, and businessmen. She's not sure she likes this old feeling of being eyed by a man, despite the surge of passion she feels flooding inside. It's all terribly confusing. She is reminded of how she felt when first reaching puberty, when sudden overwhelming sexual desire appeared out of the blue—one day playing with dolls, the next interested in boys. She had been a great student until her adolescence, when she suddenly played the piano less and wasted too much time primping for boys' attention, even pretending not to be smart to avoid threatening their fragile egos. Talk about stupid.

She had felt relief when she reached menopause and became less interested in the urges that sprang from below, and more interested in those that sprang from above. It almost felt like she was picking up her life where it left off at age twelve, before puberty took her brain away. Now staring at Priscilla, she sees herself back then, a bright and earnest girl happily making her way through a world of innocence not yet lost. But then she realizes Priscilla has just lost her mother and the loss of innocence is well underway. What kind of a future can she expect with her father, who most likely will remarry, and will Priscilla be loved as much by a stepmother as by Michelle?

She sighs in full acknowledgment that the old sexual desire is back, a mixed blessing, a necessary part of her being young again. Richard is looking lost in the kitchen so she helps him unpack the groceries and pulls out the cooking pots and skillet he will need. He is wearing khaki shorts and she sees he has nicely shaped legs, muscular thighs connecting to thin calves and delicate ankles. If he were a horse, he'd be a thoroughbred, not a heavy horse.

He catches her admiring his ankles. "Something interesting down there?" he looks amused. She notices what a beautiful smile he has, white teeth flashing from behind full lips. He has a strong square jaw, his beard neatly trimmed, and she fantasizes about feeling that beard rubbing against her cheek.

She flushes with embarrassment. "You caught me. I was just noticing what nice legs you have. Not many men do, you know."

"Can't say I've spent a whole lot of time admiring other men's legs, but thank you for the compliment," he is boiling water on the stove for the pasta. "I might add your legs are lovely, too," he is feeling emboldened. He carries himself with a degree of self-satisfied swagger, with the cockiness of a high achiever accustomed to getting what he wants, despite the recent wounds from his lost love. "So, tell me, are you nervous about playing in public tonight?"

"No, I'm fine. I've been practicing this morning."

"I can't get over how great you sounded last night. There's no way I'm gonna play harmonica with you, you'd shame me."

"Oh, I doubt that. Did you bring it with you?"

"No, it's safely at home where only I have to listen to my poor playing."

"Well, you should bring it over here. Maybe we can jam together?"

"That would be a *huge* mistake."

Priscilla comes in from her bedroom and announces excitedly, "I've just been on Skype with Daddy, it's seven hours later in Germany than here . . ." she pulls up short seeing the doctor, and realizes she has messed up.

He looks at them with a quizzical expression scrawled across his face. "I thought you said your father is with Mabel in Jackson?"

There is a prolonged and revealing silence as they realize they've been caught in a lie, and are uncertain how to recover. Finally, Priscilla speaks, deciding bold-faced denial is the best strategy, something she learned from observing powerful politicians on television. "No, we told you my father is in Germany at a conference."

"I'm quite certain you said Mabel is with him in Jackson at the lawyer's attending to family matters."

"I think you misheard," Mabel interjects. "My aunt is in Jackson attending to legal matters while Priscilla's father is in Germany. That's why she had to go, as John is not available to sign the papers concerning his wife's will."

Richard grabs the cast iron skillet from next to the stove and adds three tablespoons of extra virgin olive oil, a half cup of oil-cured black olives, and a can of whole plum tomatoes. He stirs the sauce, looking confused. "I'm known for having a photographic memory, and I'm positive you told me he was with her in Jackson."

"Well, I guess your photographic memory must not be clicking very well," Priscilla stands firm.

The doctor looks puzzled. "Peggy, do you expect Mabel back in time to hear you perform tonight?"

"No, she called earlier saying it's taking longer than anticipated. She wants to go to Michelle's house and bring her clothing to the Salvation Army while John's away, something he's been unable to deal with emotionally," she says, realizing as the lie escapes her lips that the doctor might not buy the idea of Mabel venturing out on her own at her age.

Richard samples the sauce.

"Look at you, mister fancy chef," Mabel attempts a redirection. "Are you going to put anchovies in there, too?"

"I didn't want to presume you'd like them."

"What kind of Puttanesca sauce doesn't have anchovies?" she reaches up in her cupboard and pulls down a small tin. "You do like them, yes?"

"Absolutely. It's just I know many people don't."

"Well I'm not *many people*," she laughs as she adds the anchovies to the sauce. "Do you know what Puttanesca means?"

"Should I?"

"Well, you know what puta means, right?"

"Not exactly."

"C'mon, doctor. Where've you been hiding out?"

He looks embarrassed. "I suppose it has something to do with the female anatomy?"

Mabel breaks into laughter. "I *suppose* you're close. It's an ancient Italian dish, translated literally as pasta of the whores. It's a simple peasant dish."

"Hmm," he's not sure how to take this. "I trust I haven't insulted you with my choice of dish."

"Not in the least. It's quite a treat having a man cook for me. You might be the first, come to think of it," she reaches across him and takes the wooden spoon so she can sample the sauce. She adds a pinch of salt.

Priscilla is tapping away on her phone. "Look at this," she holds her phone up for Mabel to see. "Wade's is promoting your concert tonight on Facebook and there are already thirty-four people saying they're going."

"Let me see that," Mabel takes the phone. "Good lord, listen how they're hyping me," she reads from the phone: "Mabel Johnson's niece to perform all week as part of the blues festival. Come hear the piano and vocal stylings of Peggy Winston, playing many of her famous aunt's classic tunes, this week only."

"Hey, that's pretty cool," Richard gives the al dente pasta a quick rinse from the sink, and then dumps it back into the skillet with the sauce, tossing it well. He loads the Puttanesca pasta onto three plates and sprinkles fresh parsley and parmesan cheese on top. Mabel finishes making a salad of arugula with endive, pear, and goat cheese. They sit in the kitchen and Mabel smiles as Richard eats her salad.

"Nice to be eating fresh produce," he says. "Where did you get these greens?"

"From the Farmer's Market."

"I didn't know there was one. Where is it?"

"It's right there in the town square, across from your office."

He looks up, puzzled. "How do you know where my office is?"

She recovers quickly. "Okay, I'll admit it. I've been snooping on you. I was curious to know where you worked so Priscilla showed me. That's how I discovered the market."

"She made me do it," Priscilla adds. "I think she really likes you."

"So, you've been snooping on me, huh?"

Mabel sees she has successfully appealed to his vanity, an old trick she has not forgotten and used many times. "Yes, I didn't think someone as handsome as you could *possibly* also be a doctor," she winks in a way that makes it impossible to tell if she's being facetious. She's having fun, once again manipulating men, using her good looks the way she used to in an effort to gain some leverage in her mostly powerless relationships. She knows this isn't right and feels a tug of guilt, aware that times have changed to some degree and this young doctor is probably not one who views relationships as sport—as battles where there must always be a winner and a loser. Richard, for his part, is enjoying being toyed with by this attractive woman, who he figures must be ten years older than him. He has mostly dated women his age or younger, frankly finding many of them to be less interesting than this worldly Peggy Winston.

"Do you like the pasta?" Richard turns to Priscilla.

"Very much, thank you."

"Can you spell Puttanesca, dear?" Mabel asks.

Priscilla sounds it out and spells it correctly, looking proud.

"Richard, Priscilla is in the state spelling bee championships representing her school district. Isn't that something?"

"Yes, indeed," he is eating carefully, trying to avoid spilling sauce down his shirt front.

"She's the youngest person in the competition, isn't that right, dear?"

Priscilla shrugs.

"Do you need to practice?" Richard asks.

"Always."

"How are you with medical terms? I know those can be very difficult."

"I'm okay with them. Ask me something."

Richard puts his fork down and says: "Laparoscopy."

"Lap-ar-oscopy," she sounds it out and then spells the word correctly.

"Very good," he is impressed.

"That was easy. Ask me a hard one."

Richard searches his mind. "Okay, how about oophorectomy."

She sounds it out and spells it correctly.

"I told you, she's good," Mabel smiles.

"Hmm," the doctor looks challenged as he struggles to find a word to stump her. "Okay. How about horripilation."

"Repeat it please," Priscilla asks.

He says it more slowly this time. They can see the wheels spinning in Priscilla's precocious head. "H. O. R. R. A. P. I. L. A. T. I. O. N." She looks up, hoping she got it right.

"So close," the doctor smiles. "It's got an I after the second R, not an A."

"Shoot. What's it mean?" Priscilla looks disappointed.

"It's what happens to the hairs on your skin when you see a Stephen King movie. Or when you are out in the cold."

They finish lunch and put the leftovers in the refrigerator. Richard loads the dishwasher, whistling as he does so. The doorbell rings and Mabel wanders off to see who it is. It's the neighbor, Alice Kramlich, who is standing there accompanied by an awkward boy dressed in a red and brown striped T-shirt. "Ah, you're here still," Alice and the boy push their way inside. "Is Mabel home yet?"

"No, she's still in Jackson," Priscilla replies. "Hi, Joey, I was wondering if you'd be here this summer."

"Yup, I'm back from camp and just hangin' around. I was hopin' we could ride bikes and maybe go for a swim or something."

"Sure," Priscilla hasn't seen Joey since last summer. He's Alice's son, and when Priscilla visited in the past, the two of them played together even though Priscilla had been less than keen to do so. Priscilla has never had more than a friend or two and is accustomed to entertaining herself, more interested in logical books than illogical humans. As an only child, she's never been eager to share her time with other children, and Joey has been competitive with her in the past, preferring his loud video games to her quiet books. But she can hear her mother whispering in her ear not to be rude, so she smiles at Joey.

"I got a spare bike at the house if you wanna come with me now."

Priscilla checks to make sure this is okay and Mabel nods yes.

Priscilla grabs an Atlanta Braves baseball cap from the coat rack and follows Joey outside, where the adults can hear him saying: "I shoulda went to camp for another week but my mom says it's gotten wicked 'spensive."

Priscilla corrects him: "should have gone." Their voices trail off as they descend the stairway.

Alice looks embarrassed. "That's not true, I would have happily paid for him to stay another week but he wasn't having a good time." She continues snooping around the house, running her hand along the end tables next to the sofa. "Still can't get over how fast Mabel hightailed it outta here. That's not at all like her."

"Well, it was an emergency so she had little choice," Mabel replies with a hint of irritation in her voice.

"But still, I mean, how did *you* show up so fast?"

"As luck would have it, I was in Atlanta on a flight layover and had some vacation days I needed to use."

Richard joins in the conversation. "So . . . you're a flight attendant?"

"Yes." She can sense his disapproval and wonders what he had possibly imagined, if indeed anything. Neurosurgeon? Gastroenterologist? Genomic scientist? She soldiers on with her lie. "I typically fly between San Francisco and Asia so it's unusual for me to come East. I'm filling in for a sick friend."

"Well, that's too bad," Richard is already thinking about their future together.

She mistakes this as meaning it's too bad she's a lowly flight attendant. "Well, we can't all be doctors or marry NFL quarterbacks like Luther Buck."

Ouch.

He is caught off guard by her comment and attempts to clarify. "Not that at all. I guess this means I won't be able to see much of you after this week."

She realizes she's been infected by a sudden attack of jealousy, which has arisen from some long-buried place she has not missed. "Well, that's true, but at least we have this week together so let's make the most of it," she does her best to recover, seeing the sad look on Richard's face. She remembers he is still getting over a broken heart and worries she is leading him on in a way that can have no possible

82

acceptable outcome for him. It's been a long time since she's had to give any thought to hurting a man's feelings, especially such a kind man as Richard.

He shrugs. "Sure, why not enjoy ourselves while we can."

Alice is wandering around the living room rubbing her hands along the dusty piano surface with a look of disapproval. Mabel sees her lift the magazine pile on the far table, the one with all the dust on it, as she emits a judgmental sigh. "Can't believe how filthy Mabel keeps this place," she mumbles.

"Excuse me?" Mabel looks cross.

"I'm just saying you'd think someone with all her money could afford to hire a house cleaner."

"Maybe she does and the house cleaner is taking advantage of her?"

"Oh, I doubt that. Although her gardeners are definitely doing a half-assed job. Why, I saw three fellas out there last week, one doing some raking while the other two flipped their cigarette butts in the hedge. I had to run out there and chew them out. Coulda started a fire, those imbeciles. Coulda burned down the entire neighborhood."

Mabel wonders what else this nosy neighbor must think of her. "Well, I'm going out there this afternoon to do some gardening myself. It will feel good to get my hands dirty."

Richard overhears this. "Might I join you? I've been missing working in a garden. I enjoyed the community garden back in medical school."

"Sure, please help me if you want. In fact . . ." she gestures toward the front door eager to get Alice out of her house ". . . let's head out now. Just give me a moment to put on some work clothes." After she changes, she is dismayed to see Alice still standing there gabbing with Richard. She hurries them out into the early afternoon sunshine, the day less humid than it's been, with puffy thunderheads building off to the west. They practically have to push Alice away as they begin weeding the garden bed out front. Thankfully, she finally leaves them in peace. Mabel has brought a trowel and two pairs of gardening gloves from the tool shed and they get to work.

"The nerve of that woman. Commenting about all the dust."

"I actually think the place looks well kept," Richard replies.

"You sound surprised."

"No, it's not that, but I mean Mabel is very old to be living on her own out here. I've suggested she get live-in help."

She looks up with a trickle of sweat on her upper lip. "Really? You think she's too old to live here alone?"

84

There is something threatening in her tone that causes Richard to back down. "No, no, not at all. She's just fine." He does not want to argue about Mabel and is caught off guard by how defensive Peggy is of her. But she's eager to get the truth from him given her disguised younger self so digs deeper looking for more truths not otherwise to be revealed by the doctor.

"She told me you think she eats poorly. That's why her blood pressure is too high."

"Well, it doesn't help. Just yesterday I saw her out at the diner with Priscilla packing down some fries and a cheeseburger—"

"Packing down?"

"Yes, packing down. I've told her to avoid all animal fats if she wants to live longer but there's only so much we doctors can do. The patients need to take better care of themselves, and frankly it's upsetting to see in our Emergency Rooms and hospitals how much obesity, diabetes, drugs, alcoholism, and recklessness there is."

"Well, maybe she is entitled to her few remaining pleasures given how old she is. All those years she worked herself to the bone to support her bloodsucking husband and all those managers and hangers-on who counted on her for their incomes—"

"Whoa," he looks up and wipes some dirt from his cheek.

"All I'm suggesting is she should watch what she eats. Do you realize how bad the fats are for us, the ones in french fries and animal meat?"

"What . . . you want her to eat veggie burgers that taste like cardboard?"

"They don't taste like cardboard. But look, why are we even having this discussion, Peggy?"

As Richard bends down close to her, she smells that long-forgotten odor of a man's sweat and masculinity combined into an appealing mixture. His forearm brushes against hers and she shudders at his touch. They work quietly together pulling weeds and patting soil back into place where the rains have washed it away from the lilies. They enjoy being together in silence and this continues for several minutes before he speaks again. "That neighbor is quite a piece of work, huh?"

She smiles, her hands smoothing soil around the lilies. "Tell me about it."

Richard adds: "I mean, I couldn't believe the way she just barged in and began touching all of Mabel's stuff. Very disrespectful if you ask me."

She continues tugging at stubborn weeds and then leans back, looking contemplative. "These weeds, the dust in the house, all of life is just an ongoing struggle to apply order to chaos. Eventually we will be overrun, just like these bushes and trees doing their best to survive. Yet, we toil on, doing what we can to meet the daily requirements for maintaining fleeting control: making the bed, keeping up with the laundry, the gardens, the dusting, the cooking. It's all quite exhausting, isn't it?"

"I know what you mean. You don't want to see the laundry piling up at my place. I spend most of my time as a physician doing my best to apply control to chaos. I enjoy trying to maintain order, and that's why I think I chose to go into medicine. But, yes, the powers of nature overwhelm us all eventually."

"We're just like ants with breadcrumbs tottering on our backs," Mabel says.

Richard is gazing off toward Alice's house where he sees Priscilla and Joey riding bikes. "I get the impression that Priscilla is not keen on hanging out with Alice's boy, am I right?"

"She's always preferred playing by herself. Or so Mabel tells me. Raising a gifted child like her can't be easy."

"She seems incredibly strong, considering her mother just died."

"Children tend to repress those kinds of tragedies I think."

"Did you ever want children of your own?"

She looks away, doing her best to avoid tearing up

remembering Violet. She sighs and says: "No, I decided not to have children."

"Well, I'd like to someday," he is sprawled out on his back, arms behind his head. "I think I've reached that age where one becomes thoroughly bored concentrating solely on oneself. I suppose I'd benefit from having a child in my life, someone else to focus on, to love. Priscilla is so adorable; I enjoy hanging out with her. Why, the way she talked to Wade at the club, she sounded like a grownup. Anyway, I had hoped—"

"Yes?"

"Well, I had talked about having children with my ex-girlfriend. She wanted them, I wanted them. But I guess she just didn't want them with me."

"I'm sorry," she is now gazing down upon him as he lies on his back. "I think you need to have faith that this is all working out as God wants, that had you ended up with her, your lives might not have been so great. It's been my experience that oftentimes it takes unexpected and unwanted events to redirect us in ways that turn out to be positive for us."

He smiles. "You sure have a lot of wisdom for such a young woman. I thought wisdom only came with age."

"Some of us are wise beyond our years," she laughs. "Some of us have experienced more hardships early on than

88

others."

"And what hardships have you faced that have made you so wise?"

"Nothing much, really. I consider myself to have been very fortunate. Any day not in a hospital bed is a good day as far as I'm concerned."

"Amen. So, you sure you're leaving on Sunday?" There is a tinge of sadness in his voice.

"Yes, I'm afraid I must."

"That's too bad. I really enjoy spending time with you, Peggy."

"You're sweet. This is fun, isn't it? Getting our hands all dirty like this. It's been a while."

"No garden in San Francisco?"

She realizes she's in danger of drifting away from her assumed role, so pauses and replies, "No, what with all my travel I'm rarely home. It wouldn't be fair to the plants."

"I imagine your job has its perks as well as disadvantages. What's your favorite city in Asia? I've always wanted to go but haven't had the opportunity."

She searches her mind for an answer and responds with one of the cities she most enjoyed performing in during her heyday. "Tokyo, I suppose. It's very cosmopolitan and clean. Sort of an Asian London, if you will."

"Yes, I imagine it's a lovely city."

"It is, and the food is outstanding. Not just Japanese, but food from around the world. There are many talented chefs, and a fabulous seafood market, one of the biggest in the world. Have you travelled much?"

"Not since I was a kid. My family took some European vacations back then."

"Was your family well off?"

He hesitates before replying, "Yes, my father is the former Attorney General of New York and my mother is a surgeon working in Brooklyn."

"Wow, that's impressive," they take a break from pulling weeds and sit back on the lawn. "I imagine you grew up with great expectations and pressures for yourself."

"I did. And I'm thankful for that pressure. It's sad to see how many children are raised in homes with no expectations. Despite the fact my parents were busy professionals, they made time for me and sent me to excellent schools. How about you?"

Mabel pauses, and then for some reason decides to portray Peggy Winston as a less fortunate character. "I struggled as a child in school, was a slow learner. No one in my family had been to college so no one pushed me to go. I worked as a waitress right out of high school in Las Vegas and then began working at strip clubs to up my income."

"Excuse me?" he is caught off guard. She isn't sure

where this came from but now that she's said it, is perhaps thinking this might help push him away once she returns to her old haggard self at week's end.

She continues building her fantasy. "On a good night I could earn two thousand dollars, especially when the large conventions were in town. So, I danced for five years and saved up enough money to travel the world. That's when I decided to become a stewardess." She can see him now looking at her differently, with a judgmental, disapproving expression, and realizes she has succeeded in pushing him away. That is, until he calls her bluff.

"You know what, Miss Peggy Winston? I'm calling bullshit on that little story of yours. I think you might be a bigtime bullshitter."

She puts her hands on her hips. "What, you don't think I'm attractive enough to work in a strip club?"

"Yes, no, I mean, of course . . . but—"

"I was the most requested girl for the VIP room."

He's shaking his head, smiling, pretty sure she's toying with him. "I just can't see it, honestly."

Mabel stands up and pulls her hair into a bun, as she starts swiveling her hips and pursing her lips above him. But she can't pull it off and breaks into laughter. "Okay, you got me. I'm a notorious bullshitter."

"Phew," he looks relieved. Although he's growing

concerned he might be falling for a pathological liar. "So, tell me the truth."

She returns to the garden bed and yanks a few more stubborn weeds. "I worked as a waitress in San Francisco and then became a flight attendant. I was just checking to see how gullible you are. You don't want to be gullible in this world, Doctor Richie Roberts, or the ladies will steamroll you."

"They already have," he says.

"So I gather. Maybe I can help toughen you up."

"Or harden me off," he answers using a gardening analogy with unintended double meaning, causing her to smile.

Wade's is doing a good business when Mabel, Richard, and Priscilla arrive that afternoon shortly before five o'clock. This despite the fact a line of thunderstorms is passing through, with torrential downpours of a weighty rain that bounces off the steaming pavement. Mabel has unearthed a red gown from her touring days and is pleased to see it fits. She's gotten all dolled up for her performance, Priscilla assisting as make-up artist, which explains why Mabel's red lipstick is on thicker than she realizes. But she feels sexy in a way she hasn't for a very long time, and follows the many eyes affixed upon her as she sashays into the club. Richard stands close behind and helps slide off her Burberry raincoat. It feels wonderful to wear her stowed-away clothes after so many years of saggy sweatpants and workout clothes. Wade Ferguson, the club owner, greets them.

"Welcome, welcome, please come up front here where I've saved you a table." Mabel, Richard, and Priscilla make their way through the crowded small tables, doing their best not to knock into the seated patrons. Wade points to their table where they see a young man sipping a beer, and Mabel pauses, unsure why he is there. Wade makes a hasty introduction. "This is Joel Swillens, he's the arts reporter for the Clarksdale *Beacon*."

The reporter leans back in his seat and puts down his iPhone. "Hey, cool to meet you, Peggy. I heard you tore the joint up last night so wanted to come listen for myself. Maybe write a review. I can't get over you being related to Mabel Johnson. She's one of my all-time favs, an old-time legend, truly awesome." Joel is picking at his trimmed beard, bobbing in his seat like an absent-minded professor, apparently not one to rise when in the presence of a lady—not just any lady, but a musical legend, although she realizes he doesn't know that. Still, she doesn't appreciate the absence of manners in modern society, and is accustomed to gentlemen rising when she approaches a table in a club setting. They all sit at the crammed circular table upfront while Mabel eyes the stage, noticing a Ludwig drum set and a double-bass behind the piano. Wade sees her gazing at the stage and says, "I'm hoping a couple of musical friends might swing by later to accompany you."

This is news to Mabel. "I agreed to perform solo. I'm not ready to perform with others."

Priscilla sits up straight in her seat. "We had an agreement. Peggy will play two sets of solo piano and that's what it will be, or nothing at all."

"Chill out, little lady," Wade can't believe the strength emanating from this girl. "Man, no one is sayin' she has to play with anyone, it's just with the festival starting this week we might have some musicians in town looking to play. But if Peggy doesn't want to play with them, that's cool."

The reporter is nervously twisting his beard while gulping down a tallboy of some local beer Mabel doesn't recognize. The can is brightly illustrated with psychedelic artwork that reminds her of the 1960s. Wade sees her staring at the beer and says, "Hey, can I get you somethin' to drink?"

Priscilla says: "Yes, please. Our agreement calls for complimentary beverages and food. I'd like a root beer and a cheeseburger, please." Wade casts a puzzled look at this sassy girl, who reminds him of the many pushy music agents he's tangled with over the years, the sort of people he does his best to avoid. There is something slightly off about her, but he moves onto the others and takes their orders. The jukebox against the far wall is playing modern songs Mabel doesn't know. She sits there thinking about how quickly musical tastes change over time, yet some artists manage to find new listeners generation after generation, like J.S. Bach, his music still universally loved. But most are forgotten, many never appreciated at all during their lifetime. She recalls how vain she became early in her career when she first became popular, getting swept up in the glamour and prestige of the industry. With the passage of time, she came to better understand that most artists fade into obscurity, passed over by an unstoppable procession of new generations and new music. She's proud her music is still appreciated, but wonders how many years after she's gone her hit songs will be forgotten. Fame and fortune are fleeting, it's love that matters most. She gazes at Richard as these thoughts come to her.

Richard, who has been gazing across the way where Lizzy and the street person Colin have just come in, turns and sees Peggy smiling at him. He smiles back as they make intimate eye contact. She looks so beautiful. There is something special about her eyes, a rare depth and wisdom, unlike what he sees in younger women. He feels she is gazing directly into his soul. He clears his throat and asks what she would like to drink.

"A Manhattan, please."

"And I'll have a rum and Coke," Richard adds. Wade heads off and returns a few minutes later with their drinks. The hipster reporter asks her a few questions, his spiral-bound small notepad now open.

"I gather you're visiting from the West Coast."

"Yes, just for the week."

"And did you study music with your famous aunt?"

She sips her Manhattan, realizing she needs to stay in role as she attempts to overcome her negative first impression of this pretentious man, in full realization it's unfair to judge someone without actually knowing them. "Yes, I took a few lessons with Mabel when I was young, but I'm mostly self-taught. I'm not really all that good, so I don't see any need for there to be a review."

Richard is stirring his drink. "You sounded great to me last night, but hey, I'm no music critic." She gazes at him noticing how handsome he looks in the low red light of the club. His lashes are longer than hers. Not fair. He possesses the assuredness of a young man who has not yet begun losing his virility, who mostly looks ahead, confident of an unlimited amount of time, not realizing how fast it all vanishes. Richard is wearing a black T-shirt that hugs his body, revealing nicely toned arms, strong but not overly so. The shirt is untucked and tapers just below his waist, over his blue jeans. The reporter presses on. "Well, you know, I might not write a review, but

96

Wade suggested I come, so here I am. Man, am I ever busy covering the festival this week." It's clear he feels she should be honored he deigned to come at all. She wonders just how busy he really is. She has her doubts.

Priscilla interjects, "I'm quite sure she's going to blow your socks off, *Man*." The way she emphasizes the last word makes him wonder if she's gently mocking him, which is indeed the case. He squirms in his seat, wiping a bead of sweat from his brow.

Wade returns and asks if she's ready to play. Mabel gets up and steps onto the stage, making herself comfortable on the piano bench, gazing out into the crowd unable to see most of the faces through the stage lights. She likes it like this, remembers clearly the intimacy she prefers so it feels like she is playing alone in the room. Wade joins her onstage, taps the mic to make sure it's on, and then makes the introduction. "Ladies and gentlemen, friends of Wade's and those visiting for the upcoming festival, it gives me great pleasure to introduce Peggy Winston, a fine vocalist and pianist, as you will hear shortly. Peggy is the niece of the Grammy Award-winning Mabel Johnson, who lives in nearby Sardis. Peggy is in town visiting for the week and has agreed to perform for us. Please join me in welcoming Peggy Winston to our stage." There is brief applause and then the club falls silent. Mabel waits for the street person to stop coughing—he is seated at the table with Lizzy toward the back of the room and is struggling to contain a consumption-sounding wet hacking—and then once he stops, she speaks softly into the microphone. "Hello, and welcome everyone. I will be playing some of Mabel Johnson's famous songs along with a few new compositions of my own. It's been a while since I last performed in public, so I appreciate you bearing with me." With that she adjusts herself on the piano bench, making sure her gown is not in the way of her pedal foot, and begins playing Peggy Lee's hit song "Fever." Her sulky voice begins "Never know how much I love you . . ." and she finds herself singing the song exactly the way she did years ago. She loves this song and her mind drifts back to good memories of Peggy Lee—the other Peggy, she smiles inside as she plays and sings—recalling how kind Peggy had been to her over the years, introducing her to influential people in the industry. It seems right to be playing Peggy's hit song and she gives it her all. When she finishes, there is no applause and she fears she has played badly, when in fact the audience is awed by her artistry and is too emotionally stunned to interrupt the lingering notes that hang like dew on grass. Mabel sees Priscilla eating a cheeseburger, shaking her head, mouthing the words *you're playing too well, don't blow it.* A few more awkward moments pass and then the audience breaks into enthusiastic applause. Mabel smiles, excited to be back in the limelight after all these years. She knows she played that song as well as she ever has.

Priscilla is reminding her to play less well so she launches into a version of "Going to Take a Miracle," and hits a few clunker notes, going so far as to pause for a moment after a mistake, and then restarting from a previous place in the song. She can see the reporter scribbling notes in his little pad as she moves onto one of her new compositions from that morning, again pausing part way into the improvisation, unclear how to proceed with this inchoate tune. It had come more easily that morning at home, but now in front of a crowd she realizes live experimentation is a mistake. Part of this is due to her comfort at home with her Steinway grand, this Baldwin upright piano nowhere near as good an instrument. She no longer feels like playing and realizes this is all a huge mistake. What was she thinking? She hurries through the rest of the set and rushes back to the safety of her table, faint applause circling the club.

"How nice," the reporter says in a smug tone.

"Thank you," she replies. "I'm afraid I was more nervous up there than anticipated."

"Well, that's to be expected," Richard says. "I can only imagine how nerve-wracking it must be to perform in front of a large crowd, putting your heart and soul on display for all to judge." This comment seems directed at the journalist.

Mabel is disappointed in her playing, especially considering this reporter is bound to light her up with a scathing review. She knows the type all too well, the ones who feast on others with real talent while they write small-town stories designed to appeal to their readers' lowest appetites. She bites her tongue, on the one hand wanting to reveal she has played in front of huge crowds at Carnegie Hall and Royal Albert Hall, has won many Grammys, but instead shrugs and says, "Yes, this is a bigger turnout than I expected."

Lizzy and Colin come over. "You play beautifully," Lizzy says.

"Thank you, that's kind. I'm a bit rusty."

Colin adds, "That version of "Fever" was *so* similar to the way Mabel used to play it back in Bah-stin, I thought I was seeing a ghost, but then—"

"Yes . . .?" Priscilla knows where he is heading and cuts him off.

"Nothin', I liked it very much."

Mabel worries she might have intentionally flubbed her playing too much, and this concern is made worse when the reporter hastily excuses himself saying he needs to go interview the young blues singer Gary Clark, Jr.

Wade approaches. "You're not staying for the second set?"

"No, thanks, but I need to prepare for my interview with Bobby Higgins tomorrow."

Priscilla's expression bunches up in a mix of confusion and mistrust: "I thought you said Gary Clark, Jr.?"

There is an awkward pause as he searches for a reply. He clears his throat. "I'm interviewing Gary this evening, and then need to prepare for my interview with Bobby tomorrow. I've got many interviews to do this week—"

"Right," it's clear from Priscilla's tone that she's not buying it. Joel departs and Priscilla mumbles "local hack," leading Mabel to smile at her adoring and brilliant great-granddaughter. Michelle would be *so* proud.

Mabel plays a more polished second set and continues working on her improvisations, which are coming together better now. But she's losing interest with this performing in public, largely due to the annoying fake ivory key on the middle C of the piano, which is coming loose and making annoying clicking sounds each time she strikes it. She's been doing her best to play while avoiding this key, even though it's oftentimes the correct one. Back in the day, her Steinway was shipped to all her major performances and tuned before each concert. They even shipped her Persian rug to be placed beneath the piano, recreating her home setting as closely as possible. She's a long way from those days now performing in this dumpy Mississippi club, something she ceased doing

101

shortly after her career launched and she was discovered. Mabel draws upon her decades of professionalism in completing the set, bows to the enthusiastic crowd, and then strolls over to Wade to inform him the piano needs work and she expects it to be done before tomorrow night. Priscilla is standing off to the side and mouths the words *get it done* to him. Mabel grabs her raincoat and they exit the club in such haste that Wade is unable to pay her. She just wants to get home and go to bed and certainly does not need his money. Richard drops them off and asks if he can come by in the morning to go swimming, and they all agree this is a great idea.

TUESDAY

Richard is up early the next morning, awakened by yet another disturbing rejection dream. In the dream he approaches his ex-girlfriend, who doesn't seem to know who he is despite the fact they have been in love for several years. He withdraws, wounded. Then he sees her racing away with a new lover, her hair blowing in the breeze, the wry smile he fell in love with evident across the verdant expanse stretching down to an unfamiliar ocean. Richard loathes how pathetic he feels upon awakening to the present realities of his lonely life, curling up with his sad little pillow, shrinking into the fetal position beneath the cool cotton sheets. Why is he still having this dream so many years after the breakup? When did he become so weak? Why can't he get back up on that proverbial horse and fall in love again?

He wanders into the kitchen dressed in a T-shirt and boxer shorts and makes a cup of coffee using his French press, then puts a slice of whole wheat bread into the toaster. He cuts a ripe avocado down the center and removes the pit, tossing it at the nearby trashcan, but misses, so leans down to where the

103

greasy pit has rolled—beneath a cupboard with two inches of clearance above the old pine flooring, requiring him to get down on hands and knees and grope among the ancient food bits lodged between the floor boards—and after considerable straining and cursing is able to extricate the pit with a butter knife, properly disposing of it in the trash. "So much for my basketball skills," he mumbles, unaware of how much talking to himself he does these days living on his own. "Never was much of an athlete," he returns to the counter where the avocado awaits the lukewarm toast, and he spreads it carefully, covering every inch with a doctor's precision. He sits at the butcher block kitchen table, disappointed with his toast. Now that he's been on his hands and knees and discovered the unexpected food crumbs beneath the table, his eyes are open with full visual acuity, as he gazes around this once-proud but now decaying Greek Revival house and realizes just what a mess it is: peeling paint hangs in strips from the old plaster ceiling in the living room, the ceiling faded in several spots by old water damage from the clawfoot bathtub above, a tub he enjoys given it is deep enough for him to fully submerge his entire body, unlike the shallow tub back in his Baltimore apartment. He spies what he assumes to be vestiges of fire damage along the baseboard in the parlor, the trim blackened in several sections and then apparently painted over in a failed attempt to conceal the damage. The agent who rented him the house had informed Richard that a fire had damaged most of the downstairs back at the end of the Victorian Era. At first Richard did not want to live here, and continued looking, but this neglected house was the only one available near work, which meant he could dash home for lunch, which he does most days. His laundry basket has not budged from the black sectional sofa in the parlor, which is all wrong for this period house, but it's what he owns and he's not yet settled enough to invest in new furnishings. He's hoping to buy a house in the area once the prices come down. The laundry has been piling up and he realizes he needs to get it done before he runs out of clean clothes. It's not that he's lazy or a slob—quite the contrary, he has always been fastidious—but he avoids venturing down into the dank basement where the washer and dryer sit sweating in the summer humidity, made worse by the occasional torrential downpours that seep through the stone foundation. There are old newspapers in damp cardboard boxes along the far basement wall, and he's been meaning to take them to the dump, but is afraid of finding a mouse nest buried within, so hasn't yet tackled that project. He's been considering taking his laundry to the laundromat and decides that's what he'll do. Tomorrow.

He gazes out the bow window behind him as details from his recurring dream return: an unspoken feeling of inadequacy—sexual inadequacy—lurking within his own damaged basement. Was he not good enough for her? What did he not possess that she found in her NFL quarterback? Money? Sexual prowess? Courage? He knows he should not go down this defeatist path, and mostly has avoided doing so in recent times, but just when this dream seems finally buried, it rears its ugly head. He desperately wants to be in love again, to feel the ecstasy of that heaven-sent union that is so rare yet critical to human survival and happiness. "Please, God, if you are there, send me someone to love again," he mumbles. God apparently has other plans for Richard, as he finds himself addictively grabbing his iPhone, playing back a message he never deleted from his ex-girlfriend, a message in which she flirtatiously invites him over for dinner, an ordinary everyday message that has taken on a life of its own following the breakup. He misses the sound of her voice and seems to crave more humiliation, so logs into his laptop and opens up her football hero husband's Instagram account, where he sees he is live-streaming about their beautiful life together and their two perfect children. Richard knows he shouldn't watch but cannot stop himself, delighting in this odd form of masochism that simultaneously hurts and feels good, the way heroin must feel, all this destructive conflicted pain and pleasure undermining him. Their youngest daughter, Jasmine, is prancing around the kitchen in a cute pink tutu, singing happy little songs, delighting in being the center of attention. This could have been him, *should* have been him. "What a loser I am," he closes the laptop lid and gazes out into the beautiful Mississippi morning.

He recalls how much fun he had last night with Peggy, the first time he's had fun with a woman in a long time. He has gone on a few Tinder dates but the matches have been all wrong. He's skeptical that a computer algorithm is capable of deciding who we love and why. He likes Peggy very much, there seems to have been an instant chemistry and that's a promising sign. He's not up for being hurt again, yet feels some piece of his old self-esteem rising within, a ray of hope struggling to escape the layers of defeat that have buried him in his current situation, in this sad sarcophagus of self-pity. "I'm not getting any younger," he speaks in the direction of a black cat with a splash of white on its chest that has jumped onto the outside picnic table, digging its claws into the splintering wood, no doubt in search of mice to slap around. He's missing out on a lot of fun, the kind of fun one only can have in their youth, before our short time on this earth returns us to the dust from whence we came. Maybe this Peggy Winston can help him rediscover his old confidence? He can't help but notice the way she looks at him when she thinks he's not paying attention, with that look of love mixed with lust he misses. "No, it can't work," he remembers she is leaving at the end of the week to fly far away to Asia. "Long-distance romances never work out." As he speaks these words, the cat perches on her hind haunches, licking her paws, then shoots him a look of disapproving disdain as she jumps from the table and scampers across the lawn.

Richard gazes away and sips his coffee. He has two options: cut the relationship off before it gets going and stay sequestered within the shelter of his sad solitary existence, focusing on his work where he feels important and in control, or let himself go for the week and enjoy the time they have together. He looks at the wall clock above the sink and sees it's already nine. He told Peggy he'd come by at ten, so he slurps down the rest of his tepid coffee, tosses the few dishes into the sink, takes a shower, shaves, and then packs a bag for the beach containing suntan lotion (spf 60), a Baltimore Orioles baseball cap, and the book he's been reading about the history of Mississippi. He stares for several moments into his closet and eventually finds a pair of khaki shorts and a black T-shirt with white shell artwork on the front. The T-shirt has a small coffee stain on the front but will have to suffice. It's just the beach after all.

He arrives to find Peggy standing out front by the mailbox looking distraught. He parks and walks over to where she is reading the newspaper. "Look at this bullshit," she grabs him by the shirttail. He sees she is reading a review of her performance written by the local journalist. She begins reading out loud in a sarcastic know-it-all voice in imitation of the journalist she took an instant dislike to and now has confirmation why. "Headline: Mabel Johnson's Niece No Mabel Johnson. Last night I spent a mostly disappointing amateur hour listening to Mabel Johnson's distant relation, Peggy Winston, stumble through a piano and vocal set at Wade's, where she made a plethora of mistakes. Miss Winston's set opened auspiciously enough with her rendition of Peggy Lee's classic hit "Fever," but then degenerated into an awkward performance for the assembled crowd, a performance marred by several clunkers and even moments where the pianist paused and restarted, unable to find her place. This had the deleterious effect of causing the audience to sit nervously, concerned whether she'd actually be able to complete her set, when in fact they deserved to hear a compelling performance and not some high school piano recital, which as it turns out, might have been superior. It doesn't take a music critic to arrive at the obvious conclusion that Peggy Winston may be Mabel Johnson's niece, and indeed bears a striking familial resemblance, but not artistic. She will be performing for the rest of the week, but given the many all-star acts in town for the blues festival, I suggest music lovers prioritize those performers over any shilling Wade's may be doing to hype Miss Winston."

She looks up stunned and angry. "Deleterious? Plethora? Compelling? What . . . did a dictionary of empty adjectives hit him upside the head?" she mutters. "I'd like to smack him upside that pretentious little head," she is steaming mad. "Can you believe this crap? Does that piss-ant, alleged reporter have any idea who he's dealing with, how many awards I've won . . . ?" she trails off realizing she's lapsed into Mabel mode.

Richard looks puzzled but then takes the newspaper and tosses it into the outside trash barrel on their way up to the porch. "Don't let him get to you. I thought your performance was terrific. He should have done his job and stayed for the second set, the lazy jerk." Mabel realizes she needs to be careful not to let her pride give away the ruse. Priscilla greets them in the living room where she is working on a puzzle. Richard strolls over and helps her for a few minutes while Mabel sits at the piano and plays a beautiful Bach fugue, calming her nerves from the hurt. She's now determined to play better tonight, to let it all hang out and not give one hoot if someone thinks she sounds like Mabel Johnson—because *she is* Mabel Johnson. She has her pride. She only has this one week of being young again. She's won more Grammy Awards than that local hack will ever know. When she finishes her practice session, Richard approaches and rests his hand gently on her left shoulder, eager to console her. His touch sends a charge through them both, and she stands up and squeezes his hand in recognition of the conflicted emotional pain apparent in his chocolate brown eyes. They stand like this for a few moments of unspoken human connection, when the doorbell rings and she goes to see who it is. Alice is standing there with little Joey by her side, his shirt splattered with peppermint ice cream dripping from his sugar cone.

"I'm wondering if Mabel's home yet?" Alice asks.

"No, she's still away. In fact, she'll be gone for the rest of the week."

"Hmm, that's odd. I can't imagine why she didn't tell me. It's not like her to just up and leave without letting me know."

"Well, it was an urgent matter so I'm sure she didn't have time—"

"Yet somehow she managed to reach you all the way in Atlanta and you just showed up."

Richard has to admit her appearance was quick, as he stands off to the side while Alice continues.

"I mean, she's not an impulsive person. I've known her for many, many years now. And she's not been well lately, so I can't see how she just up and left."

"Well, she did," Mabel replies with increasing irritation.

Richard doesn't help her cause when he chimes in: "I'm surprised too. When I saw her at the diner on Saturday, she seemed so excited to go touring the old clubs with me. And her memory is so shaky these days I'm surprised she left the familiarity of her home—"

She shoots him a look that stops him in his tracks.

Alice is on her tiptoes, peering over to where Priscilla is trying to hide, but Alice cannot see her as Mabel stands in the way. "I was hoping Priscilla might want to play with Joey this morning while I'm at the dentist. I'm sure he'd rather play with her than wait for me at the dentist's office."

Priscilla nudges her way behind the door so only her great-grandmother can see her, shaking her head no. But Mabel either misreads or overrules her, "Of course, no problem at all. We're going for a swim shortly."

"Are you sure it's not an inconvenience?" Alice asks.

"We're happy to help," Mabel is aware of Priscilla's issues with socialization, and is eager to encourage any interaction with others, confident this will serve her well as she makes her way in the world. A world of people and complicated emotions and all the messy aspects of life Priscilla needs to be prepared to handle. She shoots her great-granddaughter a knowing wink, and Priscilla's shoulders slump in resigned acceptance.

"It might be nice for Priscilla to have a sleepover at our place if you'd like," Alice offers. "I read in the paper you are performing at Wade's so imagine you are out late for her."

Priscilla slips out from behind the door. "No, she's done by nine, so not late at all."

Mabel likes the idea of having some alone time with Richard. "Why, isn't that kind of you."

"But I'll miss your show!" Priscilla protests.

Mabel speaks under her breath, "We don't want to be ungrateful and ignore her kind invitation."

Priscilla is staring at her feet, and then mutters, "All right. If you say so."

Mabel turns to Alice. "I hope you didn't believe a word of that idiotic review."

Her neighbor pulls a strand of hair from her mouth and says, "Well, it certainly wasn't very nice. I like to think if you don't have something good to say you should keep your mouth shut. C'mon, Joey, let's go get you into your bathing suit and put on a clean T-shirt."

Priscilla looks downcast after they've departed.

"What's the matter, honey?" Mabel asks, knowing the answer. "Don't you like Joey?"

"He's okay. In small doses."

"What is it then?"

"I wanted to see you perform and now with me sleeping at their house I'll miss the show. And he's always *so* messy and competitive. Did you see the ice cream all down his front?"

Mabel stares at Richard and notices for the first time the stain on his shirt. "Well, boys can be slobs, and the sooner you accept it the easier your life will be." Richard gazes down at his front and crosses his left arm over the stain he had hoped she wouldn't notice. In hindsight, he should have selected a different shirt, but it's too late now. "Plus, I hadn't thought you would care about this evening. I mean, I'm playing all week so you can come tomorrow night, okay? I expect I'll get better as time goes on, anyway."

Priscilla's phone starts buzzing and she hurries off for the sofa, taking a Skype call from her father. Mabel joins her but then realizes she cannot be seen by John as a young woman, so grabs Richard and hauls him off to the kitchen.

"Hi, Daddy," Priscilla is excited to see her father's face on the screen. "How's Germany?"

"Hot. I miss you terribly. There's a heat wave in Europe and I wish I could be there swimming with you."

"Have you given your presentation yet?"

"Yes, yesterday."

"How'd it go?"

"Tough to say. You typically don't get much feedback at these academic conferences. Frankly, I'm not sure many people here are interested in my latest work."

She sits like a frog on the sofa, legs tugged underneath her. "Well . . . their loss."

114

"Is Grammy May nearby?"

"No, she's in the kitchen."

He lowers his voice. "How's she doing? I felt badly leaving you alone with her seeing how much pain she's in. I'm sorry I had to rush out so fast, and as it was, I almost missed my flight."

"She's doing great. We've been swimming . . ." she stops short.

"Come again?"

"I mean, she's been sewing . . ."

"Sewing what? I thought you said swimming there for a minute."

"A button came off my blouse."

"Is she taking her meds?"

Priscilla realizes her great-grandmother hasn't needed her medications this week and slips up again. "It's strange, but she doesn't seem to need them anymore—"

"Whaaat?" he leans in closer to the screen. Priscilla sees he is sitting in a hotel lobby, a bellboy passing behind with a cart loaded with luggage. There are several chic women looking stylish in the ways of Italian women, with fine handbags and luggage. A winding staircase off in the distance features what she assumes are Old Master reproductions hanging on the walls of the grand mezzanine. A large fern can be seen behind her father's head near the front desk.

She takes a deep breath. "I mean . . . she's in less pain and not taking so many ibuprofens. Hey, Dad. That looks like a nice hotel. Do you have a mini-bar in your room?"

"Who are those people behind you?" he leans in again.

Priscilla turns and waves at Richard and Peggy to hurry past. They had thought they could sneak by for the porch, but have been spotted.

"I don't see anyone," Priscilla realizes she's becoming an expert liar.

"I most certainly just saw a young man and woman pass behind you. What's going on there?"

Priscilla is quick on her feet once again. "Oh, that. I can't see it myself. I'm using a new app that adds in backgrounds. You know celebrities, places, those kinds of things. I think that was my Cardi B background. Pretty cool, huh?"

"Hmm," he's skeptical and feels something is wrong. He's fairly certain he saw a young couple walking behind her, who bore no resemblance to Cardi B. He sighs, assuming he is just exhausted from all the travel and the conference. "It's becoming increasingly difficult these days to distinguish between what's real and what's computer-generated," he leans in even closer, so close in fact that she can see a cluster of nose hairs extending out from his left nostril.

"Dad. Lean back, I can see your nose hairs you're so close. Gross."

"You sound just like your mother," he manages a smile as he drags his hand across his face.

"I'll take that as a compliment," she hopes she has distracted him from the mistaken appearance of Mabel and Richard. There is a lengthy silence, which she breaks with a redirection that startles him. "I'm hoping you'll take me to Sunday church when you return."

"Really?" he leans forward again, perplexed.

"Yes, really. I know Mommy would want you to, even though she knew you didn't believe in God the way she did, and the way I do. I'd like to try and go every Sunday."

"It's not that I don't believe in God. I just don't believe we can know who or what God is."

"That's because you're a sociologist who believes more in philosophy than religion," her reply amuses him, as this is a conversation he had many times with Michelle, who was raised a devout Catholic and who took Priscilla to church every Sunday in Oxford. She never gave up trying to get him to join them, but the most he could manage was to come for major holidays. The fact that his daughter now sounds like his wife is an unexpected development.

"Did you go to church on Sunday with Grammy May? I know she was excited to show you off."

Priscilla realizes in all the hullabaloo of Grammy May being young again, they were too busy swimming and playing music to attend church on Sunday. Mabel didn't even mention it, which shows just how excited she was with her resurrected youth, as she never missed church, even when the weather was horrible.

"She wasn't feeling up for it, but I'd like to go with you when you return."

"Well, that's not like her. Frankly, it's not like *you*. I hadn't thought you truly believed in God. I thought you went because your mother made you."

"Well, I *didn't* believe in God back then, but *now* I do. And I believe Mommy is in heaven with him and she is able to help us, to make great things happen for us."

"Interesting," he mumbles. "Well, I'm happy you feel that way as we're going to need all the help we can get. Sure, if you want me to take you to church I will, even though it makes me feel like a hypocrite given I'm not a true believer."

"Thanks, Dad. I appreciate it. Have you thought about what's going to happen to Grammy May once you return? Are we going to move in with her up here the way you discussed with me?"

"No, I really don't want to do that. You have your friends and school in Oxford, so if anything, we might need to sell her place and she can move in with us."

"She definitely won't want to do that," Priscilla looks out at the porch where Richard has his arm around Mabel.

118

"Well, no point worrying about it now. I'm relieved to hear she's doing well and that you're having a good time. If you need me for any reason, at any time, even if it's the middle of the night, call me. I'm not sleeping well so would be happy to Skype with you and take my mind off this conference."

"Sure. But I think we're going to be just fine." His daughter sounds so mature, as if she's grown up in just the few days he's been away. It's as if a miracle has taken place and all his worries about her and Mabel have been unfounded.

"That's great to hear."

"Don't worry about us. Just make sure those idiots over there appreciate your brilliance." She laughs. He laughs.

"Speaking of which, I need to go now as there's a dinner reception honoring a colleague from California. Someone I don't especially like. He's exceedingly pretentious. I'll try and call you later this week and can't wait to be home with you."

"I love you Daddy."

"And I love you more than words can express. Are you looking forward to your birthday party when I get back?"

"I am."

"Good, me too."

"Okay, talk to you soon. Love you," Priscilla waits until the screen goes blank and then closes up her phone.

119

*****

The four of them spend the afternoon swimming and sunbathing until it's time for Richard and Peggy to leave for Clarksdale. They drop Priscilla and Joey at Alice's, and Priscilla's mood improves upon learning Alice wants to teach her how to make biscuits from scratch. Now that Peggy and Richard are alone, they feel an unspoken excitement about the possibilities for later that night with the house all to themselves. Richard is nervous about this unforeseen opportunity dangling over their evening.

When they arrive at Wade's, the club is more crowded than the previous day, apparently the local review kicking up interest in Peggy despite being so negative. Maybe press of any kind is better than none, she is reminded of what her late-husband used to say when she was first starting out and her music was dismissed as being too racy. She checks her coat at the door and looks for Wade. All the tables are taken near the stage so Richard joins Colin and Lizzy at the bar while Mabel snakes her way up to the stage and begins performing. Mabel is determined to let it all hang out tonight, and as Richard sips his cocktail, he loosens up in the realization that she is playing very well and the audience seems enamored. In between songs, Richard attempts to strike up conversation with Colin and Lizzy, despite the noise at the bar and the brief breaks between songs.

"So tell me, Colin. How'd you become interested in philosophy?"

Colin is wearing a patchwork of mismatched clothing: a red shiny polyester shirt untucked over his brown trousers, and black Converse sneakers with holes in the toes. The doctor is concerned how wound up Colin seems tonight, fairly certain he has been mixing booze with uppers. He knows from experience this is a deadly mix for the heart.

Colin answers in a boozy slur of words. "Just wuz always curious to try and understand what this is all about."

"This?"

"Yes, this. The human condition, why we're here, what's the point of it all, you know, the lodge-ah matters of life."

"Of course. Did you go to college?"

"Me? College?"

"Yes."

"It's all kinda a blur back then to be honest with ya Doc," Colin answers in a way that leads Richard to drop the topic. Mabel plays another tune and they all sit quietly until she finishes.

Lizzy leans in between the two men and speaks over the applause. "Wade told me Colin used to be a press operator."

Colin looks puzzled. "A what?"

"He told me you told him you worked at a printing press in Massachusetts a long time ago."

121

"Hmm, I spose that's true," he points to his glass and the bartender pours him another whiskey shot, on the house.

Richard asks, "What kind of printing press did you operate?"

Colin seems to be remembering a forgotten past. "Man, I was the only one who could run that old German-piece-of-crap-whatever-the-heck-it-was-press, which printed large signs for depahtment store windows and the like, you know the signs: 50% Off Sale, Buy One, Get One Free, really dumb shit but lots of volume given how often these signs were changed out. What a bitch that press was. Woohee! It was like wrangling a wild horse the way I had to constantly adjust those old levers to get the ink to spread in the right places at the right time, the machine wanting to do its own thing once you finally got the dang thing warmed up and runnin' at production speeds. I was the shop's master cowboy, that's what some of the best customers called me, as they spent the night on press watchin' their jobs come off. That press was so old we couldn't get pahts for it so a local machine shop did the best they could to keep that beast a runnin'. It was huge, about twenty yahds long, so I was always dashin' from one end to the othah. I tried apprenticing some youngstahs, but they were rightfully wantin' to learn the newah presses, so I was on my own a lot. Always dark as can be, working the graveyahd shift. I guess I understand now why they called it that, cuz it was my own personal graveyahd looking back. It was screen printing and let me tell you, the inks we used are now outlawed. Lots of nasty shit in those inks. Toluene and so forth. The clients wore masks given how toxic the plant smelled, but I couldn't do that and run around the way I had to."

"I can only imagine," Lizzy pats his hand. "Sounds horrible."

Colin looks sad, staring off into a vacant distance, sweat trickling down from his silver sideburns. "You know, I used to be somebody."

Mabel launches into "Summertime," which brings the club to complete silence, her rendition soulful and loaded with feeling. Thunderous applause rocks the club as she finishes and Richard spies more people cramming into the back of the club, which he sees is now standing-room only.

Richard looks at Colin, the classic song causing him to grow more disconsolate as he recalls his mostly forgotten past. "You know, I grew up in a good family. A prominent old Boston family. But my fathah died when I was sixteen and then my mother remarried a man I just couldn't stand, so I ran away from home. Got a job on a street crew in Cambridge, and that's when I met Earl Hoskins, who was like a surrogate fathah to me. He let me stay at his nice home in Brookline. I told him I was abandoned as a child and grew up in New

123

Hampshire. I didn't want him knowin' the truth, cuz he might hand me back to my mothah and stepfathah. Earl was a professor of theology at Haa-vid and had an incredible collection of books, so I spent much of my time being homeschooled by his wife, who was a social workah. I took the SATs even though I hadn't gone to high school and aced them. Earl used his influence to get me a scholarship to Haa-vid, but then my mother up and died and I stahted gettin' into drugs, bad drugs. I ran away again and got a job in Waltham at the printing company, where I was trained to operate that lahge-format press no one else wanted to lewn. Lars Janssen, that was the old man's name. He musta been going on seventy and wanted to retire, so they hired me to be his understudy. I did this for several years but then, well, I had a mental breakdown. Just blew a gasket, I guess, me and my press. I was on the streets of Bahstin until winter came and it was just too damned cold, so I scrounged up enough money to buy a bus ticket to Jackson, and I've been here in Clarksdale evah since."

"How sad," Lizzy rubs him on the shoulder. "You know, my grandmother toward the end of her life frequently could be heard saying: *life is just one damned thing after another*."

Colin guffaws. "That's good. I need to try and remembah that one. You know, as I reflect upon my mostly forgotten years at that printer, I think it was the inks that did me in. But then I think no, that's not right, as othah people workin' there were just fine. Lars did it for years with no ill effects that I was aware of. No, I think it was all the drugs and drinkin'."

"Or maybe the pressures you were under being on your own so young," Richard adds. "Listen, I'd like to help if you'll let me."

"How? I don't want no handouts."

"Yes, I realize that. I've been meaning to read more philosophy and would like to propose a trade with you. If you can find me ten books you highly recommend, I'll give a free checkup at my clinic in Sardis. I'm sure it's been ages since you saw a doctor and I worry about what all your drinking is doing to your heart. We should run some tests."

"That's nice, Doc, but there's no way I'm givin' up the booze. And I really don't need your charity. But I'll happily sell you some books if you want. What I really need is cash."

"So you can buy more booze," Lizzy shakes her head.

Colin smiles and Richard realizes he's probably a lost cause, one of the many who will show up in the Emergency Room to die alone. He dealt with people like Colin when doing his residency in Baltimore, working in the ER where homeless people would show up, usually too late. He sighs and glances at the stage where Peggy is playing an upbeat Samba tune he doesn't recognize. He's impressed by how well she's playing tonight, and so is the crowd. Refocusing on her reminds him of what awaits, Mabel's house all to themselves. He pushes his drink aside, not wanting to dull his own pending performance, reminded of how he felt as a high schooler waiting his turn backstage for the school play. Peggy finishes up her set with a rousing version of "When the Saints Go Marching In," a song she recalls playing as a girl back when she played a considerable amount of gospel music in church. The crowd loves this upbeat, familiar song and breaks into thunderous applause, clamoring for an encore. She returns to the stage and plays a sexy slow version of "Someone to Love," a song Richard feels is being directed at him and no one else. This only serves to heighten his anxieties.

Now they are driving home through passing thunderstorms on this steamy southern night, and Mabel places her hand on his thigh as he does his best to keep his eyes focused on the dark road ahead. He is caught off guard by how forward she's acting, but passes it off to the knowledge they only have this one week together before she returns to California, and Priscilla is conveniently off at her sleepover. Little does he know how short time truly is for Mabel. She had been mulling over how the night might play out throughout her performance, concerned about taking advantage of him, in full realization he doesn't know he's falling for an old woman. How can this possibly end without broken hearts? Imagine his revulsion upon seeing her as the real Mabel Johnson once the week is over? She knows what she's doing is all wrong but as the song goes: "If loving you is wrong, I don't want to be right." He'll get over her. He's young, will have plenty of opportunities to meet a suitable woman his age. It is with this inner rationalization that she squeezes his thigh as they speed through the night.

When the BMW pulls into her driveway, they step from the car into a sudden downpour pelting them with heavy raindrops as they dash up the stairway and stumble inside soaked head to toe. Peggy races into the bathroom for towels and returns to the entryway where Richard stands like an obedient black Labrador, unsure of what to do without his master's lead. She wipes him down from head to waist, laughing as they stand dripping onto the floor. On the drive home, Mabel had been plotting how to lure him into her bedroom, but now it becomes clear they will never make it that far, Richard pulling his shirt over his head revealing a six-pack of abs unlike anything Mabel has seen in decades. She hurriedly unbuttons her blouse and the two of them kiss passionately, fumbling with their clothes while stumbling to the sofa, naked bodies entwined.

WEDNESDAY

Mabel awakens early to sunlight streaming in through the living room windows. She rolls off the sofa drawn by the smell of pancakes coming from the kitchen, where she finds Richard making breakfast. She feels drained in the most therapeutic way, and has completely forgotten who or where she is, floating on the magical cloud of lovemaking, a feeling she has not known in a long time. Richard is dressed in boxer shorts covered with colorful puppies, the shorts partly concealed by the XL button-down shirt he must have found in her closet. He flips four pancakes in the frying pan and reaches over to kiss her as she leans in.

"Been a long time since a man cooked breakfast for me."

"Somehow I find that difficult to believe." He pauses, unsure of himself, much of last night a foggy memory as he senses a new complexity in their changed relationship. "Was last night . . . you know . . . as good for you, um, as it was for me?" he stumbles through the words.

"Well, there is no honest way to know for sure, now is there?" she enjoys toying with him. He looks down, disappointed in her reply, and she sees this and quickly strokes his ego as required. "If you felt *one-tenth* of what I felt, then all I can say is, well . . . I'm still shakin' all over, look at me." She holds out her hands and he can see she's trembling, much in the same way an overused muscle spasms following exertion. He smiles, relieved by her reassurances.

He turns down the heat on the front burner. "Well, give me some time, and with practice, I'll only get better. It's been awhile."

"Are you kidding? It's been like several decades for me—" she slips up and he glances at her, confused.

"Decades? Somehow I doubt that."

She recovers. "Well, it *feels* like decades."

He pauses, once again sensing something is amiss with this strange woman. She refuses to look him in the eye, and he recalls feeling an otherworldly urgency to her lovemaking last night, somehow both exhilarating and supernatural, certainly much different than his previous experiences. He's made love to a handful of women, but Peggy took things to a whole new level. He woke up feeling like a mortal who had just been used for unknowable reasons by a vengeful goddess from ancient mythology, like Aphrodite settling a bet with one of her adversarial gods. He can't fully explain the feeling, but their lovemaking, as great as it was, also felt wrong at times.

"Surely a beautiful woman like you has taken many

lovers," he flips two pancakes onto a plate for her and turns off the stove, pondering his unexpected usage of the word "taken," puzzled by whatever she may have taken from him last night. Mabel walks with her plate of pancakes to the kitchen table, where she waits for him to join her. She notices a certain guarded apprehension to his manner this morning, something she hasn't noticed before. Maybe making love was a bad idea? Certainly, theirs would not be the first relationship complicated by sex. These are all distant emotions for her, long forgotten matters of the heart and body, ones she senses have been a relief not to worry about since she became too old for any man to notice. Being young again might not be all it's chocked up to be, she chuckles on the inside, not certain she truly means it. Most definitely not. Being young again has been amazing. The way she performed last night at the club and, later with Richard, there can be no regrets. She knows it's best for a woman eager to enjoy a man's continued company to not confess the full extent of her amorous affairs, remembering how the mention of previous lovers can lead to petty jealousies. She replies: "I've only been with a couple of men before."

"Wow," he exclaims in surprise, head jerking back slightly, brow furrowed in confusion. "I mean, your lovemaking, your passion, your performance . . . just struck me as something only an experienced woman would be capable of. I can tell you for a fact, I've never been with a woman like you before."

She blushes. If only he knew what it was like to have the wisdom of an older woman inside a young body, capable of making love after so many years. She had done everything possible to prolong their pleasure last night, knowing all too well how quickly pleasure turns to regret. She knows she was more forward than she should have been, but found herself in a passionate dream state that overruled her rational mind. "Richard, you're flattering me and making me blush. Speaking of performances, I wonder how my performance at the club last night will make that shitty little journalist feel once he hears about it?"

Richard drizzles syrup onto his pancakes. "Well, you certainly took *all* your playing to a whole new level last night."

She smiles at his little joke. She likes him very much, he's so intelligent, funny, and handsome. If only she could stay young for more than just this week. She does her best not to worry about the future, thoroughly enjoying being in the moment.

Richard continues. "I was chatting with two musicians playing at the festival who said you sound just like Mabel Johnson. They were awed."

"Really? What kind of musicians?"

"Not sure, but I got the impression they are well-known. One said his name was Leroy something or other. They were totally groovin' on you, that's for sure. Everyone was."

The phone rings and Mabel gets up to get it. It's Alice from next door. She's bringing Priscilla home around ten and wonders if they could take Joey for the day. Both kids are hoping to go to the Neshoba Fair, and that's too long a drive for her, plus she's hoping to get her hair done. Given that Alice took Priscilla overnight, Mabel knows she should reciprocate so says that sounds fine. She hangs up and tells Richard the news. "I guess we've got a couple of hours to work on our *performances*," she smiles and they head off for her bedroom.

At ten o'clock, the four of them set off in Richard's BMW for the Neshoba County Fair, more than two hours south from Sardis. It's a beautiful day with fair weather clouds providing intermittent relief from the sun as they drive into the slick mirages disappearing ahead of them. Joey and Priscilla sit in the back seat while Richard and Mabel listen to a pop music station, and they make good time to the fairgrounds. The Neshoba County Fairgrounds greet you with a small settlement of cabins decked out with American flags and patriotic bunting, children playing in the dusty streets as their parents and grandparents look on from porches. The cabins remind Richard of an old Hollywood set, appearing almost as temporary as the rides off in the distance, despite the fact many have been here for a very long time. Local and national politicians have used the fair to launch campaigns stretching back to before Richard Nixon, and sure enough they see political signs littering the road near the square. Mabel and Priscilla have been here before so have a good idea what they want to do: stop by Lindsey's Lemonade for freshly squeezed lemonade, pass through the small exhibition hall to see what local wares are being hawked, and then hit the rides. Off in the distance they see brightly colored hot air balloons and the Ferris wheel.

"Can we get our ride tickets now?" Joey asks as they emerge from the row of cabins.

"Sure, right after we get some lemonades," Mabel leads them to Lindsey's where she buys four lemonades. Joey and Priscilla tag along behind Richard as they wander into the exhibition hall. There are small stands with sweaty older men and women selling patriotic cups and dishes, calendars and books, and homemade spicy sauces. Mabel buys some hot sauce and then they exit, eager to be back out into the fresh but hot air. "Cain't we hurry up and go on some rides?" Joey pleads.

Richard nods, "Sure, let me get your tickets and then Peggy and I'll sit out front while you two go on the rides." He buys several tickets and they head toward the Ferris wheel, which has a short line given the midday heat. Most people will be coming tonight when it's cooler.

"Keep an eye on Joey," Mabel calls out to Priscilla, as the kids race to get into line, and the adults head for a bench in the shade of an ash tree. Joey and Priscilla share a seat on the Ferris wheel, which begins its slow ascent, halting on the way up as others board below. "I wish we'd get goin'!" Joey yells into Priscilla's ear and she slides over in the seat to gain more distance from him.

"Be patient."

"I sure do love the Ferris wheel," he exclaims, lemonade stains on his shirt. "Especially at night when all the lights are on. Too bad we cain't be here tonight instead of durin' the day. I can ride this a zillion times and not be scared at all, even when hangin' up on the top waitin' for others to hurry it up and unload down below. I like it even when it's windy, like it was last time I was here when I got stuck up top as a thunderstorm was comin' through. Momma was so scared. But I liked it. I could see way off in the distance where a funnel cloud was movin' along. Ain't nuthin scare me."

Priscilla is recovering from the long car ride with Joey, realizing he is inappropriately competitive and talks too much. Yesterday, he bragged how he could beat her in the backstroke as they dove from the float in Sardis Lake, and

135

then at his house for the sleepover he became competitive playing a video game, which she had no interest in, preferring to read, but doing her best to be a polite guest in his home. Now, as the Ferris wheel finally begins making several uninterrupted circles with all seats occupied, he leans over the side waving his hands and screaming into the air. "C'mon, you do it too, Priscilla. Don't be a-scared-e-cat."

"Get back in your seat, Joey. That's dangerous."

"Ah, don't be such a sissy."

"I'm not a sissy," she pulls on his shirt to make sure he stays seated.

"Are too. I totally nuked you in *Counterstrike*. You're like the worst player I've ever seen."

Priscilla had not enjoyed playing this violent video game with Joey, which glamorized violence in Iraq or Afghanistan—she couldn't be sure which, possibly both—but at any rate some place where real American soldiers were being killed while they played that game. She had done her best to get through it, managing to redirect Joey's wandering attention back outside, where they rode bikes and she could pedal ahead and enjoy some space. "Who cares if I'm the worst player you've ever seen. That game is violent and disrespectful of our troops fighting overseas."

"Well, it's true. You're nowhere near as good as Toby."

"Who's Toby?"

"My uncle. He gave me the game for my birthday. You should see his game room, he's got like tons of games at his house. I shoulda went there today instead of comin' to this stupid place."

"*Should have gone,*" she corrects him.

"That's what I said."

"No, you said *shoulda went.*"

"They're just words. They mean the same thing," he looks away.

By the time they get off the ride, Priscilla is steaming mad at Joey, who is ruining what is normally one of her more fun outings of the summer. Why did they have to bring him? He doesn't even want to be here. They head over to the swing ride where they will have seats to themselves. As they start spinning around, Priscilla can see Richard and Peggy sitting close together on the bench, holding hands and sharing sips of their lemonade. As the ride begins circling faster and faster, the scenery all blends into a montage of hot air balloons, horse races, fading screams, and Richard and Peggy whizzing by on the bench below the trees.

Richard has one eye on the ride and the other on Peggy, who is laughing at something he has just said. "Are you sure you can't just quit your stewardess job and stay here with me?"

"If only. I'm afraid it's not that simple."

"Why not? I earn enough for the both of us to live comfortably. You could just compose music and work on building your musical career."

"Are you proposing marriage, my good doctor?"

He smiles. "Would that help you stay?"

"We've only known each other for a few days," she laughs and he loves how she lights up with her beautiful smile.

"Don't you believe in love at first sight?" he asks.

She's flattered and has to admit she might have fallen in love with Richard when she first woke up in the hospital following her stroke with him seated next to her bed, holding her hand, his warm smile reassuring her. Lust or love, she's not sure which. She cannot deny the effect he has on her, how when he's close she feels her heart racing, her temperature rising. There is a prolonged silence as they watch the kids twirling and screaming on the ride. She can think of little else than being in bed beside him, as they were just hours ago.

Richard leans in and kisses her on the neck and Peggy forces herself to pull away, not wanting Priscilla to see them. She changes the subject. "Do you think that ride is safe? It's making me nervous."

"I doubt it," he replies.

"Really?"

"I mean, I wouldn't get on that rusty old thing. Would you?"

"Now you've got me worried."

"Don't. I'm sure it's fine. Sort of."

"I'll be glad when they get off."

Richard resumes his pitch. "But, listen, I'm being serious. Why don't you at least hang around longer than this week so we can see how we're feeling? You have so much talent as a singer, it seems to me you should be pursuing music as your occupation and not flying the not-so-friendly skies."

Again, she laughs. "Right. Like I am anywhere near good enough to have a music career. Methinks you're going a bit batty, Mr. Richie Rich."

"Think of how much fun it would be living together."

"We just met," she is concerned how quickly he is falling for her, wishing with all her heart she could be with him for more than this week. She's terribly conflicted, on the one hand wanting to be with him forever and on the other thinking it will be best if the spell wears off this weekend. The poor man has suffered enough and she doesn't want to add to his suffering, even though she is finding him to be irresistible.

Richard leans over to tie his left sneaker lace and his arm brushes against hers. "Well, don't move in with me. Move in with Mabel. She can't be living on her own much longer given her dementia."

She pauses, caught off guard by this redirection, but senses an opportunity to test him honestly about what he thinks of her condition. One of her chief frustrations in recent years has been the inability to get a straight answer out of any of her doctors, all of whom are understandably concerned about lawsuits, so always careful about saying anything with certainty. She has asked Doctor Roberts more than once what to expect now that she's had a small stroke, a lacunar stroke as he refers to it, and all he ever says is to eat well and stay active, to take things one day at a time, which sounds to her like he's holding back something. What she really wants to know is how long he thinks she has before she completely loses her marbles.

"Are you all that concerned about Mabel's health?"

"Yes, I am."

"Why? She seems fine to me."

"Well, for one thing, she's far too old to be living alone. I discussed this with Michelle before she was tragically killed. Michelle and John were planning to move in with her, but now John doesn't want to take Priscilla out of her school where she has a couple of friends and is happy. He knows she'd be upset to leave her piano instructor there."

"You've spoken with John?"

"He called me three weeks ago curious to get my opinion on Mabel's situation."

"What did you tell him?"

"I told him Mabel should not be living alone, that her

vascular dementia will only get worse now that she's had a lacunar stroke. That she's liable to fall and hurt herself."

"But she has that Life Alert necklace, don't you think that's good enough?"

"It helps, sure, but what if she forgets to put the battery in? What if she forgets to wear it? What if she slips in the shower and doesn't have it on? Trust me when I tell you, it's exceedingly difficult to manage one's physical health when one's memory fails. Plus, as she loses her memory, her anxiety will only get worse, and the drugs she takes to offset that unfortunately contribute to memory loss. It's a vicious cycle. I finally insisted she at least hire in-home care to make sure she's actually taking her pills. It was a requirement for her to go home following her rehab stint and one she resisted. Honestly, I would not be surprised if she had her stroke because she lapsed in taking her pills."

"I see," Mabel looks away, not sure knowing the truth was such a great idea, but unable to stop probing him given this unexpected opportunity. "What if she hired full-time live-in help?"

He continues. "What with her dementia only bound to get worse, she can't be living on Sardis Lake all by herself, and probably should sell the place and move into a memory care facility nearer to John and Priscilla. I doubt live-in help can provide everything she'll need if she completely loses her memory and begins exhibiting psychotic behaviors commonly found among certain types of dementia. That's what I told John. I told him I'd authorize sending her to a memory care center if he asks."

"Sell the house?" she is feeling betrayed by her lover doctor.

"Yes."

"Move into a memory care center?"

"Sure, why not?" he senses her reticence and is once again surprised by how strongly she feels about Mabel.

"What did John say when you told him this?"

"He said he'd rather not but I warned him how difficult taking care of an invalid with dementia can be. I sense he's leaning toward having her sell the house and move in with Priscilla and him in Oxford. But he has no idea how much of a burden that would place on him. If she totally loses her short-term memory, she will have no choice but to be admitted to a facility."

"Hmm. Well, I'm glad he's not in a great rush to ship her off like refuse in a trash truck. From what I can tell, memory care facilities are dreadful places where the elderly are essentially locked up until they mercifully die. For what it's worth, I think she seems sharp as a tack. We had a great conversation when I arrived before she departed for Jackson. I think you may be overreacting."

"You probably caught her in a good moment. Vascular dementia is like stepping down stairs. You lose something, but plateau for a bit, and then continue down. It varies from patient to patient, but in general as one ages, there are what I call pockets of wellness, when someone will feel surprisingly well for a couple of hours, maybe even a full day, but then relapse. Aging is a narrowing of possibilities."

"Tell me about it," she sighs.

"Well, you certainly have nothing to complain about, Peggy. You're still young and in great health."

She recovers, reverting to her Peggy role. "Yes, I know. But even at my age you start to notice the losses coming."

"Well, to bring us back to Mabel, this is why I suggested you move in with her, to help her stay at home as long as possible. You both can play the piano. She can pay you to care for her, something I'm sure she would greatly appreciate and enjoy. John can get back to his life, which clearly he needs to do." He is doing his best to make the case and now has Mabel cornered in a way she doesn't like. Funny how when a man wants something, like a pretty woman as his pet prize, the truth finally emerges. He'd never be so frank with the old hag Mabel. She is astonished to hear this assessment of her condition, coming from him with such conviction and honesty. She wants to doubt what he is saying, attribute it to his interest in coercing her to stay in Sardis, but cannot in good conscience deny the frankness with which he now speaks. She realizes her life, and that of John and Priscilla, has become far more complicated in recent months with the death of Michelle, whom she had counted on as a blood relative to care for her. She likes John and trusts him, and is relieved to hear he is not eager to send her off to a nursing home. But now that she's young again, these concerns have mostly evaporated along with her pains, but if her spell does wear off after just one week, then she'll be back as an old woman facing God knows what—a memory care center! She has always figured she would die in her beloved home, but now that seems threatened by recent events.

"Oh, Michelle, how I miss you," she blurts out, tears streaming down her cheeks. She collects herself, realizing she has once again slipped out of role.

The doctor looks confused. "I hadn't realized you were close to Michelle. I'm sorry—"

"We weren't *terribly* close, but I did enjoy her company. Plus, now, what's to become of Mabel?"

"That's my point," he smiles. "This is why *you* are the answer. *We* are the answer. You can move in with her and that way I'll see more of her than I do now as just her physician. I'll have a good excuse to come visit as your friend. That way I can give her more attention than she would otherwise receive, as we assess how the dementia is progressing. It's

144

conceivable it won't progress so rapidly that she can't enjoy her remaining time."

She sighs. What a mess. There is no good way out of this conversation cycle, and she's relieved when Joey and Priscilla run toward them. Priscilla wants to go listen to the bluegrass band playing in the nearby tent and take a break from the rides, so she and Joey head that way and take a seat at a long picnic table just inside the tent.

"I wish I could play the banjo that good," Joey says, bouncing in his seat.

She looks at him condescendingly. "It's a simple instrument to learn Joey. Even *you* should be able to figure it out."

He looks down, hurt. She is unaware that she has wounded him. "I've been learning how to play Chopin sonatas and they are far more demanding than that simplistic banjo strumming."

Joey is scraping his right foot through the dust like an irascible donkey. "I bet I can beat you at Mumblety-peg," he jumps from his seat.

"What's that?"

He pulls a Swiss Army knife from his pocket. "Follow me around back and I'll show ya." She wants to stay and listen to the music but Joey disappears around the corner so she follows after him. She catches up behind the tent and Joey

145

explains that you have to reach as far as you can to one side and stick the knife in the ground without it falling out.

"What a stupid game," she says.

"Is not. Betcha cain't do it."

He stretches one leg to the left as far as he can, reaches across and sticks his knife in the ground with his first attempt, about two feet away. Clearly he has done this many times before.

"Go ahead. You try, now, Miss Smarty Pants."

She tries several times but the knife lands each time with a thud, bouncing off the hard-packed soil. Joey laughs, enjoying seeing her fail. She tries again and again with the same result until she finally gives up.

"See, you ain't so smart after all," Joey jabs her in the arm.

"Hey, watch it. This has nothing to do with being smart."

"What's the matter? You don't like losin' or sumthin'?"

"I don't mind losing something as stupid as Monkey-Peg, or whatever you call it."

"It's Mumblety-peg," he corrects her. "Cain't you speak right? You think you're all that just cuz you can play Chop-IN snot-ers?"

"It's Chopin, like Show-Pan. And they are sonatas, not *snot-ers*. You should listen to them sometime; you might just like them."

146

"Who cares? No one listens to that dead music no more anyhow. Why, I bet you couldn't play that banjo even if you tried for months and months."

Priscilla is fuming, arms pressed tightly across her chest, trying to hold in the building fury. "Bet I could learn that dumb instrument in a single day."

"Could not."

"Could so."

"Could not."

"Well," she stands with hands on her hips, "I bet you couldn't wish for your great-grandmother to be young again and have it come true."

Oops.

"Wud you say?" Joey tilts his head in confusion, looking like a perplexed chug.

"You heard me. I prayed that my great-grandmother would be young again and it came true. Peggy isn't my aunt, she's Grammy May, who *I* made young again. So chew on that for a bit, you dolt."

Joey squints, not sure he is hearing correctly. "You're a bigtime fibber."

"Am not."

"No one can make someone young again," he is kicking his sneaker into the dust, putting his knife back in his hip pocket. "You think I'm that dumb?"

147

"Well, I did make it happen. So take that you dirty little stupid boy." Priscilla charges off with tears in her eyes, heading back to where Richard and Mabel are chatting on the bench.

"What's the matter?" Mabel looks concerned.

"I'm sorry, I'm sorry, I messed up."

Joey walks over and looks long and hard at Mabel but says nothing, still trying to process what Priscilla just told him. Surely, she's got something wrong in the head. But Peggy does look a lot like Mabel, he takes a closer look.

Richard glances at his watch and suggests they head home, so they will have enough time to get cleaned up before the performance that evening.

Mabel, Priscilla, and Richard arrive at the club that evening and Mabel is introduced to Leroy Mullens and Buzz Stanley, young musicians making names for themselves in recent times. "Very nice to meet you both," Mabel is flattered they have sought her out.

"We heard you play last night and are totally in awe, man," Leroy says. "Buzz and I were wondering if we could sit in with you on your second set tonight? He plays bass and I play drums."

"Oh, I've heard of you. But, I don't know. I'm not sure I'm ready to perform in a trio. I mostly play solo."

148

"Well, it's not like we're playing Carnegie Hall," Buzz smiles and she sees a large gap between his two front teeth.

She smiles politely, thinking if only he knew.

Leroy continues, "And it's not like many of these folks in the crowd would know great playing if it hit them across the head."

She laughs. It's been decades since she's performed live with other musicians. She's feeling more confident about her playing and is curious to see how she would hold up performing in a trio after all these years. She exhales and says: "What the heck, let's give it a try. We'll play a couple of Mabel's hit songs, which I imagine you know."

"Ab-so-LUTE-ly," Leroy exclaims.

Richard and Priscilla are seated at the front table with Colin who has come for the show. Leroy and Buzz join them as Mabel begins her first set. She plays a perfect set of solo piano and then grabs a glass of white wine at the bar during intermission. She overhears Leroy deep in discussion with Colin about Ralph Waldo Emerson. "Emerson had it right," Colin says. "We all need to be self-reliant and then everyone else will benefit. We cain't be livin' in a welfare state where the weak suck too much strength from the strong."

Leroy shakes his head, breaking into a perplexed grin. "Man, you are one strange duck. I mean, here you are of all people, a street person standing up for power and privilege.

Don't you believe we all have an obligation to help the less fortunate?"

"Of course, but that's the point. It's like that old fishin' aphorism: you need to teach others to fish, not put the fish on their plate. That way they'll be able to catch their own fish."

"Sure, but not everyone can afford a fishing rod," Leroy fires back.

Buzz joins in. "Not to mention white folks like you get a huge head start. Can't you see that?"

"Sure, I spose," Colin leans back in his seat, nearly toppling over, high once again, talking too fast. "It's a balance. Everything's a balance, a continuum, that's what makes the world work. But I feel like lately that balance has swung too faah toward a welfare state."

"Are you crazy, man?" Leroy leans in. "All that's been happening for the past decades is wealth has been transferring from the working class to the wealthiest among us. You've got the balance all wrong. But whatever, you're a strange dude. Emerson. Tell me about it. You might want to spend less time reading dead white authors and try some living Black ones, like Colson Whitehouse and Ibram X. Kendi."

Richard winks at Mabel who approaches their table from the bar. Colin gets up, rising like a true gentleman, which leads her to chuckle in the realization the street person is more of a gentleman than the local arts reporter.

"Why, thank you," she says to Colin, who pulls out her chair.

"The pleasure is all mine. The way you play, you move a man to tears."

"Aren't you kind."

"I still cain't get over how much you sound like Mabel back in the day. I dunno, you might even be bettah than her."

"Now you're going too far, but thank you."

"Still, I was sittin' here havin' flashbacks to when I saw Mabel play. Some of those early small venue shows of hers were off the charts great."

"Well, you know how music runs in families," she replies.

"I do, I do. But still."

Mabel spies Lizzy sitting alone at the far end of the bar and gets up to keep her company. She sees mascara running beneath her left eye and worries she's been crying.

"What's wrong, dear," she sits next to her at the dark end of the bar.

Lizzy feigns a smile. "I'm fine," she attempts to pull herself together.

"You don't look fine to me. If you want to talk, I'm happy to listen," Mabel takes her delicate hand in hers, noticing how long and slender her fingers are.

Lizzy lets loose a deep exhale. "It's just my father, he's

so bigoted and angry. I had forgotten how mean he can be."

"I'm sorry."

"He sees me as his personal servant, the only one left in the family, and waiting on him hand and foot while he becomes abusive when drinking, well, it just isn't right."

Mabel nods knowingly. "Can't you just leave and go back home?"

"Oh, I wouldn't be able to live with myself if I did that. And truth be told, my home life isn't so great either."

They sit in quiet as the jukebox plays Patsy Cline.

Lizzy continues: "My boyfriend of two years is having an affair and keeps denying it. I found texts on his phone. Some waitress he met. I had a hunch but it still hurts when you find out for certain."

"Oh . . . I see."

"I'm not sure which place is worse, back home with my cheating boyfriend or here with my drunk of a father. At least at home I don't feel I'm regressing to the extent I am here. It's a mess. I feel trapped. And I want to have children but fear I'm getting too old and am stuck with the worst possible man as a potential father."

"Does your boyfriend have a drinking problem, too?"

Lizzy turns to the side and whispers. "Yes."

"Oh, dear."

"I know, I know. It's all so clichéd. The daughter of a

drunken father lacking self-esteem, repeating the pattern in her many failed relationships."

"Well, awareness is step one."

"I have a good therapist. Or had. But now I'm feeling middle-aged and aimless."

"You're not middle-aged, are you kidding me?"

"I'm turning thirty-two this year."

Mabel laughs. "If you think thirty-two is middle-age, then I must be ancient. Do you know how to tell when you've reached middle-age?"

"Apparently not."

"Middle-age is when you spend an equal amount of time looking back with regret as you do looking ahead with anxiety."

Lizzy lets out a loud laugh. "That's a good one!"

"Well, I think it's true. But the larger point is you don't want to spend your life caring for undeserving people. There are givers and there are takers, and the takers will suck the life out of you until you stand your ground. Trust me, I know."

"Easier said than done. My father wasn't *all* bad. I have some good memories. I can't just abandon him now."

"I'm not suggesting you flee. I'm suggesting you fight for yourself. Demand more from him if you are going to help him."

"That's just not who I am," the left side of her thin lips

tilt with regret.

"I know, trust me, I know," Mabel is thinking about her ex-husband and how he took advantage of her. She's also thinking about the music agents who negotiated bad contracts with their own interests in mind, not hers. She feels her blood pressure rising.

Lizzy's eyes well with tears. "I always wanted to be a musician but my parents couldn't afford to keep me in college."

"Where'd you go?"

"Oberlin. I loved it very much. I had an excellent voice instructor who seemed to genuinely believe I had talent. When I dropped out, she was so kind, and continued giving me private lessons until I moved back home."

"Well, she had a good eye for talent. I was genuinely moved by your playing the other day when we first met."

Lizzy perks up. "Really? You're not just saying that to cheer me up?"

"I wouldn't do that. I've heard many great performers over the years and it's the ones with distinctive voices that stand out, not the many imitators. Dylan, Joni Mitchell, Nina Simone, the list goes on and on. All unique talents. Your voice has an unusual combination of smokiness and sweetness, and that's a gift not to be squandered."

"Aren't you kind," she squeezes Mabel's hand.

"It's the truth. Listen carefully to me, dear. Life flies by and no matter how successful or unsuccessful you feel your life has been, you will have regrets. Everyone does. I think the trick is to limit those regrets, which means taking chances, chasing your dreams even though it seems everyone, even God, wants to knock you down. Don't let them. Don't let others define who you are. You are a unique individual possessed with God-given talents and you need to pursue those dreams. I have an internal mantra I call on when times get tough: *Do the work.* It takes tremendous discipline to make it through life and especially to be an artist, so you must believe in yourself and just do the work. Do it for yourself. At worst, it will help you feel better as an inexpensive form of therapy. At best, you might make a living doing what you love most. That's the goal. But to reach it you must do the work. Battle against the odds. Don't let others who are jealous drag you down."

"You speak with such wisdom, Peggy, as if you are a much older woman."

"Some of us age faster than others. I'm happy to try and help you. I hate seeing you sitting over here all by yourself. Come join the others at the table up front. It's time for the second set. I'm so nervous, I'm not comfortable playing with others I've never performed with."

"I'm sure you'll be fine. You sing and play so

beautifully, it's been an amazing treat to listen to you this week."

Mabel smiles at this innocent young woman struggling to make her way in a difficult world. She squeezes her hand more tightly and then the two of them walk to the front table where Lizzy takes a seat.

Mabel joins Leroy and Buzz on stage. They decide to play "In the Dark" as their opening song followed by "Black Coffee," and then just jam around some C blues and see how it goes. Leroy is getting comfortable behind the drum set, arranging his various sticks and brushes, when he spots Harold Barnes seated in the back of the club. Harold is the young music critic for *The New York Times* who has been very generous to Leroy with glowing reviews of his performances as part of the Buddy Grainger Quintet. It's unusual for a drummer to receive much attention in reviews of a quintet headed up by a legend like Buddy Grainger, but Harold Barnes raved about their recent album and has become a huge fan, oftentimes posting kind comments on Leroy's Twitter feed. Leroy casts a quick welcoming glance at Harold who acknowledges him with a raised glass of wine. Leroy squints through the lights and thinks he spots Charles Schmidt, the legendary music executive at Warner Music, seated next to Harold. They must have come together, he assumes. Schmidt has signed some of the top acts in the business. Yes, that's him, he gets a better look. He must be well into his eighties, Leroy figures. Wonder why he's here? Probably in town for the festival, scouting new acts. Leroy gets up and walks over to Buzz, making sure he knows Schmidt and Barnes are in the house. Their recent album was released on a small jazz label lacking the clout of Warner Music, so they are excited to give this set their all. Mabel, for her part, is clueless about any of this and is nervous about performing with a trio after all these years. Her sulky voice quiets the crowd as she adjusts the mic and begins singing: "In the dark . . ." and Leroy's subtle brushwork and Buzz's bass accentuate the bass notes of the piano, providing the gravitas the inadequate upright piano sorely needs. The music meshes in a sublime sound that has Mabel feeling that ineffable power of performing in a group at the highest levels. When the song is over, applause reverberates throughout the club. The next tune is "Fever," which sounds so much better with the drums and bass added to her solo playing. Buzz plays an extended bass solo, requiring her to comp chords in a way she hasn't done for ages, but it comes back to her as she experiments with new voicings that seem to be working well. Leroy lifts the bed with his subtle brushwork now on the cymbal. The applause is even more enthusiastic at the end of this song. Mabel sees Colin and Lizzy sitting down front with Richard and Priscilla. Richard is beaming with pride, smitten by her soulful singing.

The bass and drums start playing a C jam blues, and she joins in, splashing chords and scatting even though she knows she is out on a dangerous improvisational limb. She recalls seeing Ella Fitzgerald perform many years ago at the Newport Jazz Festival, and how impressed she was by the great singer's ability to improvise and scat, creating a unique energy onstage. It dawns on her that scat—the singing of sounds instead of lyrics—was the logical precursor to rap with its freeform improvised poetry, both art forms rarely performed the same way twice in live performance. When it comes time for her to play her piano solo, she uses phrasing she remembers from Mose Allison and others, playing slightly behind the beat but not so far as to detach from the rhythm section. She turns her head and smiles at Leroy and Buzz as the three of them merge in a fresh musical sound, different from what she knew in her heyday, these younger musicians playing in new ways. She feels challenged by their accompaniment as she strives to raise her own level, experimenting with dissonant chord structures and scat. They build to an apex and then bring the whole musical bed back down, planning their smooth landing with nods, ending in unison as the crowd erupts into applause. They play two more songs and then call it quits. The crowd continues applauding, demanding an encore as they clap in unison. Mabel returns to the stage and shows Buzz and Leroy some handwritten chord progressions she's scribbled on a napkin, which they study, asking her a few questions, then nod they're good to go. They launch into her new composition, feeling their way through unfamiliar terrain, enjoying the challenge of the music. At the conclusion, Mabel exclaims into the mic, sweat trickling down her cheeks: "All right, all right. Wow! Thank you for coming everyone!"

Back at the table she is regaining control of her emotions, wiping perspiration from her face with a napkin Richard passes to her, accepting congratulations from Leroy and Buzz. Leroy snaps to attention as he sees Charles Schmidt approach the table. He's a portly man who looks remarkably like Alfred Hitchcock, with jowls and a semi-permanent scowl on his face. It's evident from the way he carries himself that he is someone of consequence.

"That was a marvelous performance," he says. "I'm Charles Schmidt from Warner Music."

"Yes, I know who you are," Leroy smiles. "Thanks for the compliment, means a lot coming from you. What brings you here tonight?"

"I'm in town for the festival and Harold Barnes wanted me to hear you two perform before the festival gets going. I had no idea I'd be hearing a trio," he gazes at Mabel. "You must be Peggy Winston," he extends his hand.

"The one and only," she winks at Priscilla who is eating

her dinner of fried shrimp and french fries.

"What a special gift you have. Wade tells me you're related to Mabel Johnson."

"I'm her niece."

"Well, you play and sing beautifully."

Mabel remembers Schmidt from when she was looking for her first big record deal back in the sixties. He was young and working for Atlantic Records, which was a leading label at that time. Mabel had been happy with Chess Records, the label Muddy Waters and other Black performers signed with in the fifties, but her husband was pushing her to sign with Atlantic, who at the time was launching great rock bands like Yes and Crosby, Stills, Nash & Young. Schmidt made her a low-ball offer, which her husband insisted she refuse, and he actually had her back in this instance. Shortly thereafter, the great Clive Davis discovered Mabel at a club in Los Angeles, and signed her to Columbia Records, finding the perfect new popular songs that turned her into an overnight sensation. Schmidt still has that pomaded hair she remembers from back then, except now it's no longer blonde but is dyed fake orange. He was so condescending to her after she signed with Columbia Records, and later publicly denied he had made her an insulting offer, as rumors spread throughout the industry that he had missed out on a great star. Mabel long ago put him out of her thoughts, but now he is triggering buried emotions.

160

Mabel manages a forced smile. "That *was* quite a set, wasn't it? Been a long time since I played with musicians as talented as these two. Leroy and Buzz took me to a whole new level."

Buzz chimes in. "Man, I wish we could have recorded that set."

Schmidt smiles at Buzz, accustomed to being pursued by musicians looking for their big break. He returns his gaze to Peggy, noticing how much she looks like Mabel Johnson.

Leroy is enjoying his Stella Artois beer. "That was some fine comping you were doing, Peggy. I love playing with a new pianist, it's like losing your virginity."

They all laugh.

"I'm being serious. There's all this unfamiliar groping, no one quite certain what they're doing, and it's rare that it's satisfying, but when it is . . . Wow!"

Mabel looks embarrassed. "It all clicked beautifully. Great chemistry."

Schmidt says: "I imagine you're familiar with the story of Miles Davis recording "So What" in the studio from just an outline of music. Quite possibly the best live recording ever captured."

"Absolutely," Buzz smiles.

"I'd love to get you three into the studio to see if we can capture the magic of tonight before it fades," Schmidt adds.

If only he knew, Priscilla sits quietly, polishing off a slice of chocolate cake with raspberry frosting for dessert. Schmidt faces Leroy and Buzz. "I think with Peggy as headliner, we could broaden your audience at Warner Music. You both are very talented but haven't found the ideal lead vocalist, until now. I especially enjoyed the new music at the end. Whose compositions are those?"

Buzz speaks. "Well, we all kind of just played organically around some themes Peggy wrote down."

Schmidt glances at her. "It sounded fresh and contemporary, while carrying on some of the original force of Mabel's playing from her heyday. I gather you studied with her?"

"Yes," Priscilla is waking up, sniffing a record deal to be negotiated, even though she hasn't a clue what that entails.

Schmidt prepares to leave. "I'm so glad I came tonight," he addresses Peggy. "May I have your phone number so I can call you tomorrow?"

"Sure," she gives him her home number, which he adds to his phone contacts.

"I'll be in touch to discuss how we might record you. We have a studio in Jackson with a fine Steinway grand."

Leroy and Buzz are high-fiving each other while Richard is hoping this turn of events will be what is needed to persuade Peggy to stay in town. But Mabel and Priscilla know the truth, and look at each other with growing concern, realizing the fun they've been having is careening out of control toward an impossible ending, an ending that has entangled Richard, and now Leroy and Buzz, who will be crushed when she must decline the recording opportunity.

Wade Ferguson comes over to thank them all for performing. "That was terrific. Might you be willing to come back tomorrow night and play two sets together as a trio?"

Priscilla rises up like a cobra preparing to sting. "Peggy hates your piano."

"Excuse me?" he faces her.

"You heard me, that piano stinks. It's beneath an artist of her stature."

Mabel sits back smiling at her little ally.

"Is there not a better piano available?" Priscilla presses.

"I'm afraid that's all we've got."

Charles Schmidt is lingering nearby and overhears this conversation. "I have a suggestion. We're having a grand piano shipped in for Melissa Gordon's performance at the festival next week. I'm sure it would be fine to divert it here for the few days before her concert. In fact, if Wade will allow it, I'd like to come back tomorrow night and record this trio with equipment we have in town. I have a small hand recorder that delivers surprising quality, and I can send that off to the marketing people at the label to see what they think."

"Sure, no problem," Wade replies. "Just give me the morning to move the upright into storage. There's a loading dock out back where the grand piano should make it in easy enough."

"Excellent, expect the piano delivery tomorrow afternoon. I'll handle all the arrangements," Schmidt turns and leaves.

Mabel and Priscilla are pleased by this turn of events, because now Mabel can perform on a quality instrument and then have a recording to listen to once she's old again, assuming that's what will happen on Sunday.

THURSDAY

Joey wakes up and feeds Linus, his pet hamster, whose cage sits perched on the end table just a few feet from the bed. The room smells like hamster urine and his own stinky feet. Joey throws on a T-shirt and shorts and pads downstairs where his mother is sitting at the kitchen table. It's going to be a hot and sticky day and Alice has a small fan pointed at her as she reads the obituaries.

"Good morning, Joey," she puts down the newspaper. "There are Pop-Tarts by the toaster so help yourself. How'd you sleep?"

"Decent."

"Oh, isn't this sad," Alice folds her newspaper in half. "Liza Jennings passed away. Just 64 years old. I knew her from the Rotary Club. I bet it was cancer. She never could kick her smoking habit."

Joey is struggling to open the foil wrapper separating him from his breakfast treats, the packaging sealed tight by a mass production vacuum sealer. He tries for a few moments and

165

then gives up, passing them to his mother who tears them open with her front teeth.

"Are you going to play with Priscilla today?"

"Nah. I think I'll stay in."

Alice senses something is amiss. "But it's going to be very hot today. Don't you want to go to the lake?"

Joey puts two maple Pop-Tarts in the old toaster and pushes down the metal lever until it latches in place after several attempts. "She's weird, I dunno."

"Did something happen at the fair yesterday?" Alice takes off her reading glasses and leans in closer to the fan, wiping beads of sweat from her forehead.

Joey hesitates before replying. "Yeah, I guess so. She told me somethin' that seems totally crazy, but then last night I couldn't fall asleep thinkin' 'bout it."

"What did she say?"

"Well, we were having an argument after I beat her at Mumblety-peg. She was pissed off and makin' me feel dumb, in that superior way of hers. I snapped at her and then she got mad, tellin' me she made her great-grandmother young again with some sort of a spell. I know, I know, that's crazy, but then I was thinkin' 'bout how her great-grandmother just up and disappeared and that new younger Peggy showed up. And Peggy looks just like Mabel. Same eyes. Same smile. She even coughs in the same way, I noticed yesterday at the fair."

Alice is now fully engaged. "She said she cast a spell?"

"Yup."

Alice wanders over to the window and glances toward Mabel's where she sees the doctor's BMW parked out front. For the second night in a row. She's been feeling something is wrong over there, but a spell? "Hmm," she turns back to Joey who has taken his Pop-Tarts to the table along with a glass of orange juice. "I remember Mabel telling me years ago she had some New Orleans relatives in her family tree who were deep into voodoo and other magic. She even showed me a book about it that had been passed down through generations of her family. Something is definitely strange over there, no doubt."

"Well, I don't like Priscilla no more."

"Okay, don't worry about playing with her today. I'll call Billy's mother and see if you can hang out over there at their pool. You don't want to be stuck inside all day, plus I don't like all the time you waste playing those violent video games."

"Bet you don't know that many of our Special Ops forces started out playing these games, which made them smarter at what they do. Strategy and all that kinda stuff. Helped us win the war in I-rack."

Alice is back at the table reading the newspaper and emits a gasp. "Well, I'll be damned, listen to this. 'Peggy

167

Winston played a set last night as part of the blues festival in Clarksdale, Mississippi, performing with Leroy Mullens and Buzz Stanley, both recently with the Buddy Grainger Quintet. Ms. Winston is the niece of the Grammy award-winning artist Mabel Johnson, and her set with the trio was one of the best live performances this music critic has heard in years. The similarity of her playing to that of her famous aunt was startling at times. She's playing with the trio for the rest of this week, so if you are heading to the festival in Mississippi, be sure to check her out.' This is from *The New York Times* music critic. It got picked up in our local paper."

Joey has managed to drip orange juice along with maple frosting crumbs down his shirt front. He says, "I guess it makes sense then. That Peggy must be Priscilla's great-grandmother. I mean, if she sounds so similar, how else can that be splained?"

Alice gets up and walks to the breezeway where she keeps her recyclables, digging through the piles in search of the newspaper from the other day. "Found it," she brings the newspaper inside, shaking cereal crumbs off the pages.

"What are you lookin' for?" Joey asks.

"The review the local arts reporter gave her the other night."

Joey scarfs down his two Pop-Tarts and then carries his plate to the sink.

"Go ahead and wash that, don't be lazy," Alice calls out as Joey tries to silently slip away. He reluctantly returns to the sink and squirts too much dish detergent on his plate, rinses it, and then sticks it in the drying rack. Alice can see from her perch that there is still dish soap on the plate, but lets it go, figuring she'll rewash it later. She sets the newspaper down for a moment and turns to Joey: "You know what really makes no sense at all about Mabel? I mean, here is her niece, getting this rave review in a major national newspaper. Wouldn't you think she'd be goin' to her concerts? At least once? C'mon now, how important can it be to go through her granddaughter's old clothing when Peggy is in town, the belle of the ball."

Joey sits back down. "You've got a point."

"The whole situation is very odd if you ask me," Alice wipes the back of her hand across her nose with an aggressive flourish. "You know what I'm going to do? I'm going to give this local reporter a call and tell him what we're thinkin'. Maybe he can do some diggin' into this Peggy Winston."

Joel Swillens is enjoying breakfast when his cell phone receives a forwarded call from work. As much as he wants to ignore the call, he knows he should take it in case there is important breaking news. "This is Alice Kramlich, I'm Mabel Johnson's neighbor over in Sardis . . ." he rolls his eyes

169

listening to what the crazy woman is telling him, mostly ignoring her while finishing off his scrambled eggs and grits, assuming—correctly as it turns out—that he will be unable to get a word in edgewise. There are so many crackpots out there these days, with all kinds of paranoia-fueled conspiracy theories and other borderline psychotic nonsense, the kind of stuff that sells newspapers. He listens to her prattle on as he shovels food in his mouth, doing his best to be polite and listen to her totally insane story, grunting on occasion so she knows he is still there.

As she rushes through her story with increasing urgency, he is reminded of a story he was assigned to cover last year about a local family refusing to vaccinate their child, so the other families with children in the school system were up in arms. When he arrived at the home of the student to conduct an interview, eager to let them share their side of the story, he was caught off guard when it turned out the father was a physician. His wife explained he had been in a car accident, had suffered a brain injury and his personality had changed. Joel ended up writing a three-part series on medical professionals opposed to vaccinations, and took a considerable amount of abuse for it in the online comments from readers suggesting he stick to covering the arts. He returns his attention to the phone call and is finally able to speak as he hears her panting on the other end: "Sure, I'll do

170

some digging to see what I can find out about Peggy Winston. Yes, you enjoy the beautiful day. Yes, thanks very much for being a subscriber," he hangs up once again realizing it is readers like Alice who pay his bills. He groans and continues eating his breakfast, flipping to the Arts Section of today's paper. He sees *The New York Times* review of the concert at Wade's last night, a syndicated article placed where his own arts review normally would be, and realizes his scathing review will make him look very bad, assuming anyone actually read it.

He feels he deserves to write for a large newspaper, but is stuck in Clarksdale, unable to find work in Jackson after earning his journalism degree. The *Clarksdale Beacon* has been laying off staff with renewed urgency, replacing the few remaining older staffers—many of whom refused buyouts in the last round—with younger, lower-paid people like himself. Joel has become more than just the arts reporter as he's been asked to cover everything from local fires to depressing court cases. All incredibly dull compared to what he had envisioned back in college when he decided to pursue journalism. Even though he knows this Alice woman was probably phoning him from a mental ward, he decides to research Peggy Winston, something he didn't bother doing after her lackluster performance the first night she played. If Alice's story were to pan out, it might be just the ticket he needs to get out of town and into a better position with a prestigious media company. He laughs at himself. Yeah, like the *National Inquirer*. He searches online and finds many Peggy Winstons, and checks Facebook and Instagram profiles, but does not find any Peggy Winston living in San Francisco or working for United Airlines. That's strange. Of course, possibly her name is Margaret so he continues searching, finally giving up.

He rereads *The New York Times* review and is struck by the mention of her artistic similarity to Mabel Johnson. He leans back in his seat and decides to attend tonight's performance so he can ask her a few more questions, assuming she'll even speak with him given his snarky review.

Later that morning, Alice takes Joey to his friend's house for the day and then returns home, where she pretends to be working in her garden, when in fact she's keeping an eye on Mabel's house, eager to see who comes and goes. Richard descends the steep stairway to get the mail and she intercepts him, startling him as she jumps out from behind the row of rhododendrons like a leprechaun who's had a bit too much to drink. "Hey there, doctor. Do you have a minute?" she staggers forward. He releases his hand from the mailbox and looks at her quizzically. "Sure, Alice, what can I do for you?"

"I want to ask you something."

"Okay. Fire away," he is anticipating a medical question,

as those who know he's a doctor are accustomed to seeking his free diagnoses. In this case, he's thinking possibly something discreet like herpes or vaginal itching.

"I cannot understand for the life of me why Mabel has not come home to listen to her niece perform. I mean, that just doesn't make any sense to me."

Richard pauses, caught off guard by her question, realizing Mabel's absence is indeed odd. At first Peggy had told him Mabel would return the next day, then she told him maybe in a few days, and lately the topic has mostly been dropped. But Alice is onto something. Why wouldn't Mabel want to hear her niece perform, especially now that she's been reviewed in a major national newspaper? "I have no good answer," he acknowledges.

She leans in close, looking over her shoulder making sure no one else is nearby. She whispers, "Well, I think I do."

"And what's that?" he finds this odd neighbor quite amusing in her own neurotic way.

"Joey told me this morning that Priscilla cast a spell on Mabel and made her young again."

Richard bellows with laughter. "That's absurd. Joey has an active imagination, that's all."

"Laugh if you want but I think it adds up. When I look into Peggy's eyes it's like I'm looking into Mabel's. And why why would Joey make up something like that?"

"Seriously, you don't *truly* believe in magic."

"Why not?"

"Because it's just superstition, employed over the many centuries by ignorant people incapable of explaining oddities through rational thinking."

"Well, you don't have to be *mean* about it," she looks away hurt. She realizes what she is saying sounds insane, but can't stop thinking about those family journals Mabel showed her. Mabel had seemed proud of this lineage and claimed she felt her music came from some mysterious place. She confided in Alice about the stories of voodoo and spells in her family history, and said this was why she became so religious. She felt she was experiencing an internal battle for her soul.

Alice continues: "Well, don't believe me then. But you should take a look at the bound journals up in the alcove on the second floor next to the stairway landing. Those contain some mighty strange reports of voodoo and magic in her family stretching back a long time. I'm telling you, something is definitely not right over there. The way Peggy plays the piano just like her, well, that should tell you something is fishy right there. I mean, everyone who listens to music knows there is only one Mabel Johnson."

Richard can't argue with that, but is eager to fetch the mail and return inside where his coffee is undoubtedly cold by now. "I'm a doctor," he says. "I operate in a world of logic and science, not voodoo and magic. I suggest you take a sedative and calm yourself down." He turns to leave.

"Just read the journals," she calls after him. "They're on the bottom shelf in a black binding. It's the oldest stuff there."

Peggy is folding laundry when he enters the house, and Priscilla is in her room reading, so Richard leaves the mail on the kitchen table and tiptoes upstairs to the alcove where Alice claimed he'd find the old journals. He scans the shelves and on the bottom one finds an old accordion folder with handwritten journals inside. He sits on the seat built into the large vertical window, and begins flipping through the brittle pages. The earliest entry is from the eighteenth century and recounts the tale of a woman named Mathilde, a slave who cast a spell on her evil master. Her master, a notorious socialite who tortured slaves for sport, was named Madame Blanque. According to the journal, Mathilde had turned Madame Blanque into a snake after she ordered the murder of Mathilde's only son, carried out in the town square as Mathilde and her husband were forced to watch. Mathilde was disappointed that the spell wore off after just one week, at which time Madame Blanque fled for Paris. At the conclusion of this journal, there is a blood fingerprint next to a signature by a descendant of Mathilde's, a man named Earl, and then there are several subsequent entries up until the twentieth century in the other two volumes, with numerous accounts of

175

magical powers within the family, including one of another woman named Mabel, circa 1896, who was alleged to have brought about the healing of a relative who should have died from consumption, but made a miraculous recovery after being pronounced dead by his physician.

Richard sits back and gazes out the window, fascinated by these old documents and stories. Priscilla surprises him from around the corner and he awkwardly attempts to put them back on the shelf, finally able to do so in the space where he found them. He runs his hand through his hair, looking flummoxed in a way she notices, his distant eyes returning from some far-off place. They walk downstairs together and find Peggy in the kitchen arranging daisies in a vase.

"There you are. I was wondering where you both disappeared to."

"Richard was upstairs reading. I just found him there."

"I brought in the mail, and it doesn't look like anything important," he attempts to redirect the conversation.

"Isn't that a marvelous reading nook up there?" Peggy is humming little songs.

"Yes, lovely," he replies. "I ran into Alice while getting the mail."

"How unfortunate."

"Yes, she's quite the nut."

"What's she up to now?"

"She told me the most ridiculous story."

"Enlighten me."

He glances at Priscilla and then back at Peggy. "She's all worked up because that silly boy of hers told her a fantastical story that she actually seems to believe. Is there no limit to the levels of ignorance these days?"

Priscilla is growing nervous, aware that she slipped up at the fair and has been hoping Joey would not tell his mother. But now she senses he must have. She tries to cut off what she fears will follow. "Oh, Joey. He has such an active imagination. He's so annoying, always desperate for attention and making up stupid stories."

Richard looks at her. "Yes, well this one certainly was insane."

Peggy eggs him on. "Humor us, please. What did he say?"

Richard stares at Peggy and is once again astonished to see how much she resembles Mabel. Because he has examined Mabel several times in his office, he has noticed while making love with Peggy that she has the same mole in the exact same place on her upper back. The accounts in the journals upstairs are testing his reliance on science and logic to explain most everything, and he now finds himself becoming uncomfortable being there at the moment. He decides it's best not to reveal the truth of what Alice said. "It was nothing, really. Just that apparently there used to be magic running through Mabel's family."

There is a prolonged pause and then she replies, "Yes, I've heard some of those stories, but surely they are just the product of overactive imaginations."

"Of course," Richard replies.

She continues. "Many of the slaves back in the day made up stories to entertain and frighten each other. I think that's what our family stories are. Entertainment."

"Yes, that makes perfect sense."

"Well then, shall we go for a swim?"

"Sure."

"I'm going to read," Priscilla heads upstairs and Richard assumes she's going to look at the journals. He and Peggy swim out to the raft and sit side by side in the sunshine. Peggy reaches over and runs the back of her hand across Richard's furry cheek, once again noticing his eyes. "You have such lovely long lashes."

"Thanks," he releases an involuntary shudder at her touch.

She senses him withdrawing. "You seem down, Richard. Is everything okay?"

He sighs. "There's just a lot going on now. My mother phoned this morning to let me know there's a position opening up at Brigham and Women's Hospital in Boston. She

178

thinks I'd be a fool not to apply for it and likes the idea of me being nearer to her in Brooklyn."

"How exciting," her enthusiasm catches him off guard.

"I'd been hoping you'd stay here now that you've got a likely record deal in the works. You know. Look after Mabel. We could continue our relationship."

"Oh, Richard," she pulls him against her. "I'm sorry, but I just don't think that will ever work out."

He decides to probe deeper than he has in the past, now armed with the incomprehensible voodoo story and family history. "You don't seem very supportive of your aunt. Who will care for her?"

She's prepared. "Why John, of course. He and Priscilla are going to move her in with them in Oxford."

"But how sad that will be for her. She loves it here. And John is not a blood relation."

"True," she's dipping her toes in the water, remembering she's getting her hair done for the show tonight and has an afternoon appointment.

"Why in the world would you want to return to being a stewardess when you can pursue your dreams of being a musician?"

She pauses and then replies, "Oh, I don't think for one second I'm good enough to play with Leroy and Buzz. This will pass and I'll need to get back to my old life."

The words *old life* resonate with new meaning. "But they seemed to truly enjoy playing with you last night. How can you possibly not see that?"

"Well, we did play well together, but I don't know, being a touring musician is surely a lousy life."

"Lousier than being a touring stewardess?"

She sees he has her. "It's not just that. I honestly don't think I'm good enough to make it."

He lets it go and changes course. "I'm surprised Mabel is missing your shows."

She senses something is amiss and is becoming concerned. When she fails to answer, he adds: "Surely a musician of her stature would be thrilled to hear you perform as well as you have. Will she be home soon?"

"I told you. Not until Sunday."

"Well, I worry about her being away so long in this heat."

"John and Michelle's home has central air conditioning so I'm sure she's just fine."

Richard is staring at her in a new way. She feels suddenly self-conscious, as if he's become distrustful, and this is confirmed when she asks when he'll pick her up that evening.

"I think I'll skip the show tonight. I should call my mother and find out more about the position in Boston."

"I thought you liked it here?"

"I do, I do. Especially this week with you, but if you are going to leave on Sunday, maybe I should give it some serious thought. You've made it clear you see no future for us together. Brigham and Women's is one of the top hospitals in the country and I'd be foolish not to apply."

"Of course," she senses him pushing her away, which she knows she should be happy about, but finds herself conflicted, feeling rejected in a way she hadn't anticipated. But what's the point? There can be no future for them, and the last thing she wants is to stand in the way of an outstanding career opportunity. It's all quite the mess, and she looks away at the rippling currents brushing up against the float.

"I'm thinking maybe we should stop seeing each other," she turns to him, escalating matters in a way that stuns him.

"Isn't that a bit extreme?" he looks wounded. He is gazing at her with a mix of fear and love in his eyes, and she is finding it difficult to push him away. But she soldiers on in an odd tone he doesn't recognize. "I mean, there is no future for us, Richard. Don't get me wrong, this has been a wonderful week and the sex has been . . . well, it's been . . . otherworldly. But, where I'll be going home soon, maybe it will be an easier transition if we back things down a bit for the remainder of the week. We've had our fun, but maybe we should stop sleeping together and just be friends."

Richard is surprised to realize he feels relieved by her

words. "Sure, I suppose that's a good idea." He stares at his feet, a dawning smirk on his face, as he attempts to recall the last time a female suggested they just be friends. He's thinking it was back in high school. He sighs. "Listen, let's swim back and then I should be getting home."

"Are you sure you don't want to come to the show tonight?"

"No, I could use a night off. Knock 'em dead," he forces a smile, feeling bewildered by the odd events of the day. "I hope you don't mind driving yourself."

"Not a problem. I have a hair appointment this afternoon and am excited to get myself a special doo. Been ages . . ." she trails off as they dive in and swim back to the house.

After Richard leaves, Priscilla comes downstairs carrying the family volumes.

"What's that?" Mabel asks.

Priscilla shows them to her. "He was reading these when I surprised him earlier. He must know about the family history."

She takes the volumes from her great-granddaughter. "Have you looked at these before?"

"No."

"Did you look now?"

"Yes, it explains a lot. What if I have those powers?"

"Well, I was hoping to tell you when you were a bit older, but given what's happened this week, I think it's best you know the truth."

"Did our ancestors misuse their powers?"

"Yes, I suppose so. Although that depends on one's point of view."

"I can't believe Mathilde actually turned her cruel slave owner into a snake."

"Well, she certainly had it coming," Mabel laughs.

"Is what I made happen to you a misuse of power? What's to stop me from turning someone I don't like into a snake. Like Joey."

Mabel shakes her head. "You said you prayed to God so it may well be that's how my youth was restored. Don't assume it was witchcraft. Maybe it was a gift from above."

"So why when I wish that Mommy would come back does it not happen?"

"Because that must not be something God believes would be good for you, I suppose," Mabel is gazing off into the distance. "Truth be told, if I can leave you with one lesson it's this: *Be careful what you wish for, because you just might get it.* That's one of the wisest sayings ever uttered, and now I'm learning it all over again. This week has been a giant mistake, I fear."

"I'm sorry, when I made the wish, I assumed you'd want

to be young again."

"I did. I do. I don't." Mabel stands up and paces toward the piano. "It's been wonderful in so many ways but, as usual, you can't have something good without there being a compensatory bad."

"What's that mean? Com-pension-tory?"

"It means to compensate for. As in for every force in nature there is an equal and opposite force designed to maintain balance, harmony."

"You being young again for just one week can't cause too much harm, can it?"

"I fear it can. And it will. If I don't start wrapping things up in a way that avoids hurting others. As you get older, I hope you'll read the great classics, especially ancient mythology. So much of life is about losing paradise, or not being able to hold onto what seems like paradise, and the sooner you accept this, the better off you'll be."

"I still think I should turn Joey into a toad."

"Stop," Mabel laughs. "Although maybe you could turn his mother into one."

Priscilla is staring at the floor and Mabel senses something more is on her mind.

"Yes?" she probes.

"I think I messed up."

"Why do you say that?"

184

"Yesterday at the fair, Joey was being so annoying and we got into an argument. I let it slip that I made you young again."

"Ah," Mabel says. "That explains it."

"Explains what?"

"Why Richard was acting so strange just now. I think Alice must have mentioned it to him. She also has seen the family history journals, which I never should have shown her, but did years ago in a moment of weakness. That was stupid of me."

"How was Richard acting strange?"

Mabel pauses. "It's actually a good thing. We're going to take a break from seeing each other, and there's a position in an excellent Boston hospital he should apply for, so I'm actually feeling somewhat relieved. Now maybe I won't break his heart when I up and disappear for good on Sunday."

"We don't actually know for certain that will happen," Priscilla says.

"True, but if I do become an old woman again, I don't want Richard to be there to see it. And I'm starting to look forward to being my old self again. All this deceit takes a toll. I forgot that being young isn't all it's cracked up to be."

"So . . . what now?" Priscilla asks.

"I'm going to shower, and then get my hair done at Becky's Salon, that's what. Might as well before I have to shut down this charade. Are you okay staying here for a few hours by yourself?"

"Sure, I'd like to read more of the journals. Do you mind if I take photos of some of the pages?"

"I'm not sure that's such a good idea."

"Why not?"

"What with Google and Alexa and nosy Alice and the NSA and God knows who else listening in to everything we say and do, I think it's too risky. Best to keep these family matters a secret."

"Okay," she looks disappointed. "There's something else."

"Yes?"

"What are you going to do about that record producer and Leroy and Buzz? They'll be devastated when you simply disappear on Sunday, assuming you do."

"I know. I'm still trying to figure that out. I might have a plan, but I'm still noodling on how to make it happen. I might need your help."

"I'm sorry I told Joey."

"It's okay. In fact, it might end up being a good thing."

"I really like the doctor and will be sad to see him go to Boston. That means you'll be losing your doctor. Won't you be sad, too?"

Mabel hasn't thought this through. "Yes, of course. But

one good thing that's come from this week is I got to know him in ways I never would have otherwise, and he's just running away from a bad relationship and needs to overcome that. He shouldn't be here in the first place; he's far too smart to be hiding out in sleepy Sardis because some idiotic woman broke his heart, dumping him for a football player."

"But aren't you breaking his heart, too?"

She sighs. "I hope not. Truth be told, it's making me sad, too. I hadn't fully appreciated how close we've become so fast. He's a terrific friend. I will miss him very much."

"Maybe if you told him the truth he'd stay in town."

"Oh, puh-leeze. If I told him the truth he'd be thoroughly repulsed. I sense he's already weirded out being with an older woman in a younger woman's body. It's been great for me but I'm not so sure about him."

"If he really loves you, wouldn't he want to stay with you, even if you do become old again?"

"You have a lot to learn, my precious." She runs her hand through Priscilla's braided head. "Men fall in love with women they are physically attracted to. Lust before love, that's the truth."

"I just don't get that."

"Give it time and you will."

*****

187

Mabel and Priscilla arrive early at the club that evening to allow Mabel time to practice on the new Steinway grand piano and to plan the performance with Buzz and Leroy. Lizzy is seated at the piano doing sound checks with Charles Schmidt, who is standing toward the middle of the club, fiddling with a small portable recording set-up he keeps in his car when on the road.

"Try playing something in the lower octaves for me Lizzy," he calls out as he adjusts knobs on the recording device. She plays a few thundering octaves and he smiles in approval. "Go ahead and just play and sing anything you'd like so I can make sure the balances are good. I'm thinking maybe I should set up a little closer to the stage." Lizzy plays a soulful version of the Nora Jones hit tune "Don't Know Why," as Mabel listens at the rear of the club, marveling at her talent, wondering if Schmidt is even listening or is solely preoccupied with his recording equipment and the sound levels. Mabel approaches, startling him as she says: "Doesn't she have the most interesting voice?"

Schmidt is happy to see her. "Peggy. I'm glad you've arrived a little early as I'd like to make sure these levels are balanced. Lizzy, thanks," he calls out. "We're all set. Let me check Peggy now."

Lizzy looks up, the dream of the song interrupted. She stops abruptly.

"Keep playing," Mabel calls out, too late, as Lizzy passes on her way to the bar where Colin is seated with Priscilla.

Schmidt is fidgeting with dials. "Peggy, play a few bars of "Fever" and then just some of your improvisations from last night. She sits at the piano, adjusting her red gown, running her fingers along the cool ivory keys without actually striking them. The piano looks brand new and she looks at it like a new lover, eager to play but reticent in not wanting to move too quickly. She grins, reminded how similar playing the piano is to sex, with the same intimacy, the same sensual touches. Schmidt is growing impatient, observing her going through her process, aware from working with so many temperamental musicians that each has a creative ritual, not unlike that of professional baseball hitters.

Mabel finally strikes the A below middle C, listening to the overtones, the tuned instrument sounding perfect. She then plays an ostinato octave in the left hand, the firmness of this marvelous instrument resounding around the club. She pulls back and smiles at Schmidt, nodding with approval, and then launches into "Fever." The piano sounds simultaneously firm and tonally even from bottom to top, but still not up to the standards of her 1890s Steinway, which was built using parts no longer available, the old alpaca felt on the hammers providing a subtlety not reproducible on newer pianos. She played Steinways for most of her career but also liked the old

Mason and Hamlins from the nineteenth century, which were renowned for firmness in their lower octaves making them the choice of Ravel and Rachmaninoff. As great as this new Steinway is, it is lacking something important. Character. A certain amount of flaw is important to all the arts and this piano is just too perfect, as if designed by computers as opposed to musicians. She stops playing and Schmidt asks her to pause so he can move the equipment five feet farther away from the stage. Once he has the equipment repositioned, she begins playing her improvisations, stopping on occasion to scribble notes on her notepad to share later with Leroy and Buzz.

"I'm good to go," Schmidt says. "You sound fantastic."

"Thank you," she gets up and heads for the bar to join Priscilla, Lizzy, and Colin. She calls across the room to Schmidt. "Thanks so much for delivering the lovely piano. It makes a huge difference."

Colin pats the bar stool next to him, "Speakin' of lovely, don't you look all dolled up this evening."

She smiles. "I splurged and had my hair done in town this afternoon." Mabel takes a seat and orders a Manhattan for herself and a root beer for Priscilla. When the drinks arrive, Mabel turns to Lizzy and says: "Your playing is special, Lizzy. I can't get over what an extraordinary voice you have. It's like a mixture of hard cider and sweet honey, harsh and soft simultaneously. I don't believe I've ever heard another voice like yours."

"Stop, you're making me blush."

"I mean it."

"You're too kind, but thank you. Are you nervous about tonight?"

"Not really. I just hope Leroy and Buzz show up with enough time to go over what I'd like to play. I've got some changes in mind."

"Where's Rich-id?" Colin asks.

Her pause is revealing. "He decided to take a night off."

"Hmm, that doesn't sound good. He's been your biggest fan from what I can tell."

"He's applying for a new position in Boston," she adds.

"What a shame," Lizzy joins in, aware of Peggy's feelings for him.

She doesn't want to talk about Richard and is feeling that old empty lump in her stomach brought about by only one thing: love. Is it possible she has fallen in love with him so quickly? She is feeling confused and gazes at Priscilla, who seems to know what she's thinking, that there can be no possible future for them.

Mabel soldiers on in full denial and rationalization. "I think it will be great if he gets the job in Boston. He's too accomplished to be stuck in little ol' Sardis."

"But aren't you two in love?" Lizzy places her hand on Mabel's.

"Oh, dear," Mabel sighs. She feels awful for the way she pushed him away that afternoon, but sees no other way out of this predicament. She is reminded of what she said earlier to Priscilla and repeats it now: "Be careful what you wish for."

"Excuse me?" Lizzy swivels on her stool to square up with her.

"You heard me. Be careful what you wish for, because you might just get it. That's the best adage I can impart, and I cannot begin to tell you how many times all those wishes have come back to bite me in the you know what. Truth is, we don't know what's best for us, only God does."

"Ain't that the truth," Colin is nursing a shot of whiskey.

Lizzy turns to him. "What do you wish for, Colin?"

"Damn, I stopped wishin' for anything ages ago. I'm not sure if it's just my life or true for everyone, but whenevah I made plans, I got blown off course so fast I just stahted livin' day to day and let the flow carry me where it may."

"Surely there must be something you want," she persists.

"Not really," he shrugs. "I suppose what I most want is to be free from pain."

"Are you in much pain?" Mabel asks.

"I have my days. Back hurts, stomach hurts. You know—"

"Indeed, I do," she cuts him off. "Why don't you let Richard help you?" she looks puzzled. "I mean, just let him take you to his clinic to get checked over. He won't bite."

"I hate takin' freebies from people."

"It's not your fault what happened to you," Lizzy says. "We all need help at some point."

"*Fault.*" he says. "Interesting choice of words. Like the San Andreas fault, a deep wound."

Mabel spies Leroy and Buzz entering the club and gets up to greet them. They sit at a table up front with Schmidt as she goes over her notes for the evening. "I was thinking we open with "Fever," then play "Black Coffee," then I'd like to try a couple of old spirituals with you. Before we play the improvisations."

Schmidt interjects, "Spirituals? No . . . I don't think so. I want to be sure we capture the improvisations from last night. It's your own music I'm hoping will grab the attention of the marketing people at the label. So maybe not spirituals, at least not now."

She looks upset. "You do realize how much of our American songbook is derived from spirituals?"

"Yes, of course, but I just don't think they're a good idea for you. The marketing people are always eager to reject quickly as it creates less work for them. So let's not make it easy on them, okay?"

"Ah, yes. The good ol' record label marketing geniuses. I remember them all too well."

Schmidt looks at her strangely, not sure what this is all about, but senses some inexplicable baggage. Mabel, for her part, is remembering the battles waged over the years to play what she wanted and not what she was advised to play. Schmidt is unearthing forgotten wounds. She should have fought harder for her own music.

Leroy tries to keep the peace, "I'd love to play some spirituals with you another time, Peggy. I arranged a few myself back in school and miss that powerful old music."

"It was powerful because it came from real pain and oppression," Mabel replies as she turns to face Schmidt and says: "Something you are incapable of relating to."

Schmidt, ever the pragmatist and worn down from battling strong-willed artists over the decades, says, "Well, then, you both can work on your spirituals *after* I sell you to the label."

Mabel sits there bristling over his insensitive use of the word *sell.* Her ancestors were sold into slavery, her music was sold to appease the marketing geniuses, her body was sold to her abusive husband. She's tired of all the selling and just wants to return to her old self, a spent cow happily out in her pasture, away from all the constant selling of everything, especially our souls.

Leroy senses her resentment over Schmidt's insensitive choice of words and changes the topic. "How much recording time do we get tonight?"

"Around an hour," Schmidt replies. "If I send too much material it makes it easier for them to focus on something they don't like and say no. And we don't want that."

"So should we play mostly the new music?" Buzz suggests, realizing they are lucky to have Schmidt, who seems to know how to play the perilous inside game.

"Why don't you open with "Fever" so they can hear how much you sound like Mabel, and then go into the improvisations," he suggests.

"Fine," Mabel exhales a bit too forcefully, sounding like the words *be that way* should be appended. "Since we've played together once already, let's just do the same piece from last night following the outline I gave you. I'd just like to make one change, modulating from the F# to the ninth in the third section."

"Sure, that should work well," Buzz nods. They're interrupted by Joel Swillens who has arrived for the evening. "Hello, Peggy. I hope you'll forgive me for that review I wrote the other day. I'm afraid I projected some of my own frustrations from work onto you, and that was uncalled for."

Mabel is locked and loaded. "Well, it's not like anyone actually reads that local rag."

Priscilla has wandered over, and with hands on hips says to Joel: "You didn't have to be a jerk, you know."

"Excuse me?" Schmidt overhears. "And who might you be?"

"This is Priscilla, Mabel's great-granddaughter. I'm babysitting her for the week," Peggy says.

"She doesn't sound like any baby I've ever known," Schmidt is chuckling at this mighty little girl.

"That's because I'm not like anyone you've known," Priscilla stands with arms folded tightly across her chest. She turns to face Swillens. "Why do you have to write hurtful little reviews, when they serve no purpose? Isn't your job to drum up local business, not kill it?"

The reporter is gazing at his feet as Priscilla reloads, "I was taught that if you don't have anything good to say, then say nothing."

Swillens looks up and sighs, "Look, I know, I made a mistake. People make mistakes. I came here to apologize."

"Well you should be more careful in the future," Priscilla is laying it on.

Swillens faces Mabel. "I must say, I find it puzzling that your aunt hasn't come to hear you perform this week. What can she possibly be doing that's more important than supporting her niece?"

Priscilla is prepared. "She doesn't want to distract from

the attention Peggy deserves. She knows she would be a sideshow and is too sensitive to hurt other peoples' feelings, *unlike someone else I know*."

Swillens has retreated to behind Schmidt, who is nursing a glass of Chardonnay. "But here's the thing," he presses. "When I wrote my article I decided to research Peggy Winston and have been unable to find any trace of you. You say you're from San Francisco and work for United Airlines, right?"

Mabel doesn't like where this is heading. "Yes."

"So why is there no public record of you anywhere? Why does United tell me they have no Peggy Winston employed with them?"

Priscilla comes to her aid once again. "Because either they, or more likely you, are imbeciles."

"Now, Priscilla. Let's not take things too far," Mabel says.

Schmidt is enjoying this unexpected bit of theatre and joins in. "Considering I flew here on that lovely airline, and the fact they managed to lose my luggage, you have a point there, little lady. But enough of this, I need to get a sound check of the three of you playing together so let's get going."

Mabel takes her place at the piano and no longer feels much like playing. Everything is cascading down upon her and the weight is becoming suffocating. What to do about

197

Richard? What to do about Leroy and Buzz? What to do about Joel Swillens, and that busybody neighbor, Alice Kramlich? She feigns a smile, noting the earnestness of Leroy and Buzz, appreciating how much is at stake for them with this opportunity. She remembers her first big break and how lucky she was as the various pieces miraculously fell into place, her career launched without too much struggle. These two have been playing for several years now, mostly in obscurity, and she knows they deserve better. What a mess. She launches into "Fever" and sees Lizzy smiling at her from the bar, nodding in affirmation of how great they sound.

FRIDAY

Richard is swamped within a sea of disturbing dreams. He's wandering unfamiliar hospital floors in search of patients calling out for him, tapping his unresponsive tablet. He then finds himself unable to remember which patient is in which room. Now he's in a dark cave and sees Colin Lodge slumped on the floor next to a hospital bed. He helps him off the cave floor, searching for a nurse but realizing no nurses would be in a cave. An unfamiliar corridor stretches into bright sunlight—possibly a dorm corridor from college or summer camp, he thinks, the smell of cafeteria food off in the distance. He follows the light and emerges into a field of ragweed, which sends him into sneezing fits. He looks down at his tablet, which is melting in his hands. He jogs—away from something, toward nothing—no longer in a hospital but back in his college dorm room. It dawns on him that he's late for his final exam, and his lackadaisical attitude about taking the exam is offset by the realization he hasn't attended a single class, let alone bought the textbook. Panic sets in. He's walking down a sloped floor into an unfamiliar theatre-style classroom, which has the feel of a Las Vegas casino, gravity sucking him downward toward the slot machines, the carpeting garish as he shields his eyes from bright lights and annoying chiming from the slots. He's in a classroom of medical students, except it's a philosophy course being taught by Colin. The professor asks if he thinks he's up to the challenge. Richard glances down to see he's naked. He runs away while classmates laugh, and then he's at Wade's, Colin bleeding from his eyes and ears, as Peggy plays the piano looking like a she-devil, her snake of a tongue circling ruby lips. Richard awakens, mumbling Peggy's name, his T-shirt drenched in sweat, evanescent images and emotions from the nightmare receding within his subconscious. He swings himself out of bed and stumbles into the bathroom, staring at his reflection in the mirror. He splashes water on his face, slurps a few parched gulps from the faucet, vestiges of toothpaste lingering. When he gazes back at the mirror he has two people on his mind: Peggy and Colin.

He makes an impulsive decision, one that will alter his destiny, skipping breakfast and running out of his home for the BMW, destination unknown but needing to get away. He pulls onto the highway heading for Clarksdale. A few miles down the highway, his phone rings. It's his mother.

"Good morning, dear. How are you this very fine morning?"

"Hey, Mom. I'm in the car at the moment."

"Are you okay to talk? I can call back."

He hesitates, not in the mood to talk now, but says, "I've got you on the hands-free."

"Where are you heading so early in the day? I hesitated before calling thinking it might be too early, but I woke up worried about you. A mother's worries never cease."

"That's strange, because I woke up from disturbing dreams."

"Must be the full moon," she says. "It's so hot up here, I can't imagine what it must be like down there."

"I've gotten used to it and have AC in my rental. Anyway, I'm driving to Clarksdale, about an hour from here. There's something I need to do."

"What can possibly be so important to have you out and about so early?"

"Nothing, really. I just want to check on someone I'm worried about."

"A woman?"

"No, Mom. Not a woman."

"Who then?"

"A patient. Or at least someone who should be a patient. I met a street person who used to be a professor at Harvard, I think. It's difficult to know for sure but I like him and he's had some tough luck."

"Isn't that nice of you. You always were a good boy."

"I guess I'll take that as a compliment."

"It is. But I trust you're not putting yourself into a dangerous situation, are you?"

"No, he's harmless."

"Did you look at the Boston position yet?"

"I did."

"And?"

"It's complicated."

"Meaning?"

"Meaning I'm not sure I want to go for it."

There is a prolonged pause as he visualizes her expression on the other end, one he knows all too well, a look combining superiority and irritation, with a dash of disappointment.

She finally speaks. "Well, you're a grown man, so of course it's up to you. I just wish you hadn't gone to Mississippi, of all godforsaken places."

"Why's that?" he knows the answer.

"You mean other than the rampant racism?"

"Maybe I prefer rampant racism to the quiet northern version, you know: 'We love our Black friends. Just don't move into the neighborhood.'"

"That's not true."

"Don't deny it. At least Black folks and white folks here live and work together."

202

She knows there is some truth in what he's saying.

He adds: "I'm curious what you and Dad had to do to get us into our fancy old neighborhood?"

"I didn't call to get you worked up. You sound agitated Richard. Are you sure there isn't a woman problem?"

Good grief, he thinks. Why is it mothers can read our minds even when they're thousands of miles away? He remains silent, focusing on the road as he takes an exit.

Thankfully, she is back to the Boston job. "I just always envisioned you working up north in one of the better hospitals. Not in some sleepy southern town. I don't like not seeing you. What with your father and me in Brooklyn, and you in Boston, we'd see more of one another. And it's not often a position like this one at Brigham's opens up. I don't want you to have regrets later in life wondering about the choices you made."

"Well, Mom, maybe they need me here? Have you considered that? Instead of being one in a million doctors, as I would be in Boston, I can be the only one in Sardis, where they really need help."

"Sure, but what do *you* need. You've never been especially good at selfishness and I worry you've been adrift ever since the breakup."

He exhales so loudly that she can hear, but she continues undeterred. "Sometimes I worry we pushed you too hard and on some level you're pushing back against that pressure. In hindsight, I wish we hadn't been so demanding with you, all the time."

"Sure, you applied plenty of pressure. But I don't hold that against you and don't want you to feel responsible for the decisions I make as an adult. I might apply for the Boston position, I just don't know yet."

Another pause and then she asks what's really on her mind. "Have you met someone new?"

He sees he is now speeding, so slows and pulls into the right lane.

"Have you?" she repeats.

"I'd rather not discuss my love life with you mother."

"So . . . I'll take that as a yes. Is she nice?"

"Very nice. And also quite talented. She's a jazz musician. In fact, she was reviewed in yesterday's *New York Times*."

"My, that's quite something. What's her name?"

"Peggy Winston."

"I'll have to look for the review. That's great news, honey. I'm happy for you."

"I'm afraid it's not so simple. She travels a lot and doesn't seem to want to get involved with me."

"Oh, I see," she replies in a way that makes him think she might be relieved, not wanting him to derail his promising medical career for a woman, at least not until he is working in a better job, like the one in Boston.

"I'll figure things out, Mom. Please don't worry about me."

She laughs. "There isn't a mother in the world that doesn't worry about her precious babies until the day she dies. I hope someday you'll learn this by providing your father and me with a grandchild, or maybe even two?"

"Don't push your luck. Why would anyone bring a child into this crazy world?"

"Oh, the world has always been a hot mess. There's always some war raging, or a plague, or other horrible event, but there are also beautiful things. Trust me when I tell you, children are the most precious gifts of all. They help you feel young again, take your mind off your own trivial anxieties."

"Yet, you're disappointed in me."

"That's not at all true."

"Well, it feels that way at times. I don't know, I guess maybe I'm disappointed in me, too."

"Don't be so hard on yourself. You've been adrift ever since your breakup. It's important to move on from life's many wounds."

"Believe me, I know. And here I am finally falling for another woman who turns out to be unavailable."

"She's not married, is she?" she misinterprets.

"No, no I would never do that. She just travels so much it will never work."

"So . . . maybe this would be the perfect time to make a clean break and move to Boston. I mean, you don't want to get involved with someone down there you rarely see. Plus, I'm sure there are many more women up here who would be desperate to land a fine young man like you."

"I'm not a fish."

"You know what I mean."

"Actually, not really."

"You're handsome, a doctor, a high earner—"

"Ah, the money. Yes."

"Well it's true. Women are attracted to power and money and you have both, plus good looks. You're a great catch."

"Says the mother—"

"And I'm not sure I told you that your girlfriend from high school has been asking after you. You know, Janine?"

"Well, that's too bad. She's probably feeling stuck back there, never going anywhere. That's one of the reasons I broke up with her. You can't go home again, Mom. You should know that, and so should Janine. You both need to reread your Thomas Wolfe. I like it here. It's new and I like new experiences, you know that."

Again, a prolonged silence. The siren of a state trooper

approaches fast from behind and then thankfully zips past.

"You okay?" his mother sounds worried.

"I'm fine. Must be an accident up ahead."

"Sounded like he was zooming along."

"I know, probably going over one hundred or faster," Richard checks his own speed.

"I worry about you down there, son."

"I'm okay, really Mom. Don't believe all the stereotypes. Stop watching the news."

"Well, I hope things are as advanced as you say."

"Listen, I need to pay attention to my driving so I'll give you a call tonight."

"Okay, but *please* apply for the Boston position. What's to lose?"

"I will."

"Promise me."

"I promise," he says without thinking as the call disconnects. He prefers not to lie to his mother and is hesitant about leaving warm, sleepy Sardis for the cold, harsh north. He's still hoping Peggy will change her mind and decide to stay.

Richard slows along the streets of Clarksdale, not sure why he is here but feeling some larger force guiding him. He pulls over at the Blues Museum and Googles coffee shops, and as much as he wants to grab a coffee and cheese biscuit at nearby Meraki Roasting Company, the urgency of his dream compels him to hold off on breakfast and to go look for Colin.

Richard parks and walk to Wade's, his nightmare leaving him feeling as if he is supposed to act—to do *something*, and quickly—yet he is not exactly sure what. The dream sequence of Colin on the hospital floor lingers, and Richard hopes to see him pushing his cart so he can rest assured, but the streets are mostly empty with no sign of Colin. Richard gazes around, unsure of what to do, and decides to sit in the shade of a magnolia tree across the street from Wade's and wait for Colin to make his daily rounds. A half an hour passes, and still no sign of Colin. Richard gets up to wander the block when he spies Wade walking up the street. He crosses to meet him.

"Hey, Wade!" Richard calls out.

"Richard," he looks surprised. "We missed you last night. Everything okay?"

"Yes and no. Same as always."

"Man, you missed a kick-ass show. Peggy and the boys really had it goin' on."

Richard is happy to hear this and regrets not coming.

Wade is sorting through the many keys on his belt keychain. "I'm here early because Schmidt is delivering a full-blown recording soundboard for tonight's show, so I need to rearrange the floor. How cool would it be for there to be an album: Recorded Live at Wade's? You know, sort of like the old Village Vanguard albums. So, what brings you here this fine mornin'?"

"I'm hoping to find Colin."

"She-it, man, it's like *way* too early for him to be out and about. Looked like he tied one on pretty good last night from what I could tell."

"I want to persuade him to come to my clinic for an exam."

"Good luck with *that*. Last I knew he was livin' off a back alley around the corner. Just over there, next to the old Acme building," he points. "If you see his cart, you'll know he's nearby."

"I'll probably never find him but I'll give it a try."

"If you give up, come on in and I'll serve you some breakfast."

"That's kind, I haven't eaten so that sounds great."

"Just stop by when you're ready."

"Will do." Richard walks away and comes upon a narrow alley running between two buildings. He gazes down, concerned there could be rats. Today is trash day and the dumpsters behind the restaurants are overflowing. Beyond one of the dumpsters, he spots Colin curled up in the fetal position, an empty bottle of Jack Daniels next to his head.

Richard leans down and nudges him gently. "Wake up, Colin. It's me, Richard."

Colin rolls over onto his other side, and mumbles, "Go away."

Richard shakes him again. "C'mon, let me buy you a cup of coffee and something to eat."

"Just leave me be, be, be . . ." Colin starts convulsing. Richard manages to get one arm underneath Colin's left armpit but is unable to haul him up. Colin's woolen shirt is drenched in sweat and reeks of the streets. Richard sees foam spilling from his mouth, and worries he has been having seizures and will choke. He manages to roll him onto his side and then races down the alley and finds Wade sitting out front waiting for Schmidt. "Come quick! Colin's in a bad way."

Wade looks skeptical. "How bad can he be? I mean, he's pretty messed up all the time but always rallies by evening."

"It's serious. He's having seizures and will choke on his vomit if we don't act quickly. I'm going to pull my car out front of the alley and need your help getting him in so I can drive him to the hospital."

Wade spits off to the side, glancing down the street to make sure he doesn't see Schmidt approaching. "All right, just give me a second."

Richard jogs off and returns in his BMW, parking at the mouth of the alley. He and Wade march down past the dumpsters and find Colin shivering, foam coming from his mouth at a faster rate than before.

"C'mon, Colin. We need to get you to the hospital," Richard and Wade each take an arm and drag Colin to the car, tossing him into the passenger seat where he topples over, bumping his head on the steering wheel causing the horn to blare. Richard rushes over to the driver's side and pushes Colin back against the passenger door, belting him in with Wade's assistance. Richard taps his phone searching for the nearest hospital, recalling how in the dream his tablet melted in his hands. He finds the nearby Northwest Mississippi Medical Center, and heads that way. He pulls out front and jogs inside, informing the first nurse he sees that he has a patient needing immediate assistance. A few minutes later, a gurney is wheeled out and Colin is loaded on. Richard smells urine as Colin is wheeled away. He parks in the visitor's lot and heads inside to tell them what he knows.

He sits in the waiting room observing the many family members looking concerned about their own loved ones. Shortly before noon, a young doctor gestures for him to come speak with her. "Are you the man who brought in the street person?"

He walks to where she stands off to the side of the hallway so they can speak in private. "Yes, I'm a doctor in Sardis and found him in an alley this morning in Clarksdale."

"Nice to meet you. I'm Doctor Domenica Flores. He's lucky you brought him in when you did. His blood pressure was 220 over 110 and we're waiting to get his liver test results back."

"It's odd, but I had a dream about him last night, which led me to him this morning."

"Well, it's a good thing you did. I assume he has no relatives?"

"None I know of. He's a homeless person I met at Wade's Club."

"How does a dream lead one to seek out a homeless person?" she smiles, her unusual yellowish-brown eyes reminding him of a lioness. She seems young to be a doctor, and he assumes she's fulfilling her residency requirements. He recalls working the ER back in Baltimore, where he was required to wear a large badge that clearly spelled out DOCTOR, because patients frequently mistook the young doctors for nurses and janitorial staff.

"Something about my strange dreams led me here, that's all I know. I suppose my subconscious mind solves problems my conscious mind cannot."

"Do I detect a Yankee accent?" she smiles, moving in closer than is comfortable when respecting personal space.

"Excuse me?"

"Are you from the North?" she asks.

"Does it matter?"

"No, it's just we don't have many northern doctors venturing down to these parts."

"Well, yes I am. Grew up in Brooklyn. Are you doing your residency?"

She's accustomed to this and shoots him a look, her hands on hips. "No, I am the neurologist on duty in the ER today."

He's embarrassed. "Sorry, you look young to me."

"It's okay."

"Neurology, that's a very interesting field."

"It is. What's your specialty?"

"I'm a primary care physician. You know, didn't do well enough in med school to become a specialist."

"Oh, that's not true," she gazes at her pager. "You have far broader knowledge than I do."

"Broad but not very deep, that's me."

She laughs and touches him on the arm. "Where'd you get your medical degree?"

He blushes. "Johns Hopkins."

"Wow, that's impressive. I got mine at Baylor."

"Are you from Texas?"

"Born and raised in Marfa. Took everything I had to hightail it out of Texas."

"What's so bad about Texas?"

213

"Nothing, really. I just couldn't stand to be one of those provincial little people who spend their entire life where they grew up. Too much to see and do in this world."

"Well, that's sort of my story, too. I really like it in Sardis, where I have my own practice. I enjoy being my own boss."

"That sounds nice. I went to the lake in Sardis once and spent a lovely day."

"Small world," he exclaims. "That's where I've been hanging out this week." He feels her sizing him up, as if this man is too good to be true.

"You got a girlfriend?" her forwardness catches him off guard.

"Yes . . . No . . . Maybe?"

"That sounds intriguing."

He collects himself. "I think we just broke up. She's moving away."

"How unfortunate," her tone doesn't match the words.
"And you?"

"No, I don't have a girlfriend, I like men," she laughs.

"C'mon, you know what I mean."

"As it so happens—and it's extremely rare, let me tell you—I happen to be available."

Richard is stubbing his foot nervously into the floor. "So, if I were to ask you out on a date, you'd come?"

"Depends where we're going."

"Dinner? Someplace nice around here?"

"As long as we split the tab," she's now in full flirt mode.

"Of course."

There is a lengthy pause and then she reverts to her professional doctor's voice. "Given this homeless person you've so kindly tossed our way has no known relations, would you be willing to be the primary contact? In fact, maybe you could serve as his primary care physician, as that will help with his Medicaid paperwork."

"Sure, here's my business card. How long do you expect him to be here?"

"At least a few days. And then we'll need to send him to rehab, assuming his liver is all right. He needs to dry out or next time he won't make it to the ER."

Richard sighs. "He's a fascinating man. I think he might have been a professor in his past."

"How interesting. We're overrun these days by the homeless."

"That's because the only affordable housing is now on the streets," Richard looks disgusted.

"Well, it's good of you to look after him. Here's my card. If you don't hear from me within the day, give me a call. And let's go out on a date. If one learns anything working in the ER, it's that life is short."

Richard turns to leave and smiles as he heads back for his BMW. He places Doctor Flores' card in his wallet and drives away, not quite sure what to make of this assertive new doctor friend. On the way back to Sardis he phones Peggy, who picks up on the first ring.

"Richard, how nice to hear from you," she sounds upbeat.

"I've had quite the morning," he recounts his adventures with Colin.

"Do you think he'll be okay? Should we let Lizzy know?"

"It sounded like he might have a chance if he gets cleaned up. I agreed to be his primary care physician. God knows what I was thinking."

"That's kind of you, Richard. You really are the sweetest man I know. I missed you last night. The show was a big hit. But I felt down, unhappy with the way we left things yesterday."

"I heard the show was great. I ran into Wade outside the club this morning and he told me. Apparently, that record label guy is coming back tonight with a full recording setup."

"Yes, he phoned early this morning. You sound exhausted. Why don't you come over and I'll make us some lunch and then we can go for a swim. There's something important I want to discuss with you."

Richard pulls into the driveway wondering what Peggy wants to discuss. He assumes it's about yesterday's events and the hard push away she gave him. He is feeling conflicted—on the one hand wanting to continue seeing Peggy, but on the other realizing she is leaving on Sunday. And now there is this appealing doctor in Clarksdale. Everything seems to be moving so fast. He can't get past the feeling that has dogged him all week, the feeling that something is not quite right here, that Peggy and Priscilla are deceiving him in some important way. He parks and heads up the steep stairway, where he finds them in the living room seated on the sofa. He notices the family history journals spread out on the coffee table.

"Richard, come on in and have a seat," Peggy gestures to him. "Tell us what's going on with Colin. It sounded serious."

He sits between Priscilla and Peggy. "I think it is serious. I had strange dreams last night and one of them involved Colin. I found myself driving aimlessly this morning, and ended up going to Wade's looking for him. I found him passed out in an alley."

"It's a good thing you found him," Peggy looks concerned.

"We should know more later, but assuming his liver condition is not too far gone, he'll probably be off to rehab and get the chance to clean up. It looked to me like he was having seizures."

"Oh, dear," she pauses before adding: "Priscilla, would you be an angel and give us some alone time."

Priscilla looks disappointed but does as instructed and disappears around the corner for her bedroom.

Peggy waits a moment and then takes Richard's hand in hers. She runs her thumb along his palm, as if inspecting his life lines. "I think I'm falling for you."

Her words catch him off guard, as he was expecting a continuation of their previous day's conversation about just being friends.

She continues. "And I'm afraid you've fallen in love with me, too. Am I right?"

Richard's arms dangle loosely between his legs, as he stares at the floor. "Yes. I can't stop thinking about you. This week has been so much fun. But we can't fall in love, with you leaving—"

"I know," she looks away.

"So, I just assumed we need to put an end to this before either of us gets too hurt," he's doing his best to move on.

She sighs. "I was up most of the night tossing and turning thinking about you. You're like the world's most perfect piece of chocolate, and I can't stop eating you up, but know I must."

He chuckles, looking away in embarrassment. "That's an interesting analogy. I don't think I've ever been called a chocolate before—"

"Stop. I just need you to listen. Come close."

He slides toward her.

"Don't I remind you of someone?"

"Of course, you look a lot like your aunt."

"You mean the aunt you sat with at the diner earlier in the week as you complained about her triglycerides being too high?"

"Why, yes. How do you know about that?"

"You mean the aunt who was so daft she kept adding sugar to her coffee without realizing it? Because she's senile and will end up in a memory care facility?"

He pulls back, frightened. "How do you know all this?"

"I think you know how I know, and I've decided to tell you the truth as the only way forward out of this horrible mess. I know you read these family accounts yesterday. Priscilla told me so."

He gets up and paces in circles. "So?"

"So . . . they are not fantasy. Not stories invented by slaves to entertain each other. These accounts are all true and, for whatever reason, Priscilla made a wish that I could be young again for just this week, and it came true. I know, it sounds nuts. But there is no Peggy. It's me, Mabel. Young again."

He stumbles backwards toward the wall of windows. "Say whaat?"

"You heard me. This is why I've been pushing you away. There is no future for us as lovers."

"But that's insane. People can't just snap their fingers and become young again," he has moved to the other side of the grand piano, as if seeking protection, rubbing his left hand through his beard.

"I'm sorry. I know I used you. It was selfish of me. Can you ever forgive me?"

"Are you high on something?"

"No, it's just me, Richard. Mabel."

He cannot process what's happening, and stomps his feet on the floor apparently attempting to awaken from a dream. When he's done stomping, he sees Peggy is still there, smiling at him.

"This isn't a dream, dear."

"I can't believe this," he remains behind the piano. "If you're truly Mabel, then answer me this. "When did we first meet?"

"Why, in the hospital, following my stroke. How could I possibly forget? Seeing your smiling face as I woke up the following morning, was like being greeted by an angel."

"And what did I tell you?"

"You told me I had suffered a small stroke. You encouraged me to go on a plant-based diet."

"And, what did you say?"

"Why, I laughed at you. Said I've made it this far so will not be giving up cheeseburgers any time soon. I recall saying dieting was not something I was any good at."

Richard is shaking. Mabel continues: "And you told me I'd need to see a neurologist in Jackson, a man you knew from Johns Hopkins you said was first rate. Doctor Alec Wilson."

It's all true. He's flabbergasted. Richard removes his eyeglasses and massages the bridge of his nose, which shows small indentations from where his glasses fit too snugly. He puts them back on, remaining safely behind the piano. He recalls how he had instant suspicions about Peggy from their first day together at the Blues Museum, when she and Priscilla seemed to be enjoying a joke at his expense. As unbelievable as her story sounds, if true it would explain a lot about this past week. As a doctor and a man of science, he struggles to put aside his adherence to logic. He comes out from behind the piano and approaches her, taking a closer look.

"I can't deny your eyes match hers exactly, and that mole on your back, same place as hers—"

"Not hers, *mine*."

"And our lovemaking. I sensed something was strange, as if I was being used by an older woman. And apparently I was."

"I'm truly sorry, Richard. I never meant to hurt you. But pretend for a moment you're an old man and have the chance to be young again. Don't you think you just might find yourself longing for the touch of a younger woman?"

"I've never given it any thought, because I never will be young again! This is all so incomprehensible," he is pacing in circles.

"Run away, if you must. But I want you to know I love you. My love for you was, and is, genuine. I never expected to fall for you, but it just happened."

"It's all so crazy," he sits next to her. "But it adds up."

She takes his hand in hers. "For what it's worth, this week with you, and playing music again, has been a marvelous gift. We've had so much fun together. I hate to see it end."

"You're positive this spell wears off on Sunday?"

"Not exactly positive, but fairly certain. The spells I've read about in our family lasted just one week."

He looks hopeful but confused, still attempting to reconcile this world of magic with his faith in science. He doesn't want to lose her. "I suppose that's something to hang on to, then."

"If you mean the possibility that I'll remain young, there is no way I want that. As much fun as this week has been, it's also been very wrong. We're not supposed to mess around with time. We're not supposed to interfere with God's will. I just hope when I'm old again I appreciate how lucky I've been and cease having so many regrets. My life has been wonderful. I've been incredibly fortunate."

Richard sighs. "I suppose it doesn't really matter to me whether you're young or old."

"Oh, stop that."

"I'm serious. I'd rather have you around as Mabel than have you gone for good as Peggy."

She smiles. "You mean, you might love old mottle-faced Mabel?"

He smiles. "Yes," he takes her hand. "I like you as Mabel and now suspect I also love you. I don't know. It's all so perplexing. You're hitting me with a lot now, Peggy. I mean Mabel!"

She runs her fingers along his palm. "If you want to run away I won't blame you."

Richard stares into her eyes. "No, I don't want to run. One thing I've learned this week is to stop running and to fight for myself. But this is just shaking up my world. I feel like I must be dreaming."

"I'm glad you don't want to run."

He lets her continue rubbing his palm. "I'll be happy to have you around, no matter what happens on Sunday. Mabel, Peggy, or whoever you are."

She has her doubts, but feels a burden lift now that she's told him the truth. "There's something else. I need your help getting me out of the jam I'm in with Leroy, Buzz, and Schmidt."

"What jam?"

"Schmidt wants to record us tonight, and probably sign us to a contract that I obviously cannot fulfill. I've been sitting here this morning hatching a plan with Priscilla."

"Another plan. You two are bad news."

"We really could use your help."

"You're not going to turn me into a cockroach, I trust," he chuckles.

She doesn't laugh and looks serious. "It's actually a plan I hope can become a win-win situation."

"I'm game, what do you need me to do?"

The club is packed when Richard, Mabel, and Priscilla arrive that evening. Schmidt has cleared out the middle section of seats in the rear and has brought a sound engineer from the festival. Mabel smiles at him as she passes on her way to the bar to join Richard and Lizzy. She sits on the vacated stool next to Richard. She sees Lizzy conversing with an attractive young woman Mabel doesn't recall seeing at the club before. Lizzy turns to face them and Richard is surprised to see the woman with Lizzy is Domenica, the ER doctor.

"Why, hello," Richard struggles to collect himself.

224

Domenica smiles at him. "What a pleasant surprise. Do you come here often?"

"Just this week, since I met Mab . . . Peggy, here."

"Mab-Peggy?" she isn't sure she heard the name correctly, and given there are so many strange hyphenated names these days, she wants to be certain.

Mabel extends her hand, "Peggy Winston, I'm performing tonight."

"Nice to meet you," Domenica says. At first, Richard wasn't sure it was her. Her black hair falls loosely around her shoulders, whereas at the hospital she wore it up.

Mabel says: "Nice to meet you as well. How do you two know each other?"

"Domenica was working the ER this morning when I brought Colin in. How's he doing?"

"I think he'll be okay, as long as he dries out. He woke up unsure of how he got to the hospital. I told him you brought him and he told me I might find you here tonight."

"Well, that's good," Richard is relieved.

Mabel can see that Richard is attracted to Domenica, so comes to his aid in keeping the conversation moving. "You're a doctor, too?" Mabel asks, knowing the answer.

"Yes."

"Isn't that nice. Richard's mother is a doctor. Right Richard?"

"Where?" Domenica asks.

"Brooklyn," Richard answers.

Lizzy is nursing her glass of white wine, looking lost in thought. Mabel orders a Manhattan and joins her so Richard and Domenica can be alone.

"How are you, Lizzy?"

"It's been a long day."

"Your father?"

"Same as always. Demanding and ungrateful. A bad combination."

Mabel sighs, "Oh, dear."

"But, Peggy, you must be so excited," Lizzy attempts to rally. "I heard Schmidt chatting with someone on his phone about preparing a contract for you. I gather the sample files he sent were a big hit."

"I was afraid of that—"

"Excuse me?"

"Oh, nothing. It's just I'm having second thoughts about becoming a musician."

"Are you insane?"

"Possibly."

"Why wouldn't you want a record deal? I mean, this is your big chance."

"Yes, of course. I don't mean to sound ungrateful. It's just I'm not convinced I'm good enough. Now you, you have real talent—"

"Stop."

"Stop what?"

"Flattering me. I'm good but you're great. The fact you cannot see that is perplexing."

Mabel sips her Manhattan. "I know, I should be happy—very happy—yet somehow, I'm feeling depressed. It could be I'm coming down with a cold as I'm feeling sapped of my normal energy."

Lizzy reaches in her purse and passes Peggy a pill. "Take this."

"What's that?"

"Don't worry, it's nothing dangerous, just something to give you an immune boost."

Mabel stares at the yellow pill in her palm. "I don't think I should."

"Go ahead. It's just herbs."

Mabel doesn't want Lizzy to think she doesn't trust her so downs the pill with a swig from her Manhattan. She then turns her attention to Domenica. "Did you know that Lizzy is an outstanding musician?"

"Cool, I did not," Domenica says.

"Did you two just meet?" Richard asks Lizzy.

"Yes, Nica joined me at the bar. We've been having a nice chat. She's been filling me in on Colin's situation."

227

Lizzy stirs her ginger ale.

"Nica?" Richard repeats the name.

"Yes," Domenica replies. "That's what friends call me. My full name sounds, well, you know, a little domineering."

"I like it, it's cute," Richard says.

Priscilla slides off her stool a few seats away and adds: "Just don't call Doctor Richard here, Richie. He doesn't like that."

"Duly noted," she laughs. "And who are you?"

"She's with us," Richard realizes she might be concerned Priscilla is his child, so quickly adds, "She's Peggy's niece, visiting for the week while her father presents a paper at an academic conference in Germany."

"And she's going to be a doctor someday, too, aren't you?" Peggy smiles.

"I hope so, I guess. But I'd rather be a concert pianist."

Nica is swiveling on her stool like a happy child. "Maybe you'll be a surgeon, then. A pianist's hands are ideal for the operating room."

"Do you like being a doctor?" Priscilla asks.

"Very much."

"What do you like about it?"

"Well, I enjoy helping sick people get better. That's the main reason. And I've always loved science. You have to constantly study to keep up."

"Me, too." Priscilla likes her and Nica senses this.

"Maybe you can job shadow me in the hospital someday, if it's okay with your mother." The ensuing awkward silence leads her to realize she's slipped up. "I'm sorry, I shouldn't have presumed—"

"No, it's okay," Peggy gazes down at her feet fighting back tears. "Priscilla's mother died unexpectedly and we're all still in shock."

Nica leans down to Priscilla. "I'm so sorry, dear. I can only imagine how much that must hurt."

"It's okay," Priscilla stays strong. "She's still with me, on the inside."

"Yes, of course."

"But I would love to come to your work and see what it's like if you mean it."

"Absolutely. It's important that we ladies stick together. Girl power!" she makes a fist and bumps it against Priscilla's, and Priscilla beams.

Richard turns to Lizzy. "I woke up thinking about Colin this morning and ended up driving here for no apparent reason."

Mabel smiles. "Except there *was* a reason."

Richard assumes this is a reference to his saving Colin, but then she adds: "Think about it. If you hadn't gone to the ER, you never would have met this delightful *young* doctor," she emphasizes the word *young* in a way that makes her intent clear.

Domenica appreciates the support. "And don't think this counts as the date you promised me. We're going out for a proper dinner."

Priscilla spies Joel Swillens approaching. "Uh, oh," she taps Mabel on the forearm.

"Good evening, Peggy. Looks like quite the turnout." When she fails to respond, he adds in a suggestive manner: "What a day."

"Why do you say that?" Priscilla asks.

"Well, I was about to give up searching for information about Peggy when it dawned on me I should go look for Mabel in Oxford. Alice Kramlich informed me I could most likely find her at her granddaughter Michelle's house, sorting through her clothes. Alice gave me the address."

Richard and Mabel place their drinks on the bar, not liking the sounds of this.

"How is Mabel?" Richard asks.

"Funny thing, I stopped by Michelle's house, but no one was there. The curtains were drawn, and the mailbox was stuffed. How odd, I thought. I asked for Mabel around town, and was told I might find Michelle's husband John Anderson over at Ole Miss. A janitor at the university told me he thought Mabel was home in Sardis, as that was what Professor

Anderson told him before heading off for a conference in Germany. Now, how can we possibly explain all this, Peggy?"

Priscilla steps in. "Because Mabel isn't in Oxford anymore, she had to go back to the lawyer's office in Jackson because she forgot to add her middle initial when signing documents." This is something Priscilla learned from watching an episode of Judge Judy.

Joel looks up, stunned. "I hadn't realized a middle initial was a requirement for legal documents."

"It's not," Priscilla adds, "unless you sign some pages with the middle initial and others without it, which is what she did."

He looks skeptical, but drops it when Schmidt waves Peggy over to the console, introducing her to the sound engineer. "Peggy, would you please play for a few minutes so we can make a final check," Schmidt motions to the stage. She sits at the piano and plays the opening bars of "Black Coffee," joined onstage by Leroy and Buzz who have been unloading equipment. She notices they have dressed up for tonight, wearing black shirts and black slacks, sporting shiny black loafers.

"Don't you two look all professional tonight," she teases.

Leroy laughs. "Not every night you get a chance like this. I've hired a videographer from town to film us," he points to

231

the front row where a young man sits.

Peggy returns to the bar and asks Domenica if she'd come to the ladies' room and help clip a thread from the back of her gown. Richard shoots Peggy a wink as he takes the vacated seat next to Lizzy.

A half hour later, Peggy is staring out at the slow-motion scene unfolding before her, noting where everyone is seated around the club. This will be her final performance. The finality is settling in, the carefree fun of performing earlier in the week now replaced with the burdens she remembers too well, the burdens of others depending on her for their livelihoods. The burdens of fleeting fame and fortune. She will not miss any of that. On the one hand, she doesn't want to be old again, with all the pains and limitations on her activities, but on the other hand is eager to return to her simple life of church and television and reading. This has been such a freeing week; so freeing, she chuckles, that she hasn't once watched a single episode of *Jeopardy!* and finds herself wondering if she missed the Tournament of Champions. She's a huge fan of James Holzhauer and has been hoping he can finally beat Ken Jennings, whose breadth of knowledge astounds her.

Wade takes the stage and his voice sounds distant to Mabel. She gazes out from the stage relieved this will be her final performance. Everything in front of her slows. She exhales, bringing herself back to the moment, switching into performer mode. She hears: "Tonight's performance is being recorded, so I ask that you please remain quiet, withholding any applause for the end of each song, And now, it is my special privilege to present the Peggy Winston Trio."

She adjusts her gown one more time and then the trio begins playing "Fever." She fixates on a young couple in the front row, singing to them, ignoring the rest of the audience. They seem to be so deeply in love and the song is her parting gift to them, a gift she is happy to be able to offer. When she finishes, the crowd breaks into applause, and she smiles at the young couple, a glint of tears in her eyes. During the second song, "Black Coffee," Mabel purposefully starts playing too slowly, causing Leroy and Buzz to struggle to stay in rhythm with her. Schmidt hasn't been paying close attention but now looks up with concern on his face. Mabel sings: "I'm talking to the shadows, from one o'clock 'til four; and lord, how slow the moments go, when all I do is pour, Blaaaack Coffeeee, since the blues caught my eye . . ." she coughs, the song sputtering to a stop like a car out of gas. She motions to Wade for a glass of water, gulping it down while the audience sits in stunned silence. She then mouths a few hoarse words into the mic. Schmidt has come onstage and hears her whisper: "I've lost my voice." Leroy and Buzz stand off to the side, their big break vanishing before their eyes. Mabel nods to

Richard, who practically pushes Lizzy up toward Schmidt on the stage.

"Let Lizzy finish the set," Richard says.

"Absolutely not," sweat trickles down Schmidt's forehead. "We're interested in the Peggy Winston Trio, no one else."

Mabel approaches and whispers. "Go ahead and record her while you've got everything set up. What else are we going to do?"

"We insist," Priscilla joins them on stage. "Otherwise, there will be no record deal for Peggy Winston."

"Excuse me?" he is taken aback.

"You heard me. Record Lizzy while she's right here or else Peggy refuses to sign with you. She'll sign with someone else."

"That's absurd. No one turns down a record deal with Warner."

"Peggy will."

Mabel presses: "Surely we don't want to disappoint the patrons who've come tonight," her voice seems to be returning.

"You're sounding better now," Schmidt looks hopeful.

She fakes a hoarse voice again uttering air words that no one can hear.

"All right, all right. Lizzy, go ahead and do the best you

234

can," he gives in.

Mabel and Richard sit at the bar as Lizzy takes her seat behind the piano. She's wearing a Black Lives Matter T-shirt and cutoff jeans, contrasting with the professional attire of Buzz and Leroy. Her face is flushed with nervous energy as she turns to Buzz and Leroy discussing what they should play. They come to an agreement, and on the count of four launch into "Come Away With Me," another Norah Jones song Lizzy adores. Her smoky, sexy voice has Leroy nodding in approval as the song unfolds. Peggy's attention is focused on Schmidt, who is sitting behind the recording equipment looking disappointed that Peggy cannot perform. She makes eye contact with him and motions toward the stage, mouthing the words *listen to her.* He sighs and faces the stage, checking the time on his wristwatch. The trio finishes the song and the crowd breaks into boisterous applause, led by Peggy and Richard who begin clapping before the final notes are struck.

Lizzy smiles, her confidence rising. "Shall we play another tune?" she faces Leroy and Buzz.

"Mos' def," Leroy says.

"Do you know Bebel Gilberto's song "Simplesmente"?

"I think so. C#7, A#, F#7 . . . right?"

"You got it."

Lizzy starts singing: "Every moment I'm near you, I try to understand . . ."

Mabel sees that Schmidt is now fully engaged, lifted by the enthusiasm of the audience as well as the performance. The song ends and Mabel mouths to Lizzy: *play an original.* Lizzy turns to Buzz and Leroy, discussing some chord progressions. She clears her throat, announcing her own composition: "When My Daddy's Gone." It's a sad ballad about forgiveness: "He may have been unkind, he may have been cruel, but he's your only daddy, so try and keep your cool . . ."

Mabel whispers to Richard: "The best art always comes from pain."

They play three more songs and the crowd rises in a standing ovation. Mabel and Domenica greet Lizzy when she comes offstage.

"You were awesome," Domenica says.

"Amazing," Mabel hugs Lizzy.

"Your voice is back," Lizzy gazes at Mabel, wondering if this was all her plan to give her a chance.

"Well, what do you know," Mabel winks. Schmidt approaches and thanks Lizzy. Buzz and Leroy are standing behind him, hoping he liked what he heard.

"Isn't she something else?" Leroy exclaims, as he repeatedly pounds his right fist into his left open palm, as if keeping the beat.

"A fresh new voice," Mabel adds in a whisper.

236

Schmidt looks exhausted. "Listen, let me see what we've got by the light of a new day. I'll check in with the Warner Music folks to see what they think."

SATURDAY

Mabel rises before sunrise and goes for a swim. She assumes this will be her last day of youth and intends to squeeze every last drop of fun out of the day. Last night at the club went better than expected, with Schmidt, Leroy, and Buzz all seemingly smitten by Lizzy's singing. Richard was able to get the local reporter off Mabel's back, refocusing him on Lizzy's performance, encouraging him as the only journalist in attendance to write about her. Mabel feels a pang of regret mixed with acceptance, recalling the attractive young doctor Richard met. Nica. Even the name sounds sexy. She knows she should be thrilled for him, and for the most part is, but cannot deny some stubborn jealousy. Why couldn't she and Richard have met back when she was a young woman? But, no, she mustn't go down this path, and has faith everything is happening for good reasons. Even that lout of an ex-husband—the faux musical agent, Jerry—had been good in ways she couldn't appreciate at the time. He pushed her when she wanted to quit. He told her she had real talent when others ignored her. She cannot deny that he loved her. It was love, she knows this, and acknowledges she felt the same way about him back then, as difficult as that is to accept now. Truth is, no one is completely evil, there is good inside us all. She sighs. "Oh, dear." Whatever love they shared vanished like a melting fog. Love, like life itself, another fleeting joy.

She sits on the float looking back at her house. It's so big, much bigger than any other home on the lake, and too big for just herself living alone. Maybe she should sell it and move to Oxford to be with John and Priscilla. But she loves it here, has lived on the lake for many decades, and the thought of moving leads her to tear up. The rising sun has poked its head up barely above the horizon, enough so she can make out shapes along the shoreline—the tops of the masts at the sailing school bathed in a hopeful light. The rectangular windows of her home's second floor, where the reading nooks await on the other side, reflect rays up to the tops of the pine trees, where birds have broken into song. What a beautiful place. What a beautiful life. She feels unburdened now that she has told Richard the truth, and he seems to have taken the news as well as one could hope given the circumstances. Maybe this Nica he's met will convince him to stay in Sardis? That would be nice. She will miss him so much if he leaves for Boston. They went their separate ways following last night's show, and she invited him to come over this morning to celebrate her final day of youth.

She swims back to shore and heads inside to take a shower. Once dressed, she fetches the step ladder from the closet and finally gets around to washing those streaky windows that have been annoying her all week. She balances on her tiptoes, reaching as high as she can, but gives up in the realization that the top sections of the windows are beyond her reach. She'll call a professional service to complete the job next week. She steps down from the ladder and fetches her old knitting bag from the bedroom. She returns to the living room and sits on the sofa, resurrecting a needlepoint pillow project she set aside years ago. She loses herself in the busywork, finding it relaxing in the way puzzles are for many people.

"Good morning, Grammy May." Priscilla emerges from her bedroom.

"Hey honey. How are you this beautiful day?"

"Good. I was just talking with Daddy. He's at the airport in London, happy to be coming home."

"Did he say how the conference went?"

"He thinks okay, but he's homesick. He was quizzing me on country capitals."

"How'd you do?"

"They were all *way* too easy."

"Well, that's because you're so smart."

Priscilla smiles.

Mabel sets her needlepoint project off to the side.

"Okay, Miss Smarty Pants, let me try a few on you. What's the capital of Turkey?"

"Duh. Ankara."

"Not Istanbul?" Mabel looks confused.

"No, it's Ankara. Trust me."

"Okay, then. How about Sweden?"

"Stockholm. Double-Duh."

"Oh, my. Okay, how about . . . North Dakota?"

"Bismarck. Triple-DUH."

"Well, you don't have to be mean about it."

"C'mon, ask me some hard ones."

"I'm going to cheat and use my phone." Mabel taps away before asking. "Okay, how about Kenya?"

"Nairobi."

"Libya?"

"Tripoli."

"You go girl. You're really great at this."

Priscilla beams with pride. "Ask me about Ethiopia."

"I haven't a clue, but okay, Ethiopia."

"Addis Ababa."

"Never heard of it. And I've traveled the globe, far and wide. How in the world did you learn all this at your young age?"

"It's just memorization. No big deal."

241

"When I was your age, I could hardly find Africa on a map."

"Well, that's sad, given we come from there."

"You know, come to think of it, I didn't have a single Black teacher until I got to college. Do you have many Black teachers?"

"Sure. A lot of my teachers look like me."

"That's good to hear."

"Miss Jackson is my gifted-and-talented teacher and has taught us a lot about Black history, including African geography."

"Do you like your school?"

"It's okay. The gifted-and-talented program helps a lot. I'm glad Mom and Dad insisted I stay in public school. They had been talking about sending me to a private school, where many of the faculty kids go, but I don't like most of those kids. They think they're all that."

"How many children are in your gifted-and-talented class?"

"There are actually two tracks: one for math and one for everything else. I'm in both. Mostly boys in the math class, around six students in total. Then it's just me, two girls, and one boy in the general class."

"It's important you do as well as possible in school. Education is the gateway to great opportunities. And Black folks like us have to work twice as hard to avoid being weeded out by standardized testing and other racist educational programs."

"You sound like Daddy."

"Well, he knows better than most."

"Why do you say that?"

"Because his research focuses on systemic racial inequalities within our educational system. The curriculums, the increasing use of standardized tests, all skew toward white European education, ignoring Black history and experiences."

"Daddy gets angry talking about the Common Core," Priscilla says.

"He should. No Child Left Behind and all the other well-meaning programs for poor kids end up penalizing their schools, leading to less money to hire teachers. It's a vicious cycle."

"I'm glad Daddy will be home tomorrow. This week has been fun, but I miss him."

"Me too," Mabel says.

"He told me he got me a teddy bear and also a book on the Holocaust."

"You're so bright, Priscilla. I imagine you'll teach yourself as much as you learn from any teachers. Stay curious. That's the best way to live."

"I'm very fortunate that my piano teacher is helping me

learn about Black history. And he taught himself eight languages, including Chinese. He can read musical scores like most people read words."

"That's remarkable. Maybe you can learn Chinese from him?"

"I'd like that. I watch as he draws the characters, which look like art. I don't know how he does it. The characters seem far more intricate than our alphabet."

"You say he's teaching you Black history *and* has you working on Chopin?" Mabel smiles.

"Sure, why not?"

"Oh, I don't know. I'm just pleasantly surprised to hear that."

"Go on—"

"Well, it's reassuring to know you have a teacher open-minded enough to teach both European classical composers like Chopin as well as Black history. That certainly was not the case back in my time."

Priscilla struggles to comprehend. "That's sad."

"It is, but back when I was your age all we studied was white history: mostly one boring war after another all the way from ancient times to now. And my classical lessons focused exclusively on white composers."

"Have you heard of Jeffrey Mumford?"

"No, should I?"

244

"Yes. He's a contemporary Black classical composer. Professor Morehead is analyzing his scores and plays some of his motifs on the piano, talking through the score while I observe."

"I'll have to check him out. I won't kid you, I do miss playing the beautiful piano pieces of Beethoven and Brahms. But I'm happy to hear Black classical composers and performers are getting chances nowadays. Progress is always happening even though at times it does not seem that way."

"Let's play something together," Priscilla motions to the piano. "You know, while we can."

Mabel sits on the piano bench to the right of her great-granddaughter who begins playing "Moonlight Sonata."

Mabel closes her eyes. "How beautiful. You play it so well, dear."

When Priscilla finishes, Mabel tries playing the same piece, conjuring up memories of her first classical music teacher, back in elementary school, Bruce Morgan. She smiles thinking of him. He was an elderly white gentleman, who was very cultured and traveled the globe in pursuit of music and fine cuisine. Morgan was very kind to her, offering free lessons once he heard her play in church, impressed by her talent. He would sit with her following lessons in his home and they would eat croissants with butter and raspberry jam as her reward for a good session. He lived in an old brick mansion, with Oriental rugs and fine furnishings, mostly from France. She had never seen a home like his. He was funny, railing against corrupt politicians and making witty remarks about the arts and artists. He was the one who encouraged her to continue her musical studies following college and to be sure to see an opera in New York, once she was admitted to Julliard. He was visiting family in New York her sophomore year and looked her up at school, insisting she come with him to see Debussy's "Pelléas and Mélisande" at the Metropolitan Opera. She recalls the cool blues and elegant whites of the music and dancers. She remembers her impression that the music was like resting your head on a soft down pillow, a thought she shared with Morgan. She had forgotten all about her old mentor, and imagines how proud he'd be if he could see her now, a famous musician. He spent hours working with her as a young student to emphasize the colorization within the best music, the warm notes and the cool notes, and how to raise and lower the wrist for better piano technique to achieve the deepest feelings evinced by the Romantic composers. She does this now as she plays "Moonlight Sonata," concentrating on improving her technique to bring out the distinctive pathos of the sonata. Priscilla slips away unnoticed and records her grandmother with her iPhone. Tears spill down Mabel's cheeks as the music transports her, her deepest artistic emotions engaged, the truths that time is short and paradise unattainable for mere mortals. She finishes up, hanging on to the lingering notes, the perfect ending to a perfect song. She gazes across the lake. She hopes she can manage her own perfect landing, her own elegant ending. She wants to die at home, in her own bed, and not be cast off and forgotten in some lonely memory care center.

The phone rings and Mabel gets it. It's Richard.

"Good morning to you as well . . . sure, bring her with you. Noon sounds fine, see you then."

"Is he bringing Nica?" Priscilla asks.

"No, why do you ask?"

"I heard you say he's bringing someone."

"He's bringing Lizzy. They're at the hospital with Colin and Nica at the moment."

"Oh, I see."

"You sound disappointed."

"I really like Nica. She said I can job shadow her at the hospital sometime soon. Don't you like her?"

Mabel sighs. "Yes, I do."

"You don't act like it."

Mabel pats her on the head. "You're too young to understand jealousy. I would rather have Richard for myself."

"Yet, you'll be old again tomorrow—"

"I know, I know. You'll just have to believe me when I tell you that matters of the heart are not rational."

The phone rings again and Priscilla gets it.

"No, she's not here at the moment. May I help?" she covers the phone mouthing: *it's Schmidt.* A lengthy pause ensues and then Priscilla says: "Both Peggy and Lizzy will be here this afternoon if you want to stop by then. We're at Mabel's home on Sardis Lake. Do you know it? Yes, that's right. Okay, we'll see you this afternoon."

"What did he want?"

"Sounds like he's bringing a contract over for you to sign."

"I can't be signing a contract."

"Just stall him until tomorrow," Priscilla suggests. "Peggy will be gone and there'll be no way to find her."

Mabel sits on the sofa, hands dangling loosely between her legs. "You know what? I think I might have an idea of how to handle this."

Richard and Lizzy arrive shortly after noon and Peggy hugs them as they stand in the entryway.

"What a fabulous place," Lizzy gazes around. She wanders over to the wall of Grammys. "May I touch one of these?"

"By all means," Peggy says.

Richard heads for the kitchen to unload the bag of groceries. Peggy follows.

"How's Colin?" she asks.

"Not too bad this morning. Nica thinks he can go to rehab sometime later this week."

"You like her, don't you."

He touches her on the arm. "I do. But I *love* you."

"Stop that. I'm just an old hag."

"You stop that. You're a beautiful woman, inside and out. When I think about what you did for Lizzy last night, well, you're just so kind."

"She deserves it. So listen, Charles Schmidt is coming over later with a contract for me to sign."

"How do you plan to get out of that?"

"I have an idea."

"Do you need my help? I must admit I enjoyed being your sidekick last night. I haven't had that kind of adventure since grade school when we'd tunnel into the gym and play basketball at night."

"I hadn't pictured you as a baller," she chuckles.

"I wasn't very good but my friends all played so I hung with them. It was Middle School. You know, too cool for school."

"You must have been quite the sight back then."

"I was. Had my hair in hip-hop Gangsta cornrows, my Air Jordans, shorts slung down low. I had it all goin' on."

She laughs.

"We almost got the school janitor fired the way we'd sneak into the gym at night using those old underground utility tunnels. We forgot to switch off the lights one night and the school figured he was letting us in. I confessed and so that came to an end."

"Lucky you didn't fry yourselves in those old tunnels. That's where they used to run electrical wires."

"I know."

She opens the refrigerator and takes out a carton of eggs, planning to make a cheddar and broccoli quiche for lunch. She cracks open an egg and turns to Richard. "Anyway, I will need your help with Schmidt. Okay?"

"Just let me know what you need me to do. I get the sense you're not crazy about him."

"With good reason."

"Why do you say that?"

"He had the chance to sign me back in the late-sixties when he was working for Atlantic Records. My husband insisted I refuse his offer, telling me it was a bad deal. Jerry sent Schmidt packing more than once and then arranged for me to sign with Columbia Records, where my career truly took off."

"I see," Richard says.

"Schmidt was insulted I signed with Columbia, where Clive Davis was just starting to expand into rock and R&B.

He did what he could to quietly undermine me at that time. It's all water under the bridge, but I wouldn't mind getting back at him, and think I know how, with your assistance."

Lizzy and Priscilla wander into the kitchen and Lizzy says: "I can't get over what a beautiful home Mabel has."

"She did well for herself," Richard is chopping broccoli.

"You can say that again," Lizzy pulls up a stool at the center island. "I've been listening to more of her music this week and—"

"And . . . what?" Priscilla cuts her off abruptly in a way that comes across as combative.

"And . . . I cannot get over how many songs she wrote. I mean, it's one thing to have a great voice, and to play the piano as well as she does, but to compose all those hit tunes? Wow. Where does that come from?"

Peggy smiles. "I think she'd tell you from up above."

"Well, I hope God can spare some of that magic for me," Lizzy twists her hair up into a tight bun.

Priscilla grins. "He's got a whole lot of magic to go around."

Peggy is reminded of an old song she loves and begins singing:

> *Do you believe in maagic, in a young girl's heart.*
> *How the music can free her, whenever it starts. And*

251

it's maaaagic, if the music is groovy,

it makes you feel happy like

an old-time mooovie. I'll tell you about the magic,

and it'll free your soul. But it's like trying to tell a

stranger 'bout rock and roll . . .

"C'mon, sing with me you guys . . . you must know this song!" She stops and breaks into laughter realizing no one has joined her. "You all need to check out the sixties band The Lovin' Spoonful," she mixes cheddar cheese and broccoli in a bowl with the eggs.

Lizzy smiles. "Hey, I'll believe in magic if it can make my problems disappear."

"You just might find out sooner than you realize," Peggy winks at Richard.

Lizzy senses something is up. "Say what?"

"Schmidt is coming over this afternoon. I'm hoping he'll want to sign you to a contract."

"Oh, get real," she dismisses the thought. "I mean, he was so disappointed when you couldn't play last night."

"I wouldn't be so sure of that. The crowd loved you and that's what matters most to him. I noticed he perked right up once he heard the applause."

"That's kind of you, Peggy. It really is. I wonder what Mabel would think of my piano playing? Is she coming home soon?"

"She should be back tomorrow. Come over and introduce yourself. I'm sure she'd love to hear you play her piano and sing."

"I'd like that."

"I'm sure she'd be smitten by you. You never know, she might even help you make your way."

"Make my way, where?"

"Why, as a musician."

"I just can't see it, sorry."

"Don't be sorry. Believe in yourself, girl, or no one else will. Success in the arts is half talent and half perseverance, or so I've heard Mabel say time and time again.

After lunch, Lizzy and Priscilla go for a swim while Peggy and Richard wait for Schmidt. Shortly after one o'clock, they hear tires on the driveway and look outside to see a stretch limousine rolling in. Peggy watches through the window as Schmidt gets out and climbs the steep stairs. He's huffing and puffing as he makes it to the door.

"How in heavens does Mabel get up and down those stairs at her age?" he asks Peggy.

"I'm sorry. I should have told you to take the Stairlift. See it down there?"

"Now you tell me," he wipes sweat from his brow and comes inside the air-conditioned house.

"You're not planning to leave your driver out there all afternoon in this heat, are you?"

"He's fine. He works for the record company."

"I insist you invite him in. He can wait in the kitchen and have a cold drink while we meet."

Schmidt calls him on his cell phone, while Peggy mouths the words: *tell him to use the Stairlift*. A few minutes later an elderly Black man stands at the door, uncertain whether he should enter."

"Come on, Reggie. It's fine," Schmidt waves him in. The chauffeur stands in the entryway looking uncomfortable.

"Let me get you a glass of lemonade." Peggy takes Reggie by the elbow and leads him to a seat in the kitchen. She pours him a tall glass.

"Thank you, ma'am," he sips his drink.

"You just relax here and Schmidt will come get you when he's done."

"You're too kind, ma'am," he removes his chauffeur cap and wipes his brow with a handkerchief.

She returns to the living room with hands on hips, glowering at Schmidt. "I can't believe you were going to let that nice old man sit out there in this heat."

Schmidt ignores her as he walks to the wall of Grammys.

"One of the biggest mistakes of my career, not signing Mabel when I had the opportunity. Is she home, by any chance?"

"She's in Oxford," Richard joins them.

Peggy adds: "I doubt she'd want to see you if she were here."

"Another time, then," Schmidt is seated on the piano bench, attempting to catch his breath from climbing all those stairs.

"Let me get you a towel," Richard offers. He returns and Schmidt wipes his sweating head and places the towel on the floor next to him.

"Well, then. Where shall we review your contract, Peggy?"

"Follow me to the study," she motions him to follow. "Richard, you come, too."

She sits behind the large mahogany desk as Richard and Schmidt slide armchairs closer. Schmidt opens his leather brief case and pulls out a contract. "I've got great news for you, Peggy. We'd like to offer you eight million dollars for a two-record deal."

"Wow," she's genuinely surprised by the size of the offer.

"It's a standard agreement," he hands it to her. "You'll find everything in order."

She has considerable experience with recording contracts, and knows what to look for.

"I don't see Buzz or Leroy included in this."

Schmidt clears his throat, and brushes his cheek with his index finger in a way she knows from experience means he's about to lie. "We can take care of them separately."

"Hmm," she mutters.

Richard gets up and walks to the far bookshelves. "I don't like the sounds of that."

"Well, it's standard practice."

"Maybe, but Peggy here isn't standard anything."

"And what about Lizzy?" she asks.

"I'm still waiting to hear from the label to see what they thought of her performance. If they like her, we'll sign her, too."

She crosses her arms and leans into the desk. Schmidt can feel Richard's breathing close behind him. She says: "I'm curious to know what *you* thought of her performance. I mean, you keep hiding behind your marketing people, when I'm sure a man of your reputation must be the most important decision maker. Am I correct?"

His vanity gets the better of him. "Why yes, that's true."

She continues. "In fact, this contract you now are offering me . . . did you even get approval for it? I would guess not."

"Well, I did let the Finance Department know. I can't just write checks carte blanche."

"I see," she sits back.

Richard is now standing next to her. "You seem to be leaving a lot open to future promises."

Schmidt feels they are tag-teaming him in a way he does not like.

She pushes the contract back at him. "Let me tell you what I'm thinking. If you want to sign me, I'm willing to accept your terms, but for the "Live at Wade's" recording you captured on Thursday—"

Schmidt sits up in his seat. "But I doubt that will be good enough to be released commercially."

"I thought you said your equipment was surprisingly good," Richard says.

"Well, I mean, it is . . . but what we will capture in the studio will be far superior. I mean, that should be quite obvious to you."

She sits there thinking. "Okay, how about we write my contract so I'll agree to record in studio, but if I'm unable to do so, for any reason within the next sixty days, you'll release the "Live at Wade's" recording first and give me more time, say two years, to record a new album. For what it's worth, I sincerely doubt what we capture in the studio will match the energy of the live performance."

"That's certainly an odd request," Schmidt looks puzzled.

"It's about to get even odder," Richard smiles, knowing what's coming.

"Furthermore, I'll agree to sign with you for only two million dollars for this arrangement, not eight."

"Whaaat?" Schmidt is not sure he heard correctly.

"Yes, I'll take less, but only if you agree to provide separate agreements for Leroy and Buzz, to each receive one million. That will include them also performing on two new albums to be produced as part of The Lizzy Smith Trio."

"Lizzy who?"

She looks annoyed. "Lizzy, from last night."

"I didn't know her last name," Schmidt looks flustered. She's hitting him with a lot all at once.

"There's more. I need you to also come back with a two-million-dollar contract for Lizzy. All of the monies, for all four contracts, to be paid within thirty days of contract signing."

"That's nuts," Schmidt rises, wiping sweat from his forehead with his sleeve, wishing he had kept the towel with him and considers going to fetch it.

"I don't think it's nuts at all. You will be signing four artists for less than you were prepared to sign me. Think how happy the marketing and finance people will be when you show up with four new artists for less than the one they agreed to," she winks at Richard.

"But . . . why on earth would you do that?"

"I'm not in this for the money. I'm in it for the love of music."

"Right. That's a good one," Schmidt spritzes them with his spit. "For the love of music," he repeats, smirking. "If only your famous Aunt Mabel had been this cooperative. Back then, I thought I made her a strong offer, only to see her sign with a lesser label."

"It's funny you mention that," she says. "Mabel told me you low-balled her. She found your offer insulting. When we spoke last night, she encouraged me to hold off and sign with someone else."

"It was good money back then," his arms are folded across his chest.

"Apparently not good enough. I can't imagine how much money you must have personally lost as a result."

"A lot," he says. "A boatload."

She loves hearing this. "Well, then, we wouldn't want to make the same mistake twice, now would we."

Schmidt moans as if in pain, confused by what's happening.

She gets up to leave. "We should be joining the others down at the lake."

"Stop, don't go," Schmidt calls her back.

She and Richard pause and then return to their seats. Schmidt exhales. "Let me get this straight. If I come back with the contracts you want, you'll agree to sign and the others will, too?"

"Yes, but with a few other modifications."

"Good God. Now what?" he leans back, exasperated.

"Clause VI in Lizzy's contract. I want you to include a marketing launch guarantee."

"We never do that for new artists."

"Well, do it for her. New artists are the ones who need it the most."

"But . . . in all the contracts? I can't do that—"

"No, just hers is fine. Guarantee a $100,000 launch marketing fund for her."

"I've worked with more than my share of oddball artists, but you take the cake. I'm afraid to ask. Anything else?"

"I want all proceeds from my contract to go to John Anderson."

"Who in the world is John Anderson?"

"He's Priscilla's father."

"And who's Priscilla?"

"She's the spunky girl from the club. You remember her, right?"

"How could I possibly forget that little battle axe."

260

"Be nice. She's very bright. I think she might cure cancer someday."

"I'm so confused. Basically, you're saying you don't want any money for yourself?"

"Correct."

"But why?"

"I have plenty of money. More than I know what to do with. Priscilla recently lost her mother and I want to make sure any proceeds from sales of my music go to her father, and then to her at age twenty-one."

"I think you're high."

"Quite to the contrary," her eyes narrow.

"How can you possibly have money? I mean, the local reporter told me you work as a stewardess."

"I used to, but just inherited a great deal when my father died," she is becoming amazed and disturbed by her facility in making up lies on the spot about the fictitious Peggy Winston.

"What did he do?" Schmidt asks.

"Is that really any of your business?"

"No, but I'm curious."

She hesitates, attempting to come up with a credible lie. "Well, if you must know, he was one of the early investors in Amazon, Google, and Apple."

"How fortunate for him," he glances off. "But, I mean,

no one ever has *enough* money. The world runs on greed. You should see some of the people I have to deal with every day."

"Have to?" she smiles. "Surely, no one is forcing you to do what you do to earn a living."

"No, I suppose not," he wipes the back of his hand across his brow, and then dries his hand on his pant leg. "Truth be told, I'm hoping to get out of this racket and finally retire. I'm thinking this might be the perfect time to call it quits."

"Well, you've certainly had a distinguished career."

He glances at his notes. "Let me attempt to recap this bizarre meeting. You get a two-million-dollar contract for two albums, one to be the "Live at Wade's" performance, the other in studio, with all proceeds going to John . . . what did you say his last name is?"

"Anderson. Here's his business card with address."

"And then Lizzy gets a two-million-dollar deal, also, for two albums."

"Correct. Her last name is Smith."

"Yes, I got that," he is scribbling furiously on his yellow legal pad, an occasional droplet of sweat from his brow causing the ink to run, which he dabs at with his pudgy forefinger.

She adds: "And then Leroy and Buzz each get a million dollars. All paid within thirty days of signing, guaranteed. Plus, the normal 10% of proceeds after the advanced monies have earned out, which I'm confident they will, especially for Lizzy."

"You sure have a lot of faith in Lizzy."

"I do. I expect you'll be back to thank me once you see just how well she does over the many years. She's young, you know, in her early thirties."

"All right, let's do it," he returns the contract to his briefcase and gets up to go.

"One other thing," she adds.

"Now what?" a vein in the center of his forehead is pulsating.

"Why don't you bring all the contracts here this evening and join us for dinner?"

"I seriously doubt I can get them all done that quickly," he looks incredulous.

"Well, I encourage you to do your best. Before I change my mind. You're getting far more than you thought when you walked through the door, for less."

"I'll see what I can do." They head into the living room.

"Bring a good bottle of champagne with you, too. Lizzy, Buzz, and Leroy will be dining with us. We can celebrate after we sign."

"I'll do my best," he glances at his watch.

"And not a peep about this arrangement to Lizzy, Buzz, or Leroy. Understood?"

"Sure. Whatever. What time do you want me here?"

"Around seven."

"I better get moving before you change your crazy mind. I thought Mabel was a nut. Artists!" he charges into the kitchen to get his chauffeur. A few minutes later, they hear the limousine making tracks.

Richard and Mabel walk outside and down to the shoreline where Lizzy and Priscilla are toweling off. "How'd it go?" Priscilla asks.

"Very well," Mabel says. "Lizzy, I want you to contact Leroy and Buzz and invite them to dinner tonight at seven."

"Sure, if I can track them down."

"Schmidt is coming with contracts for each of you, so just find them and be here at seven for a dinner celebration. Okay?"

"A contract for me?"

"Yes, for you."

"What did Schmidt say?"

"He said he's rarely heard such a gifted singer."

"Really?"

"Really."

"Wow, I can't believe it."

"I think you'll be pleased with the money, too."

"Money?"

She laughs at her innocence. "You don't think all artists

have to starve, do you?"

"I suppose I do," Lizzy slips into her sandals and they walk back toward the house.

"Well, not you. Your days of starving are done, dear."

"Do you think I'll be able to buy a new car?"

That evening, they are all gathered at home waiting for Schmidt. It's half past seven and Mabel is growing concerned he's had a change of heart. Richard's veggie lasagna is now back in the oven, warming. Lizzy is playing the piano while Buzz and Leroy explore Mabel's home. Priscilla is on the phone with her father.

"You don't suppose he's not coming?" Mabel asks Richard.

"One would think he'd at least phone."

"God, I hope he shows up. I'd hate to break Lizzy's spirits."

Richard laughs. "I've never seen someone so excited about the prospects of buying a new Toyota. I encouraged her to wait a bit."

"If this all works out, she'll be buying a whole lot more than a new car," Mabel gazes out the front window. She's disturbed to see her neighbor, Alice Kramlich, standing outside gabbing with Joel Swillens. Why would they know each other? They approach the house and she rushes to the front porch to intercept them.

"Hello, Alice. What brings you two here this fine evening?"

Alice's hands are on her hips in a combative stance. "Joel is concerned about your aunt. He's been looking all over for her and can't find a trace."

"Why, there's nothing to worry about. How do you two know each other?"

Joel responds. "Alice thinks you've put some sort of a magic spell on Mabel."

Richard has joined her outside and breaks into laughter. "Come again?"

"You heard him," Alice is standing close to Peggy, gazing into her eyes. "Mabel showed me some old books about voodoo in her family and then Priscilla told Joey she turned her into *you.*"

Alice is now just inches away from Mabel's face, squinting and shifting her gaze to see if Mabel flinches, but she holds her own, meeting Alice's stare head on. It takes everything she has to hold her gaze and not reveal the truth.

Richard releases a bellyaching laugh. "So, let me get this straight. This fine local reporter is listening to a crazy person who believes in voodoo?"

Joel takes a few steps away from Alice.

Mabel says: "Are you okay, Alice? I spoke with my aunt this morning and told her what you said yesterday. She's worried you aren't taking your meds."

"I'm taking my meds—"

"You take meds?" Joel retreats more.

"Everyone does these days! Don't let her distract you. I'm telling you, this Peggy woman is Mabel, made young again."

They hear the sound of tires rumbling up from behind and are relieved to see Schmidt's limousine. He jumps from the limousine, briefcase in one hand, bottle of Cristal in the other. "I'm sorry I'm late. Had problems with my printer."

"I'm just glad to see you," Richard takes the bottle from him. "Come on in. Dinner is warming in the oven."

"Invite your driver to dine with us," Peggy insists.

Schmidt takes a look around and senses he's walked into a situation. "Everything okay here?" he faces Joel and Alice.

"We were just wrapping up," Peggy speaks before they can reply. "Alice, you can talk to my aunt tomorrow when she's back. And Joel, please do us all a favor and take her home and make sure she takes her pills."

Alice runs after Joel, who is heading for his car. "Wait, don't go. I'm telling the truth! You have to believe me. Come back here!"

He waves her away. "I need to get back to doing real

267

work and not waste my time chasing after ridiculous ghost stories."

Peggy whispers to Richard: "Let's get this done and fast." They gesture toward the Stairlift for Schmidt and his chauffeur, as she and Richard take the steps up to the deck. They wait for the Stairlift to arrive and then she leads the chauffeur into the kitchen, while Schmidt wanders into the living room. Peggy returns and Lizzy stops playing the piano. They are joined by Buzz and Leroy on the sofa, seated across from Schmidt, who opens his briefcase. Peggy and Richard sit in the armchairs on either side of Schmidt.

"I brought you these three VIP passes for tomorrow's festival," Schmidt passes an envelope to Peggy. "It's the afternoon performances being held outside at the fairgrounds."

"How nice," she says. "Is three all you could get?"

"I'm afraid so. The festival gave me six and I gave the others to Gary Clark, Jr., for his family."

"I see, well three is better than none. It will be fun to hear Gary perform."

"So, to get started I need Peggy to sign your contract first," he passes it to her. She scans it and sees everything is in order, with all proceeds going to John. She signs, Richard witnesses, and Lizzy breaks into applause.

"This is so exciting. How much did you get?"

"That's my secret," she replies.

Schmidt continues. "And here are contracts for Buzz and Leroy. They are identical."

"Let me see," Leroy picks his up.

Buzz is scanning his agreement and then sees the million dollar figure.

"Say what?" he exclaims.

Leroy looks at him, confused.

"Leroy, look at Clause Two right here," Buzz puts his finger on the contract.

"Am I seeing that right?"

"You are," Buzz nods.

Leroy looks at Peggy. "So, we get paid a million bucks each, upfront, to back both you and Lizzy for three, maybe four, albums?"

"Correct," Schmidt is not sure if they are expecting more so adds: "Plus 10% of all sales after the advance pays out, assuming it does." He is fidgeting in his seat, trying to understand how his day turned out so differently than he envisioned when he first awoke.

Peggy adds: "And one of those albums has already been recorded. Our Thursday night Live session."

"Give me that pen," Leroy signs and Buzz does, too. Mabel takes the agreement for Lizzy from Schmidt, and looks it over carefully. She sees the marketing fund has been written in. "This one is for you, Lizzy. Looks like you can buy a new house, as well as a couple of cars."

Lizzy wanders over and takes the agreement from her. "Shouldn't I show this to a lawyer before signing?"

"No need," Peggy says. "We already took care of that. Your contract includes a guaranteed marketing fund to make sure you get launched properly. Just sign it, dear."

"Where does it say how much I'm being paid?"

"Right here," Peggy points to the figure.

Lizzy sees it and tears stream down her cheeks. "This can't be right."

"It's very right, Lizzy. You deserve it."

"But . . . two million dollars?"

"Plus 10% on top of that once your advance earns out," Peggy says. "Which it will, many times over."

Lizzy breaks down and slumps onto the sofa, wailing uncontrollably. The others become embarrassed seeing her this way. Peggy approaches and puts her arm around her. "What is it, honey?"

Lizzy blubbers: "This can't be happening, right?"

"Oh, it's happening," Peggy sits on the edge of the sofa stroking Lizzy's head.

"But, nothing good ever happens for me."

"C'mon, dear. Please compose yourself and sign your contract," Peggy helps her up from the sofa.

Lizzy grabs a Kleenex from the coffee table, sniffling and smiling in embarrassment. She takes the pen from Schmidt, whose confidence in his new artist is plummeting by the tear drop, and signs her contract. "I hope you're being paid more than I am," Lizzy returns to the sofa with Peggy by her side.

"Don't you worry about me. I'll be just fine. Now, everyone, let's eat."

Peggy heads for the kitchen and leads Reggie to the dining room table, seating him next to her. It's been a long time since she has used the formal dining room table and is excited to be hosting once again. The table is set with fine linen napkins and silver Mabel bought herself many years ago. The plates are hand-painted from Spain, with bright orange and blue fishes and gold-rimmed edges. The original set of twelve is now down to eight, the others chipped and cracked over time. Mabel's hand-blown Italian champagne glasses have been freed from the cupboard where they've been sitting idle for years. She has also brought out her high-stemmed wine glasses for the four bottles of French Bordeaux wine on the table. Richard appears from the kitchen carrying the casserole dish of veggie lasagna, which he places on a trivet. He plates the lasagna for each guest and they pass the lovely dishes around the table.

"Be sure to help yourselves to salad," Peggy pushes the

wooden salad bowl toward Reggie.

"Thank you, ma'am." He is looking to Schmidt for approval, feeling out of place and awkward dining with his boss, something he has never done, despite being his driver for twenty years. Schmidt nods his approval and so Reggie loads salad onto his plate.

Peggy says: "Take some of the Italian bread, too."

Leroy is inhaling his meal, moaning with each bite, oblivious to the others. His head pops up for air long enough to say: "Richard, this is some amazing lasagna."

"It's an old recipe from my grandmother. She studied Italian cooking and told me this is an ancient Roman dish. The trick is getting the correct cheeses."

"What are they?" Priscilla asks.

"That's a family secret," he smiles.

Schmidt looks happy as he pops the champagne cork, which makes a small dent in the wall next to him. "I'd like to propose a toast," he pushes back his seat and stands. "To Mabel for allowing us to use her lovely home this evening."

"Bravo," Buzz says as he stands. "And to the awesome Peggy Winston."

"To Lizzy!" Peggy raises her glass and stares directly into Lizzy's moist eyes. "May your future be bright, prosperous, and filled with love."

"To being rich!" Leroy lifts his head from the lasagna

long enough to clang his glass against Peggy's, and then lowers his head to his food like a dog scouring his bowl.

Priscilla is sipping her ginger ale, unaware of how her personal fortunes have also changed. After the champagne toast, Richard passes the red wine around the table where the guests fill their glasses, enjoying their dinners, and managing to dispatch all four bottles before dessert is served.

After dessert, Schmidt offers to drive Lizzy, Buzz, and Leroy home in his limousine. Lizzy is wobbling by the front door, tipsy and holding onto Peggy as they share a sloppy embrace.

"Oh-my-god-I-can't-thank-you-enuff-Peggy," the words run together. "I lurve you." Hiccup. Burp.

Peggy smiles as she pushes Lizzy's face away. "Never forget this night Lizzy. I know I won't."

Richard takes Lizzy's hand to steady her. "Lizzy, Mabel is coming home tomorrow and wants to meet you. Peggy has told her so much about you."

"Really? Mabel wants to meet me?"

"She does," Peggy says. "In fact, why don't you come over tomorrow afternoon before we head to the festival. You can say hello to Mabel and I'm sure she'd love to hear you play."

Lizzy stumbles at the doorstep and laughs as Leroy and Buzz each take an arm and guide her out onto the deck. Peggy closes the door behind them, listening to Lizzy's drunken laughter trail off as they descend the stairs. She's confident Lizzy will become as huge a success as she was, and realizes she's been seeing her younger self in Lizzy all week. In her own odd way, she senses she's been helping Lizzy in part to gain a vicarious do-over, to relive the thrill of when she first launched her own career.

Richard is in the kitchen handwashing Mabel's painted plates and crystal glasses, Priscilla helping with the drying. It's after eleven and they're exhausted.

"Well, I guess that's it for Peggy Winston," Mabel sighs.

"She was the best," Priscilla smiles.

"She still *is* the best," Richard wraps his arm around her waist.

"I'm just hoping I'm back to my old self tomorrow. Otherwise I fear Alice might think she's losing her mind, and we can't have that."

"But won't you miss being young?" Priscilla asks.

"Yes, and no. It's been fun but I miss the simplicity of my life as an old woman. I now realize I've got so many things to be happy about. I just hope I'll use this attitude readjustment to make me less grumpy when I'm back to good ol' Mabel."

"You're not grumpy," Richard says.

"Well, I think I am. I waste far too much time resenting

Jerry and what happened in my past. The past is gone, and I don't have many days left, so let's make the most of them."

Mabel puts on her pajamas and crawls into bed. Richard and Priscilla surprise her as she goes to turn off the light.

"We want to sleep with you, too," Priscilla says.

"Absolutely not," Mabel looks alarmed.

"Why not?" Richard asks.

"Because I want to be alone when I wake up. You don't want to see old ugly Mabel. Now shoo. Away with you."

SUNDAY

A loud clap of thunder awakens Mabel early on Sunday. She's been dreaming about her ex-husband Jerry, and forces herself from the dream, eyes now open just enough to see Richard gazing down on her. He is holding her hand. She smiles, relieved to be free of her ex-husband, who refuses to leave her alone, even after death, returning too often in her dreams. It takes a couple of minutes for her to remember today is the day, when she either stays young or returns to her old self. The way Richard is looking at her, with so much love in his eyes, gives her hope that she might still be young.

"Good morning, sleepyhead," he leans in close, running his hand along her cheek.

"Hey, Richard. I was having an awful dream about my ex. What a relief to see your loving face."

"You were tossing and turning so I just woke you up." He plumps two pillows behind her head so she can sit up. When she attempts to slide up on the bed, the hurts return, and she knows she's back to her old self.

"Let me give you a hand," Richard helps raise her up so she can sit more comfortably in bed.

"Oh, dear," she moans.

Priscilla is standing in the doorway. "Good morning, Grammy May. It's nice to have you back."

Mabel pats the bed beside her and Priscilla climbs in next to her. "It's good to be back. Sort of—" she winces as a bolt of pain runs down her left arm.

Richard leaves and returns with a glass of water and two ibuprofens. "Here, take these."

Mabel downs the pills, reminded of how difficult they are to swallow, and how much she enjoyed not taking any medications this week. "I suppose I should go splash some water on my face and brush my teeth." She slowly swings her legs to the side and slides off the bed. She pauses, feeling unsteady, and then ambles off for the bathroom. Priscilla and Richard follow close behind to make sure she doesn't lose her balance. Mabel flips the bathroom light switch and sighs. "Oh, dear. What a sorry sight I am. Why did I bother going to the salon when I knew this was going to happen?"

"We can get your hair styled again today, Grammy May," Priscilla attempts to cheer her up.

Richard adds: "And, don't forget, we're going to the blues festival this evening. Schmidt gave us—well, actually he gave Peggy—three VIP tickets."

"Oh, I don't feel up for that," Mabel splashes water on her face. "You should take Nica. I'm sure she'd be thrilled to go with you."

"You forget, you have some unfinished business to attend to with Schmidt," Richard says. "Plus, I think you'll actually enjoy the festival."

Mabel looks frustrated as she picks at her lopsided hair with her left hand.

"C'mon, Grammy May. Let's get dressed and get your hair done. You can nap this afternoon before we go to the festival. We don't need to be there until five o'clock."

Mabel gazes at Richard. "You really want to be seen out and about with me looking like this? I mean, look at me."

"I am looking at you," he says.

"Well, why aren't you running?"

He smiles. "Apparently I'm not quite as shallow as you think."

"I'd run from me," she leans in close to the mirror. "What a sight for sorry eyes." She turns and Richard moves in closer, putting his hands on her waist.

"I will never forget the week we've had, Mabel. I have no regrets. And, for what it's worth, I love you. Many people love you. Despite what you believe, love runs deeper than appearances."

"I love you, too," Priscilla adds.

Mabel tears up, shaking her head from side to side. "Richard, you just think you love me. You need to move on.

You need to pursue Nica before someone else scoops her up. I see the way she looks at you."

They walk to the living room and sit on the sofa. The rain is pounding on the deck outside, the visibility reduced to near zero as they sit within the grayness of dawn. The sounds of thunder grow more and more distant as the storm passes off to the east.

Priscilla checks her phone. "Shoot. Daddy's flight was cancelled. He won't be home until tomorrow now."

"What a shame," Mabel says. "It will be nice to see him again. Is it just me, or does it seem like he's been gone much longer than a week?"

"Well, this certainly was an unusual week for us all," Richard strokes his chin.

"Is it Sunday?" Mabel looks confused.

"It is," Richard replies.

"How'd you like to take us to church? I feel we all need to go give thanks to God."

"Of course, I'd be happy to. Why don't you ladies get showered and dressed, and then we can grab a quick breakfast. I need to swing by my place to put on a suit."

"We'll hurry," Mabel heads for the bathroom.

An hour later, Mabel and Priscilla walk into Richard's home

and Richard is embarrassed to see he failed to take out the trash the day before yesterday, so there is a fetid odor in the kitchen. He opens a window and takes the trash bag out into the garage.

When he comes back inside, he can see Mabel and Priscilla's surprise at his living conditions. "I'm sorry, I would have cleaned up had I known you'd be coming. Really, I would have, it's not usually this messy."

Mabel gazes around at this old stately home, now in decline, much like herself. "There is only so much cleaning up one can do with a dump like this."

Priscilla screams as a mouse darts across the kitchen floor and slips behind the refrigerator. She jumps up onto a kitchen chair.

Talk about bad timing, it's unusual for there to be a mouse out and about during daylight hours. Richard grabs a broom and chases it out from behind the refrigerator, then follows it into the living room, where it disappears behind the sofa and into the hot air heating vent along the baseboard. Priscilla can be heard in the kitchen, flapping her arms like a grounded bird. "Gross, gross, gross …"

Mabel is wandering around the first floor noticing the brownish water stains in the living room's beautifully ornate tin ceiling. "I'm surprised, Richard. You seem so fastidious; how can you live like this?"

"I spent most of the week with you, so missed trash day."

"The trash is one thing but look at these walls. The old plaster is badly cracked with water stains everywhere."

"That's the upstairs tub again," he follows her. "I've been after my landlord to call a plumber but he's been ignoring me."

"Who's your landlord?" Mabel asks.

"Gus Simmons."

"Figures," she groans.

"Why do you say that?"

"The Simmons family is notorious around these parts for being sleazy landlords. They've been taken to small claims court many times but don't seem to care. How much are you paying in rent?"

"$1,600 a month."

"Including utilities?"

"No, those are separate."

"Good God. He's taking you for a ride."

"I came to town so fast and there wasn't anything else available."

"Not even out by the lake?"

"No, this was literally the only decent rental available within twenty miles of my office."

"I cannot get over how this proud old home has been let go. When I was a little girl the Swanson family lived here and

I recall coming to a birthday party when I was probably around six years old. These living room walls had beautiful old Victorian-era wallpaper; I think it was yellow with green florals. There was a Chickering grand piano in the parlor where Mrs. Swanson could be found playing folk tunes and Christmas carols." Mabel gazes out the front window lost in memories when Richard approaches from behind and rests his hand on her shoulder.

"Want to know something funny?" he asks, eager to change the topic.

"What?"

"You still seem young to me. On the inside. Do you feel differently?"

"Now that you mention it, I am feeling mentally sharper than a week ago. Of course, I look terrible."

The doctor is intrigued. "If you wouldn't mind, I'd like to administer the Montreal memory test again, to see if your short-term memory has changed from when you last took it."

"Always the doctor, listen to you. No, I don't want to take that humiliating test ever again, thanks all the same."

"I hadn't realized you felt that way."

"So, what are we going to do about this place?" she asks.

"I'm not planning to be here long. Just until my lease is up in December. Assuming I'm even here then."

"Are you seriously considering the Boston position?"

"I've decided to apply."

She shakes her head. "I can't blame you, but you'll be sorely missed."

"Let's not get ahead of ourselves. I probably won't get it. This Sardis work experience won't look great on my curriculum vitae."

"C'mon Priscilla, let's wait outside while Richard gets showered and dressed." Priscilla hops down from the kitchen chair and scurries across the floor nearly as fast as the mouse. Relieved to be outside in the fresh air, she and Mabel lean up against the BMW, noticing the trash that has blown up against the chain-link fence surrounding Richard's rental, the original wrought iron fencing long gone. The once-proud Greek Revival porch is down to just two original columns on either end, the others replaced with temporary pressure-treated beams.

"This used to be such a beautiful home," Mabel looks pensive. "Before the Swansons, I recall being told that two generations of the Messengers lived here. They were among the first Black families to start businesses in Mississippi. It's so sad to see these old homes being neglected. I wouldn't be surprised if Gus Simmons is just waiting for this grand dame to be condemned so he can tear it down and divide it up into condos. Just what we don't need—more overpriced condos, when what we do need is affordable housing, but who cares?"

"I feel badly for the doctor having to live like this," Priscilla says. "I can't imagine sharing a home with mice. Eeew."

"I know, he deserves better, but the real estate and rental markets are sellers' markets now so it's not good timing for him."

"I'm glad we don't have to live like this. Maybe you should ask if he'd like to live with you? You've got plenty of space."

"Oh, I'd love that dearly but he's probably headed back up north to be nearer his family."

"Well, maybe if he doesn't get the job?"

"My, Priscilla, you really like the doctor, don't you?"

"Yes, he's very smart and funny—"

"And handsome," Mabel finishes her sentence.

"Um, I was going to say a doctor."

Mabel smiles. "Well, you're right, we are very fortunate to live the way we do, not worrying about food or having a roof over our heads. It's important not to turn our backs on the less fortunate."

"Our class took a field trip last month to the Oxford food bank where we helped serve food."

"Good for you."

"I was in charge of pies."

Mabel laughs. "You and your pies."

"Can't help myself. I love a good chocolate cream pie. That's what Daddy ordered for my birthday party."

"How many friends will be coming?"

"Just two. I don't like the big parties others have. And most definitely no boys, just girls."

"Well, I'm excited, too. It should be a fun time for us all. Hopefully the weather will cooperate so you all can swim. I cannot begin to tell you how much I enjoyed swimming this week."

"It was fun. I'm glad I made you young again even if it did complicate matters."

"Me too."

"I'm also glad I got to hear how well you play the piano in a live setting. I've only listened to your records, but seeing you perform live was truly special."

"I hadn't thought of that. Yes, how nice."

"I'm still working on not getting too nervous at my school recitals."

"I can probably help you with that. The trick is to pretend you're playing at home, to keep everything as natural as possible."

"Easier said than done," Priscilla kicks a pebble with her right shoe.

"It will become easier the more you perform. The key is repetition, to the point you can play in your sleep."

Richard comes sauntering down the steps dressed in a tan suit.

"Well, well. Look at you. You think you're Obama or something?" Mabel laughs.

He is happy she approves of his outfit, eager to recover from the embarrassment of her seeing where he lives. They climb into his BMW and drive to St. John's church where he drops Mabel and Priscilla out front. He parks up the street and returns, seeing them in conversation with none other than Alice Kramlich.

"I was so worried about you, Mabel." Alice won't let go of Mabel's forearm. "I thought for sure I'd never see you again."

"That's silly. I was just taking care of business in Oxford and Jackson. Didn't Peggy tell you?"

"Speaking of Peggy, where is she?" Alice spins around.

"She took an early flight home. She had to get back to work."

"She's still working as a stewardess? That local reporter told me she was about to sign a big recording contract. That's why that slick man was at your house in a stretch limo."

Richard repeats the lie Mabel has been telling as cover for the make-believe Peggy: "She's planning to give her notice. Her father died recently so she needs to look after her mother."

286

"How sad for you," Alice feigns concern, still not convinced that Peggy wasn't Mabel.

"Yes, very sad," he puts on a forced frown that doesn't look authentic to Alice. "I will miss her very much. We became close over this week."

"So I noticed."

Her eyes are bloodshot and Mabel assumes she hasn't been sleeping well, spending too much time with her face pressed up against the window hoping to catch them up to no good. "You look tired, Alice. Are you getting enough rest?"

"It's been a long week."

"Tell me about it," Mabel mutters. "And these youngsters are dragging me to the blues festival at the fairgrounds this evening. I just hope I have the energy, and that it doesn't rain."

"I wanted to get tickets for Joey and me but they're all sold out."

"Sorry to hear that," Mabel says.

"Well, I hope when Peggy is on tour somewhere nearby, we can all go hear her," Alice is leaning in a little too close for comfort, gazing into Mabel's eyes.

Mabel takes a step back. "How nice. Now, let's head inside so we can get a pew towards the front."

Richard takes Mabel's hand and helps her climb the granite steps leading to the church.

287

"Welcome, Mabel," Father James greets her. "We missed you last week. And who is this adorable young lady?"

"This is my great-granddaughter, Priscilla Anderson. Michelle's daughter."

"I didn't recognize you. My, how you've grown."

"Nice to see you again, Father," Priscilla replies.

Richard introduces himself. "Hello, I'm Richard Roberts."

"Yes, I know who you are. You're the young doctor from up north who set up practice in town after Tommy Timmons retired."

"That's right."

"I don't recall seeing you at church before."

"This is my first time."

"Ever?" Father James looks up with concern.

"No, just since I've been in Sardis."

"You've been in town for almost a year. Surprised you haven't come by. All are welcome here."

"Thank you. I guess I'm what you'd call a lapsed Catholic."

"Being lapsed is not so bad. It insinuates you might return."

"Yes, that would be nice. Now that I've met Mabel, I'm hoping we can attend together so I don't feel quite so alone."

"Assuming you don't move back up north," Mabel says.

"Oh, I hope you're not thinking of leaving us already," Father James looks dismayed.

"I honestly don't know at this point. My mother is pressuring me to move back closer to home. She and my father live in Brooklyn."

"Don't you like it here?"

"Yes, very much. It's just there is an opening at one of Boston's leading hospitals and my mother thinks I should apply."

"I see," he looks away. "The medical committee will certainly be disappointed. I know how excited they were to hire you."

"I feel badly about that. Honestly, I'm torn. Let's not get ahead of ourselves, and I'd appreciate it if you'd keep this between us. It might not happen at all."

"Of course."

Mabel joins in. "Richard agreed to bring Priscilla and me to church this morning. Wasn't that nice of him? He's such a kind man."

"Yes, indeed. I hope you'll feel comfortable coming to church now that we've had the chance to meet and talk."

Richard is gazing at his feet. "Full confession, Father, I want to return to the church but I'm a man of science, and have not been thrilled with the church's positions on certain social issues that are important to me."

"I see. Religion and science don't have to be mutually exclusive," Father James smiles at a couple passing off to the side. "And you might be surprised to see how accepting our church is to the new ways. All are welcome here."

"That's good to hear. In actuality, my faith in God is growing stronger since I've been in Sardis."

"Oh, that sounds provocative. Did something happen to change your thinking?"

"It did."

"Mind if I ask what?"

"Well, I can't say for certain. There have been so many oddities lately. For one thing, I had a dream that sent me to save a homeless person."

"Isn't that wonderful," Father James puts his hand on Richard's right shoulder.

"I'm just happy I was able to save him. But the dream did seem like a heaven-sent vision. I didn't know exactly where I was going and ended up in a back alley where I found the man."

"God speaks to us in mysterious ways," Father James smiles. "Maybe someday you'd be willing to share that story with our parishioners."

"Sure, why not."

"Please, come in. We're happy to have you with us, Doctor."

After church, Richard swings by Lizzy's father's house and offers to drive her to Mabel's, and then later to the festival. Lizzy dashes down the stairs, calling out to her father who looks to be nursing a beer on the front porch. "Are you sure you'll be okay Dad?"

"I'm fine. You run along with your fancy friends. Nice wheels, *boy*," he calls to Richard and then spits brown chewing tobacco into a plastic cup.

"Father! Really, must you?"

"Run along now, Lizzy."

She climbs into the back seat next to Priscilla. "I'm so sorry about that. He's set in his ways."

Mabel turns and smiles at her. "He's not the first racist we've encountered and won't be the last."

"Are you Mabel Johnson?" she exclaims.

"I am."

"Oh, my God. I'm so thrilled to meet you. Peggy told me you'd be back today."

"I've been away for the week."

"It's uncanny how much you two look alike—"

"Except she's young and beautiful and I'm a mottled mess."

"Which reminds me," Priscilla says. "Let's see if we can get your hair fixed."

"On a Sunday?" Mabel looks skeptical.

"I called Shanice and she said she'd be happy to see you today."

"Who's Shanice?"

"The woman Mommy went to out here. Don't you remember how Mommy was always saying what a great job Shanice did?"

"And she can take me today?"

"She's at home and said to stop by anytime."

"What will you all do while I'm getting my hair done?"

"We can wait for you. I doubt it will take long."

Mabel groans. "Just a few clips of her hedge trimmer should do the trick."

They laugh.

"I don't mind waiting," Lizzy is checking her iPhone. "I'm just killing time before the festival. Peggy must be excited to go."

Richard says: "Actually, Peggy had to fly home this morning, so Mabel will be taking her place."

"That's too bad—"

"Ahem," Priscilla clears her throat.

"No, not that. Of course, I'm thrilled Mabel can go. It's just I know how much Peggy wanted to hear Gary Clark, Jr."

"Well, believe it or not, I'm excited to see him, too." Mabel shifts in her seat, looking somewhat uncomfortable. "Michelle turned me onto his music. I'm a big fan."

"I'm excited, too. It should be a fun evening," Lizzy slips her phone inside her purse.

"Well, I suppose I should go get this mop-top trimmed so I look presentable tonight," Mabel says.

Richard drives them to Shanice's house in Sardis. He parks on the street out front and walks to the passenger side to help Mabel from the car. "Feels good to stretch my legs. They were cramping up." He leads her up the three steps to the door and they ring the buzzer. Priscilla stays behind with Lizzy.

Shanice answers the door. "You must be Mabel. Come on in."

"Okay if I come, too?" Richard looks apprehensive.

"Sure. Follow me. I've just been straightening up the living room. I apologize for how messy it is. My step kids spent the night."

They walk through the living room and into the kitchen where Shanice has a salon chair with a variety of hair products spread out on the table. She's listening to the Isley Brothers on the radio.

"I love your hair," Mabel says.

"Why thanks."

"How do you get it to be straight like that? And purple?"

Shanice laughs. "Tricks of the trade, my dear. Tricks of the trade."

"Any chance you could do that for this tangled mess on my head?"

"Your hair is beautiful, Mabel. I wish my hair was thick like yours."

"Thick, like a briar bush."

"How about I just shorten it so you have a cropped Afro?"

"That sounds good. Could you add color to my hair, too?"

Richard is sitting reading *Time* magazine and smiles. Shanice turns to him.

"Are you her son?"

"No, just a friend."

"Don't you two be making me feel any older than I already do."

"How old are you, Mabel?"

"That's a secret."

"Let me guess. Eighty?"

"If you're angling for a big tip, keep it up, girl."

"Eighty-five?"

"Keep heading north."

"Eighty-eight?"

"I'm ninety."

"Well, look at you, getting around the way you are, sharp as a tack."

"More like a dull tack," Mabel laughs. "So, can you color my hair like yours? I want to feel young tonight, we're going to the festival."

"Do you have a color in mind?"

"I've seen those Black models with blonde highlights in the fashion magazines. Do you think I could pull that off or am I too old?"

Richard looks up. "You want to go blonde?"

"Sure, why not? I've been hearing all my life that blondes have more fun."

"Haven't we had enough fun for one week?" Richard smiles.

Shanice is onboard. "Let's do it. Just one warning. I usually like to do some tests with the peroxide before going whole hog in a head of hair."

"What's the worst that can happen?" Mabel asks.

"Well, you might have an allergic reaction. I'll put a little bit on your arm and we can wait before goin' ahead."

"I'm not too worried about an allergic reaction at my age," Mabel says. "I doubt there's anything left on this planet I haven't come in contact with, so doubt I'll be allergic. I have a lot of problems but allergies have never been an issue."

"How long will this take?" Richard asks Shanice.

"Why don't you go get some lunch in town and come back in two hours," she replies. "I'll just add some highlights to your hair, okay Mabel? Nothing too radical but enough so you'll look elegant."

"Elegant sounds perfect," Mabel says as Richard leaves.

Richard returns after lunch and walks in with Lizzy and Priscilla. Mabel is drinking tea in the kitchen with Shanice.

Priscilla exclaims: "Oh. My. God. Grammy May!"

"Do I remind you of Marilyn Monroe?" she stands up and swings her hips in a slow, painful circle.

"You look amazing," Richard cannot believe his eyes. Mabel's hair is cut stylishly short, with hints of blonde interspersed throughout. Lizzy stands shyly off to the side. Mabel calls to her, "Get over here young lady. Richard tells me you just signed a big record deal. Is that true?"

"It is," Lizzy beams.

"Well, you can't go on tour looking like that, girl. Shanice, can you make her look as sexy as you made me look?"

"I doubt anyone can look as sexy as you do," Shanice laughs.

Mabel stands up and motions to Lizzy. "C'mon, girl. Get that skinny butt of yours over here and let's see what Shanice can do for you. My treat."

*****

They make it back to Mabel's a little before four o'clock. Alice is standing in front of her house and intercepts them as they step from the car. Joey is by her side, holding his bike. "Well look at you, Mabel," Alice exclaims.

"Do you like it?"

"I do."

"Makes me look younger, right?"

"Sure does."

Lizzy steps from the car, her auburn hair dyed hot pink. She's uncomfortable with her radical new look, but likes the idea of becoming a new woman and changing her appearance and starting fresh.

"Hey Priscilla," Joey says, gazing down as his feet and kicking at some dirt.

"Hi, Joey. How've you been?"

"Okay. It's been pretty boring without seeing you."

"I'm sorry we fought, Joey. And I'm sorry I made up that lie about my great-grandmother. I was just upset and trying to one-up you."

"Me too."

Mabel is happy to see the children making up. "You should come over and go swimming with us tomorrow, Joey. Would you like that?"

"Yes, ma'am."

Alice offers: "Maybe Priscilla can stay with us this

evening while you three go to the festival. She's welcome to come for dinner."

Priscilla looks hesitant. "I was thinking I'd wait for them at home and read."

"Go have dinner with them, honey," Mabel touches her on the shoulder. "We should be back by nine at the latest."

"Okay. You want to ride bikes now, Joey?"

"Sure," they head off.

"Join us inside if you can Alice. Lizzy is going to play the piano."

"That's kind of you, but I want to do some gardening and then I'll get dinner started for the kids."

"Thanks, Alice. Appreciate it."

Mabel, Lizzy, and Richard head inside and Mabel sits on the piano bench next to Lizzy. "Peggy told me you wrote a new song I should hear."

Lizzy is nervous sitting next to Mabel, a musical legend, an idol from her youth. She begins playing but then stops.

"Something wrong?" Mabel asks.

"I can't play with you sitting so close."

"Let me get up and sit behind you." Mabel moves.

Lizzy plays the song she wrote about her father, and when she finishes, Mabel claps enthusiastically. "That's marvelous. What a set of lungs you have, girl."

Lizzy smiles, confidence rising.

"Do you mind if I make a suggestion?"

"By all means, I'd be honored."

"Well, when you get to the refrain, try and hold off the A# chord just a beat or two longer, so your voice trails behind, creating more drama."

Lizzy plays that section and does as Mabel suggests. "Yes, that's better."

"You play and sing beautifully," Mabel sits next to her on the bench again. "I have another suggestion for your technique. Did you study classical piano growing up?"

"No, I'm mostly self-taught."

"I thought so. But that's perfectly fine and it shows in your originality. Your technique would benefit from some classical training. You might want to consider taking lessons and I know someone who would be perfect for you."

"Yes, I'd love that. Who do you have in mind?"

"Me," Mabel smiles.

"Get serious."

"I am serious. I can't play much anymore so it would be fun to pass along what I've learned to a younger performer with your natural ability. Let me show you a trick. When you get to the second verse . . . I think it's C#, am I right?"

"Yes."

"Lift your wrist just slightly like this," Mabel takes her hand and guides her up to the C# minor chord. "Isn't that better?"

Lizzy tries a few times but has difficulty doing what Mabel suggests. "It feels awkward," Lizzy keeps playing, making slow progress with each attempt.

"It takes practice, dear, but this will relieve some of the stress on your hand and forearm muscles. Touring will be physically draining, so you need to take good care of your voice and wrists. Last thing you want is to develop carpal tunnel syndrome as you age."

"Thanks, Mabel. Honest to God, am I dreaming? I can't believe I'm sitting here playing piano with the famous Mabel Johnson, in her fabulous home. I grew up listening to your music. My parents were huge fans."

"That's sweet. Maybe you'll be famous someday, too? Why don't we start daily lessons tomorrow and focus on some minor changes to your technique to help eliminate strain."

"Absolutely."

Mabel laughs. "I cannot get over how gorgeous you look with your pink hair like that."

"You, too."

"We're a couple of hotties, aren't we," Mabel slides on the piano bench up against her.

Richard is tapping his watch. "It's time to get going."

*****

They arrive at the festival fairgrounds and enter the VIP back stage area, showing the guard the tickets Schmidt gave them. Schmidt is off in the distance talking with an attractive young woman, who breaks away upon seeing Mabel.

"Mabel Johnson, is that really you?"

"It is," Mabel takes her hand.

"Oh, my God. I'm such a huge fan!"

Schmidt approaches. "Why, hello Mabel. What a pleasant surprise. I see you've met my client, Jesse Wilson."

"Nice to meet you, Jesse."

The young musician is bouncing up and down in excitement like a little girl at a birthday party. "My parents listened to your music for hours on end when I was growing up. My mother would say: 'You see, Jesse? Look at Mabel Johnson, who made it to the top despite all the obstacles. If she can do it, so can you.' And here I am. Still can't believe it. May I hug you?"

"Sure," Mabel has tears in her eyes.

Jesse motions to Gary Clark, Jr., who is getting ready to take the stage. "Gary, come say hello to Mabel Johnson."

"Hey, Mabel. What an honor," the young blues singer shakes her hand.

"Let me give you a hug," Mabel squeezes him tight. "I'm a big fan of your music."

"Seriously?"

"I know, I know. Probably aren't many old folks like me digging you, but I do."

"That's so cool. I don't know what to say."

"My granddaughter turned me onto you last year. She was a big fan."

He has one eye on the stage and the other on Mabel, not wanting to be rude. "Listen, I've got to go play now, but hang out if you can, as I'd love to pick your brain."

"Gary, before you rush off, I want to introduce you to a student of mine, Lizzy Smith. Lizzy just signed with Warner Music, so I imagine you'll find yourselves on tour together at some point."

"They *will* tour together," Schmidt replies. He notices Lizzy's pink hair for the first time. "Don't you look great Lizzy. Love what you've done with your hair."

Gary Clark, Jr. departs for the stage and Mabel turns to Schmidt. "Charles, what about my hair, don't you like it, too?"

"Why yes, of course, you look wonderful. Blonde is the new black. Or maybe black is the new blonde? I'm so confused these days. I'm getting far too old for this scene. Not woke enough I guess."

Mabel lets that one pass. "We both had a good long run," Mabel forces a fake smile.

"Where's Peggy?" he asks.

"She had to fly home to help her mother. Her father recently passed away."

"I'm sorry to hear that. Listen, Mabel. I want to apologize to you for how things worked out—"

"What do you mean? My goodness, everything worked out wonderfully for me—"

"I know. Believe you me, I know. But I'm sorry about the way you were treated back then. With the benefit of hindsight, Atlantic Records should have chosen a more experienced agent to try and sign you. I was in over my head and had only just started my career."

She sighs. "Yes, we both were so young."

He continues, wanting to get this off his chest once and for all. "Times were different and I know we tried to take advantage of you because you were—"

"Poor?"

"Um, no. I was thinking because you're a Black woman."

"I know."

"It wasn't just you. All the Black and female performers were paid less then—"

"And, has that changed?" Mabel leans in close.

"Why, of course."

"That's not what I hear. I hear women and people of color are still paid worse than men and whites."

He looks uncomfortable. "Well, that's not true just for the music industry."

"And that somehow makes it right?"

"No, of course not," this is not going as he'd hoped.

"So why don't you do something about it?"

"Like what?"

"Like pay equally for equal work."

"But everything is market-based."

"Then change the freaking market. Show some leadership. You're Warner Music!"

Schmidt exhales and wipes sweat from his brow. "Well, Lizzy here is getting one of the best contracts we've offered any performer, male or female."

"Yes, Peggy told me. Although, it sounded like she had to bludgeon you to get it."

"I wouldn't go that far. It's funny standing here with you Mabel, how much you and Peggy look alike."

"Yes, isn't that odd," she leans in.

He gazes at her, feeling something is not right.

"Did you enjoy the lasagna last night?"

"Why, yes. How do you know about that?"

"And I trust you will not leave your chauffeur out in the heat ever again."

Schmidt takes a step back, confused.

"Peggy told me all about dinner. She also told me about

her contract, eager for my input. I can't tell you how much I'm looking forward to hearing the "Live at Wade's" performance, which I'm told was off the charts great."

"Yes, it was special. I'm just not sure if the recording is worth releasing given the sound quality."

"Oh, I'm sure it is. People love live performances. Just look at all those old bootleg soundboard masters being digitally enhanced and released to eager fans these years."

Schmidt is picking up a hostile, almost supernatural, vibe coming from Mabel. Sweat is trickling down from his silver sideburns, with just a hint of orange hair dye mixed in. Mabel chuckles to herself in the realization she isn't the only old-timer dying her hair to appear young.

The music of Gary Clark, Jr. fills the air, and Mabel starts dancing with Lizzy and Richard in a dance circle. They smile, and Mabel sees Gary staring at her, smiling back, pointing her out to the crowd. "Mabel Johnson's in the house, folks. The great Mabel Johnson is with us tonight!"

After he finishes his set, Jesse Wilson takes the stage. Mabel goes looking for Schmidt and finds him seated behind the stage drinking a glass of water. Mabel asks: "Do you have your phone handy, or a piece of paper?"

"Sure, why?"

"Take down this advance blurb and be sure to use it. You owe me and will never know exactly how much."

"Sure," he fumbles with his phone.

"It's been decades since I've heard a voice as original and soulful."

"That's great, Mabel. I'm sure Peggy will appreciate this very much—"

"It's not for Peggy. It's for Lizzy."

"Wait. What?"

"You heard me. Use that quote to help launch Lizzy's career. You've got all that guaranteed marketing money so promote the heck out her."

"But, what about Peggy?"

"I'm family. That wouldn't fly."

"But, she's your flesh and blood," he looks confused. "Why waste a great quote like that on Lizzy when Peggy is so much better?"

"For someone with your track record of spotting new talent, I cannot believe you can't see how great Lizzy will become. Maybe it's time you called it quits and let the younger people take over."

Mabel walks away back to Richard and Lizzy.

TODAY

It's unusual, but not unheard of, for snow to fall in the South, and this January has been no exception. Mabel considers the snow to be a beautiful nuisance that will melt away quickly. Richard has built a fire in the fieldstone fireplace, and the two of them watch the snow falling on the lake through the wall of windows while the others sleep.

"Come sit with me," Mabel pats the seat next to her and Richard joins her on the sofa. She takes his hand in hers, feeling the warmth from the fire. The flames flicker in his dark eyes and she leans in and kisses him on the cheek. He pulls away slowly, eyes shut, lingering within the lost image of Peggy.

"I'm so happy today is a holiday," he withdraws. "My BMW doesn't much like the snow."

"Isn't it beautiful?" she pulls a blanket over them.

Richard leans his head against her shoulder while she strokes his hair. The house is quiet with just the occasional gust of wind swirling the snow on the deck.

Priscilla appears from her bedroom dressed in pink pajamas.

"Come sit with us, honey," Mabel separates from Richard, making room for her. "Is your father up yet?"

"He's grading papers in bed."

"How'd you sleep?"

"Okay, but Daddy snores so I was up for part of the night."

"Seems like a shame he has to grade papers on a holiday," Richard says.

"That's my dad. Always working."

"Isn't it nice, all of us together like this?" Mabel smiles.

"You didn't really think we were going to put you in a nursing home, did you?" Richard is struggling to recover from the truth he revealed back at the fairgrounds when he thought he was speaking with Peggy.

"You don't fool me. I *know* you would have sent me away in a heartbeat. You and John. I'm just glad I learned the truth with enough time to do something about it."

"Yes, how could I possibly ever do that now, with you letting me live here for free."

"Well, once I saw your dilapidated rental, and the way that nasty landlord was treating you, it seemed like a smart idea."

He rubs the back of his palm along her mottled cheek.

She feels lucky to have him so close, to be able to lose herself in his dreamy eyes. "And now I've got a doctor in the house, 24/7. And not just any doctor, but the handsomest one in all of Mississippi."

"Which reminds me, did you remember to take your morning pills?"

"I'll take them with breakfast."

"It's important you don't forget."

"How can I possibly forget with you constantly reminding me?"

"I'm just doing my job."

"Well, try looking handsome and being less of a doctor, okay?"

Lizzy and Colin wander out from the other end of the house. Mabel decided to let them live with her after Lizzy summoned the courage to ignore her boyfriend's pleadings to return home and decided to make a fresh start in Sardis. Colin completed his rehab stint in November and needed a place to stay, so Mabel kindly offered him a room of his own, something he hasn't had since he was a teenager.

"You're looking good today, Colin," Mabel says.

"Thanks, I slept like a log. But, might you turn the heat up a bit?"

"Come stand by the fire," Lizzy takes his hand.

"You must be so excited, Lizzy," Mabel says. "Today's the big day."

"I know. I hardly slept a wink."

"What's today?" Priscilla is out of the loop.

"You know, honey. Her album is being officially released."

"Oh, yeah."

Priscilla's father strolls into the living room wearing a royal blue bathrobe and matching slippers. "Good morning, everyone. Happy Martin Luther King Junior Day. Looks like we're getting more snow than they predicted," he gazes out across the lake.

Priscilla runs to her father and wraps her arms around his waist. "I'm so glad you don't have to work, Daddy. I miss being here with Grammy May, don't you?"

"I do," he replies. "I can't thank you enough, Richard, for the way you've been looking after Mabel. You've gone way above and beyond the call of duty. And it's so wonderful to see everyone living happily like this, all together under one roof."

Priscilla winks knowingly. "One might say they take the doctor patient relationship to *whole new* levels."

Richard looks away, embarrassed. His emotions are more confused than ever, enjoying the time he has been spending with Nica, who is working the ER today, but also still in love with Peggy, or Mabel, he's not quite sure which. Mabel has been pushing him more forcefully toward Nica in recent weeks, knowing the relationship she and Richard now enjoy needs to continue cooling and he must move on. She's been surprised at how affectionate he continues to be, apparently more able to overlook her exterior appearance than she had expected. The look of love is still in his eyes.

The four house guests disappear into the kitchen leaving Richard and Mabel alone on the sofa. She turns to Richard and says, "Maybe Nica can join us later this afternoon when she's done with work."

"Yes, that would be nice. I'll give her a call later."

"I want you to move on, Richard."

"I know."

"I'll be dead and gone and you'll need a good woman to love. Nica is that woman."

"I know you don't believe me, but I still have feelings for you. Conflicted as they may be."

She pauses before speaking. "Let me ask you a question. Do you still have feelings for that idiotic woman who dumped you for the football player?"

Richard is startled by this question. "No, in fact I haven't thought about her in months. What a relief!"

"See, that's what I told you the day we toured the Blues Museum. Lovers come and go, but love itself endures. We need to be loved and we need to love others. The ones we loved in the past are never completely lost, as they remain within us as we make our way. You will move on from me just as you moved on from your previous love, and maybe you'll marry Nica and start the family I know you so very much want." She squeezes his hand. He knows she is right, yet navigating all these matters of the heart has him feeling wistful.

She continues. "I hope you and Nica will help Priscilla make her way. She wants to become a doctor and I think she could grow up to be an exceptional one." Richard has become very close to Priscilla, and he and Nica have brought her to the hospital to job shadow twice since the summer. The magic of Priscilla's spell changed him in many ways, most notably his attendance with Mabel at church every Sunday morning. He wasn't sure if this magic was the work of the Devil or the Lord, but now as he gazes around the room, observing the others returning with their coffees and pastries, he knows the answer.

"Colin, have you given further thought to what you want to do now that you've cleaned up?" John sits in the armchair by the antique walnut table, resting his coffee mug on a coaster. The table smells of Lemon Pledge and shows no signs of dust.

"I've been writin' some about my life. I might try and find a publishah at some point."

"My offer still stands to guest lecture at the university. I'd love to have you speak to my Sociology 101 class."

"That's nice, profess-ah. But I'm not ready to do anything like that. I just need to focus on my health for the time being." He turns to Mabel and Richard. "And what you two have done for me, well, I can nevah thank you enuf," he tears up.

"Oh, stop," Mabel says. "You're the one who has done the hard work. And having so many people around has been a tremendous joy. I used to be so sad and lonely and now every day is a blessing."

Mabel turns to Lizzy. "So, are you ready for us to listen to your album?" Mabel gestures to Richard who connects his iPhone to the Bluetooth sound system, with six recently purchased Bose speakers mounted from the walls providing full surround sound.

They sit in front of the fire as Lizzy's music fills the room, her sultry voice backed by the firm foundation of Buzz and Leroy's playing. They listen to the first song and then Lizzy motions to Richard. "That's enough. This is too embarrassing."

"You sing beautifully," Colin says. "The recordin' quality is so crystal cleah."

"It makes me uncomfortable having you all listen to me like this," Lizzy is flushed, her pink cheeks matching her pink hair. "It reminds me of a painter in a pretentious little art gallery, forced to hear the comments of strangers."

"Well, *we* are not strangers, but I understand how you feel, dear," Mabel sits back, happy she was able to make this all work out. "Have you talked with Leroy and Buzz lately?"

"Yes, they're in Chicago. I'm flying there tomorrow to join them for the continuation of the tour."

"Are they happy?"

"Ecstatic. Plus, now they've got enough money to fund their own work. You know, play what they want to play. I think they're planning a new album with Buddy Grainger."

"That's excellent," Colin says. "So, nobody knows what became of Peggy, huh?"

"Nope," Mabel replies quickly.

Colin strokes his chin. "Sure is strange the way she came and went like that. I heard Schmidt is pullin' his hair out tryin' to find her."

"I don't know why he's wasting his time looking for her when he's got Lizzy under contract," Mabel sounds cross. "That ol' fool should retire by now, anyways."

"I wish I could thank Peggy," Lizzy leans back in her armchair. "She was so kind to me, right from the beginning. First time I met her, she gave me half her sandwich."

"And you gave me some of it," Colin remembers.

"I don't know, but I feel like she had something to do with me getting my contract," Lizzy gets up and walks to the wall of windows, gazing out at the falling snow.

314

"Oh, I doubt that," Mabel says. "She told me Schmidt was very excited to sign you."

"I'm curious, Lizzy. Just how much dough didya git?" Colin asks.

"A lot," Mabel interjects, knowing the terms of the agreement she helped make happen.

"Like, exactly, how much?" he persists.

"I'd rather not say," Lizzy looks away, not believing how wealthy she is, so accustomed to struggling to make ends meet.

"Don't be modest," Mabel eggs her on. "It's unbecoming on you."

Lizzy says, "They signed me to a two-million-dollar contract for a couple or more albums."

"SHE-it," Colin slaps his knees.

"And once my house is finished, I hope you'll move in with me, Colin. At least until you figure out what you want to do."

Lizzy glances down the lakefront where her house is under construction. The foundation was poured in December and the exterior framing is now visible through the snow. Mabel sold her the land for cheap, and Lizzy is building a large log cabin home with a basement music studio, with acoustic ceiling tiles and a new Steinway grand piano on order. The top floor will have a large deck ideal for watching sunsets. Mabel enjoys having Lizzy nearby and is still giving her lessons when Lizzy is not off touring.

"I might just take you up on that," Colin smiles. "That is, assumin' Mabel will want me out before much longer."

"You're welcome to stay as long as you want," John has joined Lizzy at the wall of windows.

"That's kind of you, but it's really up to Mabel."

"Actually, it's not completely up to me," Mabel says. "I gifted the house to John and want it to pass to Priscilla. Plus, my word, we have plenty of room here. There's over 5,000 square feet and it's so nice having people around. I cannot begin to tell you how lonely it was here before."

"And we're eternally grateful for the gift," John adds.

"Grammy May made my father swear he'd never, *ever* put her in a nursing home or memory care facility," Priscilla cuts to the chase in her own inimitable way.

Mabel smiles. "And, as long as the good doctor is living here, it's a win-win for everyone."

John is indebted to Richard. Priscilla is thriving in school this year and might be skipping a grade next year. She has an upcoming piano recital in Oxford, which Mabel is looking forward to attending.

"Hey, twist my arm," Richard laughs. "Living in this house with the famous Mabel Johnson is not too shabby a life."

"But don't you miss Peggy?" Lizzy asks. "I mean, you two seemed to be *so* in love."

This is not the first time Richard has faced this question. "Sure, I miss her, but it feels like she was a stepping stone to Nica."

"How are you two lovebirds?" Colin asks.

"We're doing great," he looks away, shyly. "She's a catch."

"Like a fish?" Mabel smirks.

"Yes, like a fish. A very special fish."

"Well, you're a keeper as well," Mabel touches his forearm. "Don't you ever forget it. You deserve only the best and I think Nica is very lucky to have you."

Colin looks serious. "I owe you both my life."

"I'm just happy I found you when I did," Richard says.

Colin gazes out at the lake. "I can't believe how low I sank."

"Hey, life's tough enough for those of us who've had it easy. What you went through would be enough to take any man down."

"Spose so, but I wish I'd been strong-ah."

"Having difficulty reconciling your love of Emerson's *Self-Reliance* with your own life?" Richard smiles.

Colin looks down at his feet. "I guess we all need help at some point."

"Exactly," John joins in. "This is why I'd love for you to come speak to my class, to share your story with the students, so they better understand the consequences of environmental policies on actual people. The way you were poisoned by those hazardous inks at the printer, it would be good for the kids to hear from you."

They sit in silence watching the snow fall on the lake.

"Let's listen to Peggy's album." Priscilla connects her iPhone to the sound system. The lush sounds of the "Peggy Winston Trio, Live at Wade's" album fill the room.

Lizzy sighs. "That girl better show up, cuz she's got *way* too much talent not to record her next album."

Peggy's "Live" album was released in December and is climbing the Billboard charts, now at number ten. They listen as "Black Coffee" fills the room. Richard smiles at Mabel, aware of how much money John and Priscilla stand to inherit from the success of her Peggy Winston album.

"Come play the piano with me," Mabel gestures to Lizzy. "We've been rehearsing one of Peggy's favorite songs at the end of our lessons. I taught Peggy this magical tune when she was a child."

"And I absolutely adore it," Lizzy beams.

They sit at the Steinway and play a duet.

"I hope you'll record this on your next album, dear. I have a feeling this could become a hit single for you."

"Don't you worry. I've been wondering if you might want to record it with me. What do you think? You can still sing, right?"

They play and everyone joins in:

> *Do you believe in maaagic, in a young girl's heart.*
> *How the music can free her, whenever it starts. And*
> *it's maaaagic, if the music is groovy* — "Come on
> Richard, sing!" — *It makes you feel happy like*
> *an old-time mooovie. I'll tell you 'bout the magic,*
> *and it'll free your soul. But it's like trying to tell a*
> *stranger 'bout rock and roll . . . Do you believe in*
> *maaagic, in a young girl's heart . . .*

Priscilla sits next to them on the piano bench, singing along, hugging her beloved Grammy May.

ABOUT

This is Valerie McKee's debut novel. An employee within the the New York City public school system, Valerie is a graduate of Tufts University and La Sorbonne. She has an MBA in Human Resources Management from the University of Phoenix.

This is Don Trowden's fifth published book. His novels include *Normal Family* (2012), *No One Ran to the Altar* (2016), *All the Lies We Live* (2018), and the non-fiction book *The Isles of Shoals Remembered* (1991).

The authors thanks you for reading *Young Again* and hope it provided some fantasy and relief from the losses and hardships experienced by so many during the Covid-19 pandemic.

ACKNOWLEDGEMENTS

Valerie would like to thank her grandparents, Jeanette McKee, and Bennie and Shirley Hudson, for making sure she spoke the "King's" English properly. Her parents, Emmit and Rosa McKee, placed great importance on education. Her brother, Herb McKee, and sister, Janet McKee, set the bar as high as they could. Many thanks to Wadleigh Scholar for giving the wonderful opportunities of expanding educational opportunities. Mr. Plummer, Mrs. Matthews, and Miss Brunson helped to push the three McKee students into New England preparatory schools, colleges, and beyond. Each of these people taught their students to follow their individual paths. Valerie thanks Ms. Brunson for preparing her for St. George's School English classes, and for letting her students tell the stories of their choosing.

Don Trowden (Caleb Mason) would like to thank the people who read drafts of this novel and provided helpful feedback, including: Paul Barclay de Tolly, Hayden Head, Anna Blauveldt, and Michael Kinnamon. Thanks also to the many dedicated teachers along the way, including Roy Penny, Sylvan Barnet, and Seymour Simches. And special thanks to

Valerie McKee for agreeing to tackle this work of the imagination as a team project. Valerie brought great intelligence and insight to this uplifting novel written during the onset of the 2020 pandemic.